ABSOLUTE VISIONS

Edited by MacAllister Stone

Visit us on the Web: http://absolutewrite.com/absolute-visions/
http://absolutewrite.com/forums/
Printed in the United States of America
ISBN-13: 978-0-9848719-0-2

To the members of AbsoluteWrite

You're the finest group of people I've ever had the pleasure of associating with.

Thank you.

Contents

Introduction

By MacAllister Stone

When she was accepting the National Book Award, Ursula K. Le Guin said:

> We who hobnob with hobbits and tell tall tales about little green men are quite used to being dismissed as mere entertainers, or sternly disapproved of as escapists. But I think that perhaps the categories are changing, like the times. . . . The fantasist, whether he uses the ancient archetypes of myth and legend or the younger ones of science and technology, may be talking as seriously as any sociologist — and a good deal more directly — about human life as

it is lived, and as it might be lived, and as it ought to be lived. For after all, as great scientists have said and as all children know, it is above all by the imagination that we achieve perception, and compassion, and hope (*Language of the Night*. New York: Perigee, 1979. 57-58.)

Le Guin gave that acceptance speech in 1975. Just about that same year, someone left a bunch of battered science fiction paperbacks on the book-swap shelf in the waiting room of my dad's auto shop. I thought they looked a little weird but pretty cool. I was one of those kids who is always looking for more books to read, so I took a handful of them home. Among those books was *E Pluribus Unicorn,* a collection of short stories by Theodore Sturgeon. It had a unicorn on the cover, so it seemed like an especially good bet. There was some Heinlein and Asimov, some A.E. van Vogt and Arthur C. Clarke, and a copy of Le Guin's *Rocannon's World.*

That beat-up collection of paperbacks changed me forever. The stories within those volumes opened entire alien landscapes for exploration. The words offered a portal to strange and fabulously rich, distant environs that turned out, after all, to be about the very nature of life and hope and what it means to be human.

INTRODUCTION BY MACALLISTER STONE

My fondest hope for this volume you're currently reading is that these stories will fire your imagination the same way those tattered paperbacks fired mine, all those years ago. My wish for you is that this anthology will transport you somewhere entirely different than and far, far away from where you're right now sitting and reading. This anthology represents some seasoned writers who've been publishing for years, and some talented newcomers who are just beginning their own journeys.

Join us, won't you?

PART 1
DISCOVERY

"Flickers" illustrated by Puss in Boots

Flickers

By Christian Crews

"You never tell me about the fairies anymore," Carlos said, swirling a stick in the rainbow storm water that ran by the curb.

"I was wrong to tell you about them," I said. "I made it up. You know how adults make up things to tell kids?"

"Uh huh."

"That's all it was. I made it up." I crushed my cigarette butt on the steaming pavement where we sat. He tilted his head like a mantis, that alien head that was too large for his small bones.

"I want to believe that one, Rose."

"So do I, Carlos." I picked up my books from the asphalt. "So do I."

6

A clotted streak of blood from his ankle to his shoe looked painted on his dirty skin. I wished I could get a Band-Aid for him, but I was already late for work. He had turned the slick of rainbow oil in the storm water into a figure eight.

"Do you think your mom and Bill will stay out too long again?" I asked.

Carlos shrugged. Then nodded. Another figure eight.

"Well, do you have food to eat?"

He made a pistol motion with his other hand. He did.

"OK, I have to go to work, and I have class tonight. You'll be fine. I know it sucks, but you'll be all right."

He didn't look up from the rainwater streaming into the sewer grate.

***

When I got home, their side of the duplex was crawling with dark figures out front near the street light. They looked like rats scurrying, the way the thin light flickered. The noise of the party was unbearable, with motorcycles and speakers in the yard, crackhead women cackling and men mumbling loud things. Stupid things. The flickers from the crack pipes were random and scattered like fireflies. My migraine was back.

Carlos sat alone, dead center under the lamp, his eye sockets chiseled into shadows by the light.

"Hi, guy. It's earlier than it must feel," I said.

"It feels like dark. That's all." He didn't even look up.

"It's only nine o'clock."

Carlos just shrugged.

"I could tell you about the fairies," I said. His shoulders started toward me while his head remained aloof and socket-eyed. He was just excited, but it was a repulsive insect movement in that light. I closed my eyes to give time for the image to shiver away under the flickers. When I opened them, he was a skull grinning like a *Día de los Muertos* pastry. I sat down beside him under the lamp.

"This is where they come. This light, this place. The fairies only come here," I said. He moved closer to me on the curb, the bone of his knee touching mine.

"They are drawn to a special boy," he said.

"Yes, I think so. We can only guess these things, remember." The ember of my cigarette glowed like lava in the grey as I took a drag. "They don't like to be seen at all."

"But you can see them. Only at night. Only here."

"Uh-huh. I may be the only one who can," I said.

"What are they telling you right now, Rose?"

I looked to his bedroom window across the veil of smoke and the cruel flickers of light, to the spot in the glass he had rubbed clean to gaze away from his life. The fairies were there. They were always there. They were screeching. Some tore at their faces — distorted faces like gargoyles in the architecture — each strobe of light catching them in a new ghoulish posture.

Gone were the flower fairies and fireflies with cherub faces, gone for a long time now. But I could never tell Carlos that. "They still want you back, they say."

"They switched me as a baby. My parents aren't really mine."

I nodded. "That's what fairies do."

"I always knew it, you know. I always knew it."

I patted his knee and stubbed out my cigarette. "Always remember you're a special boy, Carlos. A chosen boy. You aren't really from this place."

Beaming, proud cheeks softened the skeleton shadows of his face. I didn't look back to the window to see what the fairies thought of his happiness. They only existed under the flicker of this light, and Carlos would leave from here.

Carlos had to get away from this place some day.

Fireflies

By Sage Collins

When we were in the hospital, right before Troy woke up, I swear I saw his spirit, glowing like an iridescent firefly over his bandaged head. But when I blinked, it was gone. Then, he blinked too, waking up for the first time since the accident.

***

Our suite is dark when I walk in and take off my shoes. We came to this inn to let Troy recover from the TBI — that's traumatic brain injury. Mom's sister, Aunt Sonya, runs the inn. It's right up the road from the San Diego Wild Animal Park, in between the farms for Christmas trees and emus. There's usually not much more rain here than in Arizona, where our apartment is and where Dad is still home working. Only, this week the rain has been endless.

The inn has a suite ready-made with handicap equipment, unlike home, plus we're on the first floor here. Troy has trouble with stairs.

That means he can't roam upstairs at night with me. Which means he doesn't know about the ghost.

When I enter our suite, depressed by the rainstorm outside, Troy's watching television in the dark. I don't know if he's processing the football game. I peek into Mom's bedroom, where she's stretched out on her bed, her eyes covered by her hand. At first, I needed to be with Troy if she wasn't, so I babysat him at night while she slept or if she had to leave him. Now she trusts the television to babysit him. And she sleeps when he sleeps. At least they're both getting some.

As I draw closer, I realize that Troy is sobbing. He's clutching the remote between both hands. He looks like he's praying to the football gods with his head bowed over the remote.

I sit next to him and put my hand on his back. "What's wrong?"

He holds out the remote like he's presenting a gift. "Make it work."

I've shown him about twenty times how to use it, but the thing about the TBI is that Troy won't necessarily retain that knowledge. The remote is full of buttons, all with their own names and colors, but it's too much to figure out. Sometimes it's too much for people to figure out when their brains aren't swelling.

"What do you want to watch?" I study the remote with unfocused eyes to see if I can understand what it's like to not understand what the buttons do.

"There was something..." His eyes wander past me to the sliding glass windows that lead to our water-logged patio, and they stay there.

I put the remote down. I'd rather be outside too. "When the rain stops, I'll take you out."

"Not now?"

"Mom would worry if you got all wet."

Too bad we don't have an umbrella.

"Can you keep watching football while I find an umbrella?"

His eyes flick to the game, still on, where a player scored a few seconds earlier. Scenes of people cheering flicker on the screen, never halting more than a second. Who has the attention span for longer? Troy grins at me as if he saw the play and is excited by it. I lift my hand to touch his mouth, but I pull it back in the end.

The last time I had seen that toothy grin was my birthday a few weeks ago. Troy handed me a present before he dropped me off at middle school.

I wish I knew what Troy felt when he created the wooden box inside the green wrapping paper. The lid was made of a lighter-colored wood than the bottom. Carved on the center of the lid was a lonely bug with a big, round tail, three small lines bursting out from it. A firefly, all lit up.

Fireflies are my favorite insect. They have so much promise, lighting up as they fly towards the heavens. In Japan, fireflies are thought to be souls of soldiers going to Heaven. Mayans thought they had the light of the stars. It's a romantic bug as long as you don't look too closely at it.

I haven't touched that box since we arrived in San Diego. After falling in love with his high school shop class, Troy wanted to become a carpenter, to open a store one day with furniture he had made. I told him I'd run the cash register while he formed chairs and tables and bed frames, but I don't know if that's possible now.

He's not paying attention to me anymore. The game has caught his interest again. I don't know whether he'll care if I get an umbrella, but I put on my slippers and go out in search of one.

Maya, the cleaning lady, was in the lobby when I escaped the rain earlier, but now she's gone. Sometimes I wonder if she's a figment of my imagination. I take the first few stairs and run my finger along the railing. Nope, my finger comes out clean, so she really was here dusting things.

I shift my weight, and the whole stairwell echoes with the resulting creak. I don't know how the guests on the second floor sleep when every person who goes upstairs must make such a racket.

When every step I take upstairs in the middle of the night makes such a racket.

I wander up, keeping my eyes on the painting at the top of the stairwell. A girl about my age wears a frilly, pink dress that's far too old for her and her hair up in a bunch of curls. She doesn't smile as she gazes straight ahead, daring guests to approach her. I picture her as the ghost. She's waiting for someone to solve her mystery.

Aunt Sonya says there is no ghost or mystery. That doesn't explain how I can feel her when I'm upstairs at night or how I can hear her above the second floor, walking around. It's a shame I can't see her.

Sometimes I think it's only a matter of changing how our brains think about things. All we can see is what we've been trained to see.

Maya is working in one of the empty suites upstairs. I walk in and sit on the arm of the suite's couch, watching. She takes out a fresh sponge to wash the bathroom vanity. Water from the faucet pours into it, and the sponge swells up. Like Troy's brain.

When he hit the edge of the pool, his brain began to swell against the side of his skull. That's what causes all the problems. The brain gets overcrowded and can't work right, so the area that's swelled and all squished against the side—like Maya is squishing the sponge against the sink now—doesn't let his thoughts go through like they're supposed to. He can't think right. Eventually two things happen. The best one is that the swelling goes down and lets thoughts go through the brain the right way.

But some parts of the brain might never work right even after the swelling goes down. They die. So he has to train himself to find new ways to think. His thoughts have to travel in a different direction in his brain.

If not, he'll be a lot like he is now, forever.

"What are you looking for?" Maya says, wringing out the sponge in her hands. I wince. Troy's brain doesn't need that kind of abuse.

"I need an umbrella."

"Do I look like I'm made of umbrellas? Go find your aunt. Or ask Mrs. Kinomoto. She seems like the type that would have an umbrella."

Mrs. Kinomoto has everything.

"Thank you." I leave for the end of the hall where Mrs. Kinomoto is staying. I knock.

She answers the door, her black hair up in curlers. "Oh, Fiona-chan."

I bow. "Kinomoto-san." The honorifics are a private joke between us. Just before we became friends, Mom first trusted Troy with the television. He was watching an old kung-fu movie, and I joined him for a while. When I asked Mrs. Kinomoto about the "-san" used in the movie, she was delighted to tell me about honor and respect in Japan. It became a game. We pretend like she is my master and I'm her student. The curlers don't lower her status. "I must request your assistance."

She smiles at me. "What can I do for you?"

"I seek an umbrella. Can you help?" I bow again. There's lots of bowing.

She opens her door wide to let me in. She's made a home for herself here. Her walls are covered in pictures and paintings and knickknacks, collected from all over the world. Her son was in the navy and sent her a souvenir from every port. She says the plate on her wall came from Spain. A painting of the ocean from China. A piece of jade hangs from a cord on the wall. Peru, she told me the other day.

"What's this one?" I pick up a small, wood carving off her bookcase. It's like something Troy would've carved. It's a small cylindrical box with an eight-point star carved onto the top. I try to twist the lid off of it, but it doesn't budge.

"That doesn't open, Fiona-chan. But you'd be peeking into an old woman's secrets if it did, wouldn't you?"

"Oh." I put it down and search my brain for the right thing to say in this game of ours.

I change how my thoughts go.

"Most humble apologies." I say, as if following a script. Maybe for that kung-fu movie. "I meant no disrespect." I bow.

She laughs.

"How's this umbrella?" She hands me a long, pink umbrella with a curved handle.

I thank her with another bow and make a gracious exit. I swing the umbrella by its handle around my finger, like it's a pendulum counting down to an undetermined time. Maybe the time until Troy recovers. Or the time until the ghost girl's mystery is solved.

I stop to the left of the stairs and gaze up at her. It's weird how her eyes still focus on me even though they were pointed down the steps just a few minutes ago.

I follow the path her eyes made earlier and go down to my suite.

Troy is asleep in our room. Guess he's not going outside after all. I lay his quilt over him, and he immediately gathers it in his arms and hugs its soft texture against his face.

When I was little, he'd sit beside me when I was sick and tell me a story. I'd snuggle under the blanket and listen until I fell asleep.

I'm out of stories.

***

What happened to Troy is an exercise in waiting. We waited for him to wake up, now we're waiting for him to get better. This part is much longer than the first, but both seem infinite compared to the time it took for it to all crash down on us.

Troy crashed down on us.

Zero point three inches. That's the average precipitation in May in Tempe. It was raining that day. Troy was trying a daredevil stunt at a friend's party. He slipped in the rain, and his head hit the edge of the concrete as the rest of his body fell into the pool, dragging his banged-up head with it. For a full minute he stayed under, breathing in chlorinated water before someone jumped in and pulled him out.

His head was all bandaged by the time I saw him, so I never saw the wound that destroyed the brother I knew. I saw him sleep for two days while my mother prayed, clasping his hands in hers any time he wasn't getting an MRI. I sat beside her with my hand on her back when she slept. I didn't speak, I just watched Troy until he opened his eyes.

I barely sleep now. It's okay. The darkness doesn't bother me.

***

The candle is flickering because the oxygen keeps disappearing from the room. I watch the flame, mesmerized as it dances around. Troy breathes steadily, not bothered by the candlelight or the oxygen depletion.

Sometimes our bedroom is like this. The air gets all sucked into a giant, invisible vortex, and I have trouble finding it. The TBI must shield Troy from its effects.

I lit the candle to monitor the situation.

Troy faces the ceiling as he sleeps, and the shadow on the wall is that of his face. When the candle was steady, his nose looked like a mountain. Now the shadow is a stormy sea, a looming wave passing back and forth on the wall.

I blow out the candle and leave the room.

The floor creaks with every step, but neither Troy nor Mom have woken up any other time I've crept out of our suite. I trap my fuzzy socks in my slippers, and they muffle the sound once I step outside.

The hall is completely black, but it's straight, and I've walked it enough to follow it in the dark. I keep my hand on the wall, just in case, until I'm in the lobby again.

Here, the frosted glass of the door's window lets in an orange globe of a street lamp. It reminds me of the ball of light that hovered over Troy that one night.

It's better to search for the ghost at night. I keep my eyes trained on the painting until I reach the top of the stairs. All I can see are the bits of white, the girl staring down at me with blank, black eyes. I stare back at her. I thought it was her daring me, but maybe she's the one who needs the dare. Maybe it's the way to make her appear.

There's a creak from above me. I cock my head so my ear is pointed to the ceiling and listen. *Creak creak creak.* I don't know why people think ghosts float around without feet. People die with their feet intact — at least usually. Why would their feet be left behind in the afterlife?

This ghost definitely has feet. I follow her footsteps above me down the hall. Aunt Sonya says that there's an attic, but access to it has been blocked for ages. She must be there, trapped.

The creaking stops, and so do I. My hand reaches out and finds the outer wall just a foot away. She would have me walk head-on into the wall.

She disappeared into the wall.

I feel around the bricks, but there doesn't seem to be anything special about them. I stand there a long while, searching and listening, but there's no more creaking, no more signs. I've lost her.

Back in bed, after I've given up, I stare at the window over me. A bit of night sky sneaks past the clouds, a small hole in the darkness where stars can shine through. The hole is shaped like a brain, the stars, bits of thought waiting to be processed. I watch them, unblinking, until my eyes begin to water, and suddenly they're shimmering before me. They move quickly, like fireflies rising to Heaven. Like thoughts firing through the brain.

I close my eyes. Thoughts light up and fly through my own brain. I send them in another direction. I reshape my brain. I will see the ghost tomorrow, if I can find a new way to think.

I push past the part of my brain that's broken and won't let me see her.

Troy sleeps soundly, oblivious to my transformation.

***

The next morning, when I look out the front window of our suite to assess the rain, I see a new car at the top of the long, winding driveway. A family full of girls — at least one my age — is rushing between the inn and the car. Finally! Someone to hang out with other than adults and my brother. I rush with the family, taking the stairs two at a time to get to the second floor.

The door to 206 is open. A woman bustles past me, her arms full of luggage. She doesn't look at me. Inside, I can see three girls. Two are younger than me. Elementary kids. One girl looks about my age, maybe older, maybe just taller. She's wearing a red-and-gray-striped hoodie. Her dark hair hangs down in shiny waves. A pair of thick-rimmed glasses look odd sitting on her button nose. She snatches them off her face when she catches me peeking in the door.

"Who are you?" Her mouth makes the "who" with a small O, but the size doesn't match the tone of her accusing words.

"Fiona Hartwell. I'm staying here too."

She lowers her little nose at me, and I feel like a bug pestering her. Her sisters, the middle one who has similar glasses on a similar nose and the little one who has her black hair up in pigtails, have different expressions. More of wonder than of judgment.

"I thought I could show you around. I know some interesting places."

"No thanks." She turns away and picks up the television remote. Her sisters watch her, then turn their eyes to the television, except when they're sneaking glances at me.

"I could tell you about the ghost."

"The ghost?" the little one squeals.

A boy who also looks my age, wearing a brown Padres ball cap over his hair, a pair of torn jeans, and a plain blue t-shirt, peeks his head out of a bedroom. I hadn't even noticed him until now. "A ghost?"

The older girl turns and glares at me. "Stop scaring little kids." She stomps over to the door. I realize now that she's even taller than I thought, a head taller than me. Her looking down at me is more pronounced up close. "Goodbye."

She shuts the door in my face. I stagger back a bit, surprised by her abrasiveness. I go over my words carefully, but they weren't confrontational. They were just an offer to tour the inn.

But the ghost . . . perhaps I should keep her a secret. Aunt Sonya pushes aside any reference to her. The older sister seemed antagonistic about her. The littlest sister, frightened.

The ghost doesn't scare me. She never has. I just want to see her.

I don't hear the door open or his footsteps, but suddenly the boy from the room catches up to me.

"Hey, don't leave."

I turn to him. His ball cap completely hides his hair. I want to pull it off and check to make sure he has some.

"Nobody wants me there." I study his face. Cool blue eyes speckled with golden brown meet mine. His face is thin, pale, and pointed.

I cock my head toward room 206. "Are they okay with you being with me? Seems like Big Sister was the boss."

"Not of me." He looks over his shoulder at the door. "Will you tell me about the ghost?"

I point to the painting. "I think it's her."

"Her?"

I nod. "I can hear her walking at night. She's trapped here. Last night she walked right up to a wall and stopped." Without thinking about it, I've walked him to it. "This wall."

He gives me a hint of a smile and puts his hand up to the wall. "Maybe the ghost flew through the wall?"

"No," I say, exasperated. "She's trapped. We have to figure out her mystery and untrap her."

"What's her mystery?"

"If I knew that, everything would be solved, wouldn't it? That's what she's waiting for, obviously. Someone to set her free."

"You've . . . thought about this a lot, huh?" He wrinkles his nose up. "Sounds like you think you know a lot about it."

24

He makes it sound like I'm a little insane. "You don't believe in ghosts, do you? Why did you follow me?"

"I believe in ghosts. I just think that looking for a mystery that probably isn't there is kinda silly." He steps away from the wall, his hand lingering on it just a second longer before he pulls it away. "You should find your ghost and ask her what she wants. If it was me, I'd want you to do that first before you go getting all guessey on me and try a billion things that don't help me. But that's me. Good luck." He shrugs and leaves.

***

But he's in the lobby when I escape the suite the next day. I didn't say good morning to Mom or to Troy. Troy didn't notice. Troy's always too trapped in his brain to really know what's going on. Hope it's not scary there.

"Boo," the boy says.

I manage a small smile. "I'm not scared of you."

"You should be. I'm a scary boy."

"Yeah, a scary boy with no name."

He laughs, loud and obvious. I cringe a little, expecting the sound to echo around the lobby and down the hall, but it doesn't.

"I'm Luke. And you're Fiona. You said it in the hotel room."

I nod. Now that we're introduced, I suppose I can let him tag along in my ghost hunt. If he wants. "You're here for the ghost, right?"

"Yes. For you and the ghost."

"It's harder in the day. I hear her at night."

"Did you hear her last night?"

"No . . . I didn't go out last night. I stayed in my room." I don't tell him it was to take care of Troy, who was having bad nightmares. I like having something separate from Troy for once.

"Huh. I wondered." That's all he says, then suddenly he's wandering up the stairs without me.

"Wait." I catch up to him. "Where are you going?"

"To the wall she walked through. That seems like the place to start, yeah?"

I'm not so sure about that. I've already looked at it, at night and in the day. I love the idea of pressing the right brick and having a secret passage open, but I've felt all around the wall, and not a single brick has given a hint of movement. There's nothing to move, no matter how much I might wish for the mystery of it.

When we reach the wall, I push each brick anyway.

"Nothing?" Luke asks.

"No," I say sadly. "This is a dead end."

"So what now?" he asks me.

"We should go outside and look for what's behind this wall."

His eyes widen, and he shakes his head. "I can't go outside!"

"What? Why not?"

"It's not allowed. I have to stay here."

"Okay," I say softly. He's so insistent. I wonder if his bossy sister has trapped him in here like my brother trapped me in my room last night? I'm still surprised she lets him come meet me, no matter what he says about her not being the boss of him.

"Then I guess the people here are our best bet," I say. "Mrs. Kinomoto has been here forever. And Maya works here so she probably knows stuff. But today's her day off."

Mrs. Kinomoto's room is across the hall from Luke's. I expect him to be nervous outside his suite, as if his sister will come yell at him for joining my ghost hunt.

"Mrs. Kinomoto and I pretend we're in Japan when I visit. We bow, and I call her Kinomoto-san, and she calls me Fiona-chan and everything is very formal. You don't have to play, but if you're going to make fun, don't come in."

Only after his quick promise, do I knock on Mrs. Kinomoto's door.

She opens it just enough to see it's me before opening it fully. "Ah, Fiona-chan, what can I do for you?"

I bow. "Kinomoto-san, your most humble student has a question for you. May I ask what you know about a ghost in the inn?"

"A ghost?" Her mouth curls into a smile, and she gestures us in. Luke follows me into the room, but sinks back into a wall after we do. He doesn't speak at all.

"Yes, has anyone you know of died here?"

She puts her hand to her mouth. "Oh, such a question. No, there haven't been any deaths here."

"Maybe before you lived here?"

"Maybe," she says.

Luke is studying the knickknacks and paintings in the room without moving, like he's overwhelmed. His eyes stop on one painting, and I glance up at it. It's not one I've ever noticed before, probably because it's so high up, but that's a shame because it's gorgeous.

I walk slowly towards it. A geisha stands centered in the painting. Her black hair is done up in a bun with a red hair clip holding it together. She wears a kimono of teal, with white and gold cranes decorating it. Her face is painted white, but is half-hidden behind a wooden fan with an intricate design of a vine and flowers etched into it.

Her eyes are painted with the most delighted expression — so that I can guess at the wonder in her hidden mouth — as they point to a firefly making its way up the painting, lit in a soft glow.

"Where did he get this one?" I ask, my voice hushed. I have forgotten about our game.

"From Japan. It was his last trip, and he went home to Japan and bought me that painting. He said it was the second most beautiful girl he had ever seen. But that he would bring the most beautiful girl home the next time he visited, and he would marry her. This was his promise to me that he would return with her."

"But he didn't," I whisper.

"He didn't. They sent him back to sea and left me with this painting."

The geisha was watching the firefly the way I would. I've only seen one firefly, since they don't like Arizona or Southern California very much. Troy and I were walking back to Dad's car after we went to the Maricopa County Fair. During his last game, Troy tossed some darts at some balloons and won me a goldfish, then we shared a funnel cake. Sugar was all over my face and hands and the goldfish bag, much to my dad's dismay when we reached the car. But before we got there, we walked along the parking lot fence together. I watched my fish, magnified by the curve of the bag.

Through the bag, there was a strange light. I lifted my head above the bag, but it was gone.

I gasped. "Did you see that?"

He nodded, his eyes searching. Finally, he pointed. "Wait for it."

An inch from his finger, the light came again, rose a little, then disappeared.

"That's a firefly. It must have traveled with the fair people. I've never seen one here before, but remember when I went camping with my troop? There were fireflies all over those mountains."

Fireflies all over . . . I longed to see that someday.

But even this one had disappeared.

I took Troy's sticky hand with my sticky hand, and we found the car.

I wish instead of powdered sugar all over my face, it had been painted white like this girl. I wish my hair had been elegant and not in a braid going down the back of my neck. I wish my clothes had been colorful, instead of the ratty, gray t-shirt I had worn that day. I wish I was worthy to share this experience with the geisha as she looks up and thinks, "Oh, a beautiful firefly."

Mrs. Kinomoto is smiling, but it's tinged with sadness. I'm suddenly embarrassed to be here, looking at her things, prying into her sorrow, asking about ghosts. "I am sorry, Kinomoto-san." I bow out of instinct. "We shouldn't bother you. I'll go."

"No, Fiona-chan. You don't bother me. It's nice, having someone who wants to hear about my son. Don't go."

But Luke and I are already leaving the room. I shake my head over and over.

All I can think is how she told me last week about fireflies in Japan.

They symbolize a soldier going to Heaven.

I leave Luke, claiming I'm too tired for ghost hunting today.

"We could go search outside tomorrow, if you want."

He shakes his head fiercely. Oh, right. He doesn't go outside. He's not *allowed*. Well, maybe I'll go anyway. I'll bring Troy because he wouldn't care if I searched for clues while I walked around outside with him.

I really am tired right now, though. Maybe I could actually get some sleep.

But Troy is right inside the door when I open it. He startles me, suddenly in my face.

"You should be sitting," I say. It took some time for him to relearn how, but he can stand and even walk fine now. But he usually stays sitting if he can help it. Walking exhausts him, especially with nobody else around.

"Wanted to see if I could do it."

"Do what?"

He grins, a big, sloppy expression that's left over from old Troy. "Walk around the room. An' I did. An' I look normal. So you don't have to be embarrassed," he says, squishing that last word all together. "You can walk me outside, an' I look normal."

He thinks I'm embarrassed to take him out.

"Oh, Troy, that's not why we haven't gone out yet," I say quickly. "Things just keep coming up, and I haven't gotten to it yet."

"Can we go now?"

I'm tired, and he has physical therapy soon, so I look for something to distract him and finally grab a bottle of water from the mini-fridge. "Now, you drink this." I twist the cap off the bottle and hand it to him. "And soon it's lunch. And then you have physical therapy. Tomorrow we'll go, I promise."

He holds the bottle awkwardly, like it's the wrong shape for his hand. Shaking a little, he brings it to his lips and lets the liquid flow out and into his mouth.

Almost immediately he begins to cough. The bottle falls to the ground, spilling out water, splash, glug.

His eyes are wide and panicky, and mine probably are too. I hit his back, helping him cough up any water that went down the wrong pipe.

He falls to his hands and knees, gasping for breath, while fat tears fall down his cheeks and mix with the spring water, contaminating its supposed purity.

Where the salt water meets the fresh water, that's an estuary. The ocean's not that far, I wonder if there's an estuary nearby, closer than a spring? So many different types of water in the world.

Troy needs to stop drowning.

I sit Troy down on his bed as soon as he can breathe and quickly look up at the skylight and all the rain to avoid his intense eyes, but the words spill from my mouth anyway. I tell him everything. I tell him about the ghost and my search for her and Luke and his sisters and Mrs. Kinomoto's son and the geisha and the firefly and the fireflies in his brain. I tell him everything I know, I talk until I don't have enough breath to talk anymore. My mouth is empty, and I have nothing more to say. It's his turn.

He's silent.

I glance at him. He's asleep, curled up in a ball with his clothes and shoes on, right where I sat him down on the bed.

I just poured my heart out to him, and it was nothing more than a bedtime story.

I tear out of the suite, out of the inn, out to the end of the endless driveway. Who cares about the rain? Who cares about whether Troy needs someone with him?

Who? Who?

Who cares about me?

"Who cares about Fiona?" I scream into the rain, down the hill, down the road, down to the Wild Animal Park. Some animal there, some bird maybe, will look up at my scream, will flutter its wings and wonder what caused it and if it should run. Whatever it is, it will be trapped because that's what they do in zoos, isn't it? Trap animals and make them stay in hotel rooms and be too scared to leave.

And I'm running back into the inn, my wet hair in my eyes and my water-logged clothing getting rain everywhere. Maya's going to kill me, but I don't care. I'm searching for someone, but it's not the ghost. It's Luke. I'm running up to his room, and I find him on the stairs instead. He's standing just below the painting and daring me with the same look on his face that she has.

Daring me to set him free.

"We're getting you out of here," I say before he can speak. "We're setting you free. This isn't a cage, you're not an animal. You're going free."

"Wait, what?"

I run up behind him and put my hands up to his back to push him gently down the stairs and out the door, but he's walking before I touch him, looking over his shoulder at me.

"Stop. What're you doing? Hold on."

I stop. I stare at him. I'm the one doing the daring now.

"You're going outside."

"I can't."

"Nobody can stop you. Nobody's between us and the door, see? Nothing can stop you, so we're going. Worst that happens is that you get yelled at, but that's later, that's not now. There's no hidden barrier, no bricks stopping you. You can leave."

He shakes his head. Slowly, he says, "I'm not trapped. And you're not running away."

I inhale. "That's . . . That's not what I'm doing."

He looks away. "Okay, fine. It's not. I'm still not going out."

"No, Luke. You have to be free. I'm freeing you and her and . . ."

His eyes meet mine. "And who else?"

I stand there, breathing, not answering.

"Who else, Fiona?"

I can't breathe, I'm right below the surface.

"You can't free him. You know, I saw your brother out with your mom last night. I know why you're running away. You can't fix him by stepping out a door or finding a ghost."

"I'm saving you. I'm saving her. I'm going to talk to your sister." I march up the stairs past him.

"No. Don't do that."

"She's not so scary." I remember how she grabbed her glasses off her nose when she saw me. Maybe she's more scared of me anyway.

"Fiona, don't."

I pause at the top of the stairs and look over my shoulder at him. He looks genuinely worried. "What can she do to you?"

"Nothing. Just leave her alone." He stands up, and I think he's going to yell, but instead his voice is hushed. "Please, Fiona. Stop pushing."

I head to the door. My hand is poised to knock.

"I'll go outside."

I halt.

"Now?"

He nods. He looks absolutely terrified.

"We'll go out and take the next bus to the beach, how about that?" I suggest.

He squeezes his eyes shut and nods.

He still has his eyes shut when we walk out the front door into the miraculous sunshine that's burned off the clouds since I ran in. It's as if he thinks that not seeing it means he's not really leaving. Once outside, though, he peeks open one eye, then the other. Huge smile then, and I have to wonder what he expected to happen when he left the inn.

I've taken one of the pamphlets at the front of the lobby with the bus schedule on it. I throw out my arms and soak in the sun while we wait the ten minutes it takes until the bus shows up to the stop at the bottom of the gravel driveway.

"What beach are we going to?" he asks me, as we ride across town.

I look at the schedule to see where the bus stops. "Torrey Pines State Beach."

Like either of us know one beach from another. Actually, I'm not sure if that's true. For all I know, Luke grew up on the beach. I realize I don't know anything about him.

"How long have you been in San Diego?" I ask.

"Forever," he sighs, staring out at the scenery.

"So, do you know if this is a good beach?"

He shrugs, then points towards the front of the bus, where I can see the beach come into view, blue sky meeting blue water with the single, thin line of the horizon marking the difference.

The bus drops us off at a staircase to the beach, but instead of going down, I run to the end of the parking lot and climb onto a large, flat rock overlooking the shore. I put my hand to my forehead, shielding my eyes and watching the ocean.

"Have you ever seen anything so beautiful?"

He's there at my side, shaking his head. "Were you going to climb rocks all day, or did you bring me to the beach?" He does his loud laugh, then beckons me to follow him down onto the sand below us.

We kick off our shoes and run down the stairs. The brown sand squishes between my toes, even more so when I reach the edge of the ocean. However, it only takes a few instances of stepping on sharp broken shells and imagining they're bits of broken bottles before I'm watching my feet leave impressions in the sand like I'm

Troy walking across the living room. I stand, watching them sink into the mud, further and further as each little wave reaches them then retreats.

I don't ever want to go back.

Luke has run into the water, not caring about his clothes getting soaked, I guess. I stay on the water's edge, content to get my feet wet and wondering how cold he must be out there.

A seagull flies down and tries to grab something on the beach a foot away from me. Then, I watch him spread his wings out and let the wind carry him away, only having to flap every so often to gain altitude.

He's free.

For this moment, so am I.

The wind is coming stronger, and I look at the sky and realize that dark clouds are making their way back over us. My brief reprieve from the rain seems to be coming to a close.

Luke runs back to me, a humongous grin plastered onto his face. "I never thought I'd get to come to the beach."

"Well, if you hadn't been so scared of your sister . . ."

He puts out his hand to stop me. "I was never scared of her. I just didn't want you to bring me up to her. Nuh uh, this is what I was scared of. All of this." He raises his arms out and spins around once. "Funny, huh?"

I don't laugh because I'm still trying to figure out what he was scared of.

His face falls just a bit, or maybe I miss the point where he suddenly grows serious. "I was scared to move on. To leave the inn. But you've shown me it can be better. You've shown me it can be paradise."

He's free.

He leans in close, and the specks in his eyes dance around. "Thank you, Fiona."

I close my eyes, and his lips touch mine, just a second, but it's nothing like I expected a kiss to be. It's as if a light breeze has brushed across my lips, leaving a hint of salty sea air upon them.

When I open my eyes, he's gone. How long did I stand there with my eyes closed? I look around for him. "Luke? Luke?" I turn around twice, but don't see him in the ocean or on the shore.

A movement catches my attention just above eye-level. With the backdrop of the dark gray clouds, I can see it more clearly, a small glow rising up and away from me. I cover my still-tingling mouth. Oh. A beautiful firefly. It's odd though. Fireflies usually glow in spurts as they rise up. This one is steady.

Oh. "You're free," I whisper to the little bug.

The firefly rises a bit further, then blinks out.

***

A candle casts its light across Troy's bed, painting his shadow on the wall. I sit next to him and pull the blankets so they're all around him. Then I tell him the story of a ghost who was so scared of the afterlife, he imprisoned himself, and how it took a girl to set him free. Then I tell him how the ghost floated away to Heaven like a firefly.

Troy smiles from this side of his dreams.

I stroke his hair and lie down next to him, whisper thanks for not leaving us that night in the hospital, promise to take him outside tomorrow.

I blow out the candle.

I sleep until morning.

"Crow" illustrated by Marina Lostetter

Crow

By Victoria Horsham

The local herds had been shrinking for weeks, with goatherds across the village complaining of lost livestock. Our fathers did what any pragmatic men would do and posted the second-born sons, the deformed and the bastards to guard the fields at night. Wolves and poachers had been trouble enough in the past, without risking favored sons or the heads of households.

As my father's third-born, and with a lame arm rendering me unfit for most farm work, I was sent out to guard our herd most nights. Before you pass judgement, you have to remember these were different times. I bore no grudges; I was young and stupid, and pleased with the chance to make my father proud.

Still, it was cold, damp, dull work. Hardly surprising that I was half-asleep when the dragon came, swooping from the night sky to land in our field.

I froze in place, sweat on my palm making my hand feel slick against the shaft of my spear.

The dragon was an oddly stunted creature; as much bird as lizard, no larger than a horse and with a scruffy, dusty appearance that reminded me of the crows up in the bell tower. The beast even moved like a crow, folding its leathery wings at its sides and stalking through the goat-cropped grass with its head bobbing back and forth.

I tensed to attack, but a lump in my throat and the spreading cold up my spine held me in place. Dragons were known to be fearsome beasts, cunning and cruel, and capable of roasting their victims alive. But weren't they also supposed to be massive, terrifying monstrosities? Could this be a runt? Did dragons produce runts? Would it burn me to nothing the moment I leapt to attack?

A doe, bloated with pregnancy, wandered from the herd to drink in the stream that passed through the field. The dragon tensed, and there was no more time for such cowardice.

I slid from my perch in the old olive tree and landed with a thump. The dragon turned, and I threw my spear with a shout. It raked the beast's side, skittering off its flank. A poor shot. I flinched then, expecting fiery death, but none came. Squawking its displeasure like a seagull chased off refuse, the dragon fled. My hands were shaking, even my good hand, and I slumped against the olive tree.

The bobbing light of a lantern appeared out from the direction of the farmhouse. My father had come out immediately after hearing the racket I'd made. My second brother, Rob, following behind him. No wolf corpse was waiting at my feet, and my father's frown told me all I needed to know about that. When I told him what I'd seen, I was thrashed for lying, and the spear was given to Rob, who "could be trusted to take this seriously". Rob, of course, gave me a shit-eating grin at that.. I protested, but it only earned me another clip about the ear for my trouble. I was dragged back to bed, scowling at Rob who waved back at me with the cocky self-assurance of a son who knows he's loved best.

I slept terribly, and awoke in a foul mood. No breakfast for me, my father insisted, until I learned my lesson. Mother looked at me with a mixture of pity and disappointment, but knew better than to argue over it. Rob teased me over my chores. A dragon? Then how had everyone else missed a huge, fiery beast all these nights? Oh, a little dragon, was it? Of course. And it looked like a crow? We've got names for those. Birds. Rob laughed at his own jokes and smirked at me, looking back to our father every time like a puppy seeking approval for harassing pigeons. All the while my face turned a deeper shade of purple and my bad arm twitched and shook with impotent fury.

That evening, I begged my father to let me guard the herd again, promising not to make up stories again. My father knew my pleading had less to do with being genuinely sorry and more to do with shutting up Rob, but he relented with the proviso that further nonsense would merit a sound thrashing and worse. I didn't care. This time, I intended to start the night out prepared.

Mother was already in bed by the time my father sent me out to guard, and Rob was busy trying to impress our elder brother, John, with his newly invented dragon jokes, so it was easy enough to pinch a side of smoked goat from the larder and the bridle from the hook by the door. I took the spear again, but picked up my slingshot as well; a perfect weapon for a one-armed hunter and something I could be far more accurate with in a pinch.

This time, I would be ready. I'd show them; see that grin wiped off Rob's face when I dragged a monster through the kitchen and dumped it on his bed. Father would have to be proud of me, then. I'd be a hero. A dragon slayer.

I wrapped myself in an unwashed blanket that stunk of goats and crouched beneath an overturned

45

barrow. Just like stalking rabbits, I told myself. Cold sweat on my back gave lie to that.

Hours passed. Bored, aching in the cramped hiding spot and damper than the night before with my stomach pressed against the grass, I began to feel very stupid. A dragon, indeed. I'd been half asleep the night before, who knows what I'd really seen. Even if it was something fantastic, why would it return here the next night with so many fields to choose from; fields which didn't contain shouting boys armed with spears? I was just about ready to give up when a faint shadow passed over the grass, and a pair of taloned feet landed softly just within my narrow field of view.

I stopped still, breath caught in my lungs, and stared. The dragon stalked about just out of sight of the goats, head cocked.

I'd been crouched there, forgetting to breathe, for some moments before I remembered the bait. I unwrapped the smoked meat and pushed it gently out from under the barrow with the butt of my spear. The dragon started, turned and eyed my gift suspiciously, head bobbing from side to side and eyes blinking dumbly. It sniffed the air from where it stood at first, but gradually inched closer, neck craning to try and get as close to the fragrant treat without actually getting near it. Eventually, when it stopped jumping at every rustling leaf and farting goat, the dragon snatched the meat and, settling on its haunches, began to eat.

I was out from under that barrow in a second and slung a rock from my sling before the dragon had a chance to react. Hitting it squarely in the jaw, my rock sent the beast's head snapping back, disoriented. Then I was on it, wrapping my arms about its neck. The dragon squawked in shock, but I gripped it like grim death and it buckled under my weight. The dragon landed on its side and I straddled its neck, pulling the harness over its snout before it could snap at me.

It was only once I had the beast tethered to the barrow that I remembered to breathe again and realized how much I'd been shaking. My legs collapsed from under me, and I leant back against the barrow to catch my breath. No bobbing lantern-light or fatherly voice called out this time; neither I nor the dragon had made as much noise as I'd thought.

The dragon cawed and struggled against the harness, flapping its wings and trying, but failing, to take off. It was so weak; hollow-boned like a bird, and so light it hadn't even been able to stand up under my scrawny frame. I started to feel a little sorry for the beast, watching it pull dumbly against the harness, eyes rolling in animal panic.

If I called father, he'd kill it.

I blinked at that. What was I thinking? Father should kill it. I should kill it myself, and grab the glory and the pride. The village would do no less to a wolf if they'd caught one poaching goats, and they'd execute a man caught pinching livestock. I stood up and hoisted the spear. One quick thrust through the ribcage, and it would be done. It'd be easy, on something so thin.

Just one thrust. I tried and failed to swallow the lump in my throat. It'd hardly be the first time I'd killed an animal. I'd butchered pigs for old Nan in the farm across the road, who had no sons at all to tend her livestock, and I downed hares with my slingshot for the meat all the time. The dragon wasn't even impressive, really. Just a biggish, dumb bird-lizard that killed pregnant goats and got scared when a skinny boy startled it.

I took a step closer the dragon. Cornered and panicking, wings flapping futilely except for one that must have been hurt in the fall, it vomited.

My nose wrinkled at the stench. I thrust my spear into the smoked meat instead, and wrapped the reins around my lame wrist. Using the meat to tempt it, I led the dragon by fits and starts to the old cowshed at the edge of my father's land. The shed hadn't been used since the King had the genius idea to start taxing beef a generation ago, and the roof had caved in before I was born. Once the dragon was tethered securely, I dropped the meat in front of it and retreated out of sight.

The dragon took a while to calm down, but a pile of musty feed sacks made a decent enough seat, and I was content to sit and watch for a while. The more I watched that dragon, the more bird-like it appeared. It was oily black in colour, with leathery hide and patchy tufts of feathers about its face, skinny legs and wings. The beast stared about with large, dumb yellow bird eyes and chirruped with a muzzle that resembled a beak, albeit one with teeth. Scrawny, fitful and more pitiable than scary, it occurred to me that it might be just a baby. Baby birds often have bald spots, and it was certainly stupid in the way fledglings could be.

Maybe, I thought, it'd been abandoned by its mother. Maybe it was a runt, and had been pushed out of the nest by stronger, older siblings. Maybe some smirking hero, second-born and desperate to prove himself, had killed its mother in some glorious battle.

Whatever reason the dragon had come here for, it'd definitely been hurt in the fall with me; one wing hung half-open and dragging on the floor. My mind filled with ideas, then; nursing a baby monster back to health, training it, commanding it. Well, you can imagine the sort of things a boy might dream. Rob might try to compete with me for the rest of his life, but he'd never impress our father more than the son who tamed a dragon.

Presently, the dragon settled down and curled up on the floor to eat. I slumped in my seat, limbs suddenly heavy. It was tiring work, hunting dragons.

***

Dawn light and my father's voice calling for me woke me with a panic.

Startled by my sudden movement, the dragon squawked and pulled at its tethers. I stuttered and waved my hands desperately to shush it – as if it knew that wildly flapping hands meant "be calm" - while calling back to my father that I was just putting my spear away. I'd be out in a moment, I promised.

The dragon eventually shut up, I checked the reins to make sure they were secure and headed out. The side of goat was gone, bones and all, and I made a mental note to bring more meat and some water the next night.

Breakfast was already under way by the time I was in the kitchen and mother gave me a plateful along with a gentle pat on the shoulder. Good boy. Rob wolfed his food down like a boy half-starved, and was out the door before I got spoon to mouth. Some work was being offered hauling wood in town, and he meant to get there early to get ahead of the other boys. My father asked if I might be planning on heading out and earning some money for the family that day. Of course, he knew I couldn't do heavy labour with my arm, but there was always something needing doing in the village. I offered that I might do better to head out with the slingshot and try to bring in some meat for the table, since we'd lost goats. Really, I just needed a way to feed the dragon without mother noticing the loss of food in the larder.

I've always been good with the slingshot. I might be crippled, but I was quiet and fast on my feet, and my good arm was steady enough to ensure decent aim. That evening, I brought home two pigeons and three rabbits for the larder, which mother pronounced excellent before promising me a big slice of the game pie she'd make with them. Three more rabbits hung in a sack behind the old barn until I had time to bring them in for the dragon. It seemed a little less scared that night, and hungrier too, screeching at me like a baby bird begging its mother to regurgitate dinner and sniffing about the floor for more when it was done.

The next night I brought it trout from the stream, and the night after that a wild piglet, and the night after that a fox I'd caught skulking about by the hen house. The dragon gradually grew accustomed to its captivity and in time let me get close enough to splint its wing. After a few days I started training it to walk around the barn on a leash. Meanwhile, livestock losses in the village had stopped and the men congratulated their spare sons for scaring off the wolf-or-whatever that must have moved on.

As the dragon grew bigger, he shed more of his feathers in favor of sleek scales. In the barn, I taught him to sit, and lay down for food, and removed the splint to let him start stretching his wing again. I decided to call him Crow.

***

Of course, I couldn't keep hunting and fishing forever. Our larder was only so large and it wasn't much longer until my father started scolding me for "buggering off having fun all day" whilst my brothers worked so hard. Crippled arm or no, I had to help out with at least some chores around the farm.

The first night that Crow went without food, he just looked at me confused and fussed at me constantly to just give him dinner already. The second night, he refused to do what I said and kept straining at the leash to get away.

I tried shushing him and gently rubbing at his snout, but Crow was having none of it. He bucked and fidgeted, darting back from my hand. I reached for him again, and was rewarded with a snap. I pulled my arm back, cradling the hand, sucking air through my teeth. On further inspection it was just a graze, but it sure hurt like hell. Crow screeched, back arching and wings raised, backing away from me. This wasn't working.

Outside the barn, one of the goats had wandered from the herd and bleated at the night sky. I sighed, and picked up my spear.

My father blustered and shouted and grumbled when the next days herd count came up short, and made me and my brothers spend half a day searching for a lost goat that I knew we'd never find.

The night after that, old Nan lost a pig. The next night, Ginger Bill from across the lane smacked his head for being so daft as to forget to lock the door on his hen house, after three chickens turned up missing. Then, Jack Tanner lost a lamb.

Crow kept getting bigger and sleeker, and I even tried to ride him a couple of times, but he was still too small to bear my weight and his wing was still too weak to let him fly. Still, I started training him to wear a saddle, so he'd be used to it by the time he was big enough. He was starting to turn into a real beauty, especially once the last of his fluffy baby feathers fell out.

The men went back to grumbling over their pints about the bloody wolf coming back, and their second sons sat hunched and cold with spears and slings and axes in the fields. And every night I headed out after dark with an old grain sack and a kitchen knife. The wolf was more careful than before, only hunting in the fields kept by old folks without any sons, or where the boys were still young and tended to fall asleep.

One night, Crow belched in panic when a sudden noise startled him, and the tiny spark and puff of smoke almost set his tether on fire. It was but the work of a moment to throw my blanket over the rope to stamp out the flame. Not that I wasn't delighted, you understand. Crow was looking to turn into a real, scaly, fire-breathing dragon. I brought him extra meat the next night, and used the spare to try to train him to breathe fire on command, with limited success. The next morning, Rob asked me how I managed to burn my hand. I told him I messed up trying to light a fire to keep warm guarding the field, which made my father furious when he heard and earned me another thrashing. What good was it to announce myself to whatever wolf or poacher was bothering the fields?

More animals were lost in the fields, night after night. The men of the village thrashed their boys for falling asleep on the job, or strung bells and alarms along their fences, but the wolf snuck past every night regardless. Eventually, some of the men gave up on their useless boys and started guarding the fields themselves. Not that I knew at the time of course, so it was a huge surprise to me when I crept up behind Ginger Bill's barn and heard a cry of "Got you, you little bastard!".

I dropped the sack and knife, and ran for it. Bill wasn't so old, but he was half blind and weak in the knees, and nowhere near my match for speed. He wouldn't have been able to recognize what I was at night, let alone who, and he'd never catch me but oh boy, did he have a pair of lungs. I couldn't breathe for fear, running as fast as I could while all along the route lanterns were lit and men came running up their fields after Bill's shouts that something had been at his chickens again.

I ran straight back to the old barn, chest rasping and cold sweat clinging to my spine. They'd find out what I'd done. They'd find me and Crow. They'd kill Crow and hang me for a poacher. I took the harness off of Crow and started leading him out the back of the barn, my good arm reaching around his neck. He chirruped in greeting and nuzzled my hair as we walked. My legs wobbled, but I kept moving and recited the plan in my head. Get Crow away from the barn, pray his wing was healed enough to let him fly and pretend to have been out guarding all night.

I forgot that my father would have been guarding the field himself too, if the other men were. He saw me before I was even near the tree-line, calling out after to see what I had with me.

"What's that? What've you caught, boy?"

I panicked, and my panic started Crow up, who tried and failed to flap his wings to take off and fell, taking me with him. I landed heavily on his neck with a thump, my bad arm caught under him.

Ginger Bill, and Fred Thatcher, and John Weaver caught up with my father by then and all stopped short at the sight of a crippled boy wrestling a dragon on the ground. Oh, they whooped and cheered at that and called me brave, then panicked and came to help when a burst of immature flame from Crow's nostrils singed my eyebrows.

In a few seconds they were on Crow too, holding him roughly to the ground on all sides and keeping his head pressed to the floor with their boots as my father helped me up, pride and surprise in his eyes all at once.

I looked down at my hand, feeling the sudden weight of the axe as my father pressed it into my hand. Everyone was watching me, expectant, even my brothers John and Rob; staring with open mouths like a pair of fish gasping in the open air. Crow, squealing now like a panicked infant, strained under the weight of the men. Vomit speckling the side of his snout. His eyes stopped to focus on mine for a moment, and he let out a high, keening whine. Just a baby, after all.

My father laid a hand on my shoulder, and pressed me gently forward.

***

There was a big celebration in the village, the next day. Men in the pub called me "dragon slayer" and bought me pints even though I was just a lad. A couple of the girls giggled and whispered amongst themselves, and Pretty Enid dared Freckled Jenny to kiss me, which she did on the cheek before running squealing back to the other girls. Jack Tanner promised to make me a fine, dragon-hide coat, and old Nan said I should mount its skull on a staff so, wherever I went, people would know what I'd done. Everyone said I was a hero, and my father just beamed across the table at me, even when I got so drunk I fell off my stool and knocked over my pint.

I'm not so stupid I wanted to sabotage my own success, and I just kept grinning a smug, shit-eating grin at Rob, scowling at me from the door of the pub. He wasn't allowed in, our father said, since he was too young to drink, and he got a clip around the ear when he pointed out I was younger than him. I just sat and drank in their praise and let them all tell me how brave I was. A hero. The dragon slayer.

Gus

By Candace Petrik

Gus doesn't like chlorine but it's not my fault and I don't know how to fix it. It makes his tentacles shrivel and flinch. He seems mad that there isn't anywhere else, but we need the bathtub for later and if I put him in the washing machine Mom might accidentally kill him. I explain this to Gus while standing over the pool cover, leaning over so I can look through the gap in the canvas and see him churning in there, pushing angrily against the sides like he wants out.

I go back inside to the kitchen, leaning onto the bench with my elbows in the way that Mom hates.

"It's too cold for swimming."

Mom points outside, "Look at that sky and tell me that."

GUS BY CANDACE PETRIK

Dad says it looks windy.

"It is," I say. "A bit."

"He's scared of the cold, aren't you Parley?"

"Dad! I'm not scared," I don't like the way his mouth twitches, almost smiling. "I just don't wanna swim, ok?"

"You're going outside anyway," Mom says, wiping down the bench so I have to move. "Unless you want to help me mop."

Clara isn't home. If she were she'd march out there and rip the cover off, even though she mainly stretches out on the banana lounge and only jumps in and out of the pool for about a minute. She says I can play by myself.

"You're a retard if you don't know how."

***

Mom says it may seem quiet down at the storm water drain, but she once knew a little boy who was playing inside a concrete drain tunnel like the one near our house. It started raining when he was down there. He didn't hear it barreling down and flooding into the drains, hard like the force of being slapped. He got swept out to sea and was surrounded at all sides by water until he sank and sank, no matter how hard he struggled. He's dead now. So if Mom asks where Gus came from I'll have to make up a story and I'm not sure she'll believe it anyhow. I only play in the drain because you find cool stuff, like basketballs and tennis balls and bits of colored plastic that are kind of pretty but could be from anything. There's also lots of stuff like cans and plastic bottles and plastic bags and cartons and things that stink so bad like dirt does if you dig down too deep, releasing the smell of eggs. When I found Gus he was huddled in a pool, barely deep enough to do much but wade in. He was stretched out, tentacles going in every direction so he could suck up every bit of water.

"Hi."

He didn't say anything, and still hasn't. He just looked at me with one of his big eyes, blinking and red like the sun was hurting him. I had to use the wheelbarrow, and almost dropped him because he's so big and because he wrapped a leg around my shoulders, not tight enough to hurt but tight enough so I felt my arm start to go to sleep.

"Stop it, do you want to fall out?"

I was supposed to get a little brother but he died not long after he was born. He was going to be called Gus too. Angus Josiah. I was too young to remember what he looked like really well besides that he was blotchy and angry and wriggling, like everything outside stung. Mom says he would turn seven next week. Every year she knows how old he is, even if she doesn't always say so because Dad calls her 'morbid'. Which he says means

Gus By Candace Petrik

death-obsessed. But I'd say she was life-obsessed and forgets Gus never really did much but sleep a few nights in our house and cry. She won't have another brother for me, she says she tried that already and there are no second chances.

***

Gus is getting hungry, but when I ask what he likes to eat he just crawls and splashes in the pool some more. I decide to save him some of my dinner, the lamb that I don't like eating anyway. It's greasy and grey and comes from a baby sheep.

"You're weird," Clara says, when I put it into a serviette and say I want to eat it in my room. That I'm not hungry, but might be later when I'm doing my homework.

"Try to eat the carrots and beans, then," Mom orders. Dad doesn't talk, just forks bits of meat into his mouth and chews them more than he needs to, so they must be turned into a paste by the time he swallows.

"I think we should have a birthday party for him," I say after I have eaten a little of my veggies and become bored by how they taste of nothing but water, the steam rising from them when my fork sinks in.

"Whose birthday is it?" Clara asks. Mom gets up and starts clearing the table, even though we're not done.

"Gus," I say. "Mom says he's turning seven tomorrow."

"Don't be ridiculous," Dad barks. He's been very still all through dinner and the sudden blast of noise coming out of him makes me lean away.

"He's never gotten any kind of party," I say. "It's not fair. I've had them. Clara's had heaps."

"Gus doesn't get birthday parties," Dad says, like he finds even saying those words embarrassing. "Look Parley, I don't need to explain to you how upsetting this is. So we're not going to talk about it anymore. Am I understood?"

I look to Mom but she doesn't back me up, she just turns away and starts scraping the leftovers into the trash. I shove away from the table and go outside, taking the serviette of food with me.

Gus curls away from me when I approach the tank. I peel back the canvass a bit and watch him, floating on the other side of the pool. I feel bad that I haven't been able to make it nicer. That there are dead leaves and bugs and pool floaties in there, that there are pink and orange diving rings which bob as the water ripples

"Sorry if you don't like lamb either," I say. I empty out the serviette and it sinks slowly to the bottom, the sauce and oil floating off it like a trail of muck. Gus flies at it immediately, his tentacles slapping the water. He devours it with a mouth that looks like a cave full of sharp spikes.

***

Sometimes on her tired days, Mom will let me come and sit with her on the couch after she's watched an old movie that I find boring. I'm always home first after school. I can tell it's going to be a tired day because she won't be up at breakfast with us and Dad will say not to bother her. Mom isn't downstairs on the morning after I fed Gus my lamb dinner. When I come home in the afternoon she's under a woolen blanket in the living room.

"Feeling better, Mom?"

"Not much."

She turns off the TV like always and we sit there together, watching the fish tank because family time means no TV. The angelfish look goggle-eyed at me most of the time, swimming back and forth like they don't know how to belong in their small rectangle of glass. Because Dad won't be home for an hour and a half, Mom starts to tell stories about my brother. Dad's not allowed to know about this but he should. He can't just pretend Gus doesn't exist.

"Would he like swimming?" I ask.

"Well of course," Mom says, like that was too easy.

"What about collecting rocks and shells and having pet lizards?"

"He might, I think he'd prefer to collect matchbox cars though."

"Matchbox's are lame.'

'Then Gus doesn't have to share them with you."

"Would he be like a best friend or would be just be annoying?"

Mom makes sure I look her right in the face, "brothers are always the best of friends. You know your uncles, how close they are."

I do. But they always seem to be arguing or disagreeing about something, though never as badly as me and Clara. Clara slams her fist into my shoulder when I get in her way. Gus would never do that. If Clara tried to hit him I'd smack her right back I think, even though I never do anything when she hurts me. I don't even tell.

Mom leaves me for the kitchen, even though she doesn't need to cook. On her sick days Dad brings home Chinese food or gets pizza delivered. I frown when she abandons me alone on the couch. She says don't sulk.

'Start on your homework now, if you're bored.' She doesn't wait for me to argue back.

The angelfish are always moving. Pacing back and forth probably stops them from going crazy. Dad says there's something wrong with them, that tropical fish are usually 'placid' which I think means Dad's annoyed that they don't like the tank. They are supposed to sway back and forth like the weeds he planted in the pebbles. The weeds always look happy.

I grab Mom's empty coffee cup and stare at the fish. I can hear her in the other room opening drawers, dropping cutlery. She turns on the radio. Before she can come back I dip the cup into the tank, but the fish are fast. It takes me lots of goes before I catch one. It flips around in the cup because there's not enough room to move. Not enough water. I slide open the door to the backyard, hoping Gus is ok because I haven't even said hello yet. He is quiet inside the pool, like the weeds in the tank, barely moving when I push the canvas up.

"Are you all right?"

He won't say. I feel nervous, but the fish aren't happy anyway and Gus might die. I tip the cup into the pool. The angelfish doesn't really move, suddenly calm. I get a horrible, sick feeling watching it swim about like I've given it a present. I dunk my hand in with the cup, the water soaking up my sleeve, but I can't get the fish back inside. It doesn't trust me now. Gus trusts me. He coils his tentacles, shifting towards the fish. His mouth gapes, coming at it with a snap. A little piece of the fish bobs to the surface, pink and fleshy. A blob of blood ripples in the water and turns it the color of raspberry Kool-Aid. I take a step backwards, pulling the canvas lid over but my fingers don't work, take forever to do it.

Then I run. Water drips from my clothes onto the carpet in the living room.

***

Dad parks in the driveway, blocking Mom's car. I hear his work shoes clomping along the hallway and the loud thumping of him quickly climbing the stairs. He knocks on my door but opens it right after, without waiting.

"Hey Par, want to come outside for a spell?"

He is holding a cricket bat, a wicket, a ball. They're all sealed in a plastic packet, brand new for me.

"I don't like cricket, Dad."

He shakes his head like I've given the wrong answer in a quiz. "You've got to give new things a try."

"But they make us play it at school. It's slow. It's boring."

"Downstairs. We're having a hit."

It's almost dark out, the street lamps have even switched on. The paving in our backyard is uneven because of the pool, spilling water and making the ground swell. The wicket keeps tipping over by itself. Dad grabs it, slams it down with a bunch of swear words but this only makes it fall over more quickly.

"I'm cold."

"Stand right there and give the ball a whack, a bit of running will warm you up."

He bowls and I swing, but I miss and knock the wicket instead. Dad's eyes close, then open. His frown wrinkles his face like I did this on purpose. It's worse than when he tried to play football with me and I kept dropping it. He struggles with the wicket. I listen to the sounds of Gus moving about in the pool, getting worked up by the noise we've been making. I pretend not to hear, but Dad looks towards the sound, like it's something buzzing around his head.

"Come on, we'll have some dinner and give it another hit before bed. Whadaya say?" he tries to get a smile from me by prodding my shoulder playfully with the bat.

"Yeah, ok." But I can't smile if I don't want to smile.

Dad must smell it first, because he gives me a look like he wants an explanation.

Inside, the house smells like baking. He walks quickly, like he's rushing to put a fire out. He beats me into the kitchen. Mom is decorating a tea cake with passionfruit icing, the cake is still too warm and the icing starts to melt and trickle down the sides.

'What's wrong with you? The pizzas'll be delivered soon!'

Mom sticks the special birthday decorations on: a little ceramic bird, an angel with one wing chipped. Nobody ever remembers to buy new candles so we reuse the same pink and white speckled ones until they are stubs. She searches for matches.

"Shouldn't we wait for Clara to come home?" I say, but mom is busy with the cake, and Dad won't answer. "I don't feel like singing."

"Go to your room Parley," Dad orders.

"We have to make a wish." Mom lights them with great effort, a gust of air keeps snuffing them out. I go to help but Dad smacks the matches from my hands.

"What did I just say?"

Mom steps away from her masterpiece, smiling down at the candles like she produced them from the oven as well. Dad tries to push me out of the kitchen, I struggle against him.

"But it's his birthday, Dad."

Mom starts singing, her voice cracking and missing notes, going high and low at the wrong spots. Wobbling on "birthday" and "Gus". She finishes the song by herself, because I'm too afraid to join in and when she is done she looks at both of us calmly. Then she blows out the candles.

Dad sends me outside to play, even though it is past dinnertime and we didn't even get to cut the cake. I can see them through the glass door, but then Dad slides the curtains shut so I can only hear them yelling. Not in words but loud sounds, like he's put a curtain over that too. I sit on the steps and wait, but they don't stop anytime soon. The concrete is cold beneath me and I'm not wearing my sweater. Clara still isn't home, but Mom and Dad haven't asked after her. Gus is quiet, but when I walk up to the pool he starts splashing again, like he knows I'm there.

"I don't want to talk to you," I say. He splashes louder in response, I can hear it but don't want to pull the canvas away. I stand there waiting, for what I'm not sure. I think of how hard it will be taking him back to the storm water drain, how his slippery skin will feel like wet leather. I push the canvas back, hoping he has somehow disappeared. I don't even scream when I see Clara in there too, floating and bobbing like the pool toys. I only scream when she gasps, pushing out of the water as if suddenly waking, she scrambles towards me.

"Parley, you dumb-ass," is all she can manage, it sounds water-logged too.

She isn't even in her swimsuit, her school dress is soaked and her hair looks like a tangled bunch of weeds. She stumbles onto me as I help drag her out, one foot and then another onto the concrete. The weight of her is heavy, her legs unsteady.

"Gus," I glance at the pool, see him floating in there lifelessly. Clara swears at me, but she mumbles it, almost like she's talking about someone in another place. She leans on me, like I am the only thing keeping her legs from jutting out in the wrong way from under her. Her skin is the tinge of blue you go when you lose track of time, playing in the water. I examine her hand and she lets me hold it, gripping mine back tightly, her fingers are wrinkled. She coughs and coughs, leaning forward to throw up, but nothing comes out.

"Where's Mom and Dad?" she asks. I don't know how to tell her about Gus's birthday cake, how we went ahead and did it without her. I lead her to the back door without answering, half carrying her, half dragging. They're still arguing, I can hear Mom yelling that Dad doesn't understand her, that if he could just understand then maybe, maybe. I miss the rest because I slide open the door and they have to shut up, because they see Clara. And they see me.

"Daughter of the Void" illustrated by Puss in Boots

Daughter of the Void

By Fatihah Iman

Alya prayed in the cramped cabin. The plastic-alloy floor was cold beneath her forehead as she prostrated, and hard beneath her shins as she knelt. Brevan watched her from the bed.

"It's nice that you still pray," he said when she was done. "I like that about you."

There was nothing in his smile but warm honesty, but recently such comments only served to remind Alya of yet another thing they didn't have in common.

Brevan Delgardia lay on the bed and grinned at her, the earthy brown skin of his handsome face topped with an untamed 'fro of black hair. Oh yes. The hair.

Alya said nothing as she unwound the *dupata* from her head, the soft fabric of the scarf running through her hands like water. The rhythmic bass hum of the spaceship's engines vibrated through the floor of their guest cabin, and as Alya stood up it made her bare feet tingle. It was the ship's heartbeat.

"The spacewalk starts soon," she said, tucking the <u>dupata</u> away in her luggage. "We should head downstairs."

***

Sabra knelt to pray in her quarters. She was alone in the spacious family suite, a veiled figure in the middle of the hard floor, surrounded by scattered cushions and her children's discarded toys.

A huge window filled most of the ceiling above the warmly-lit space. Sabra looked up into swirls of pink and white dust, glowing softly in the virgin light of a newborn star. Her husband Hanif was at the helm, piloting their ship *Al Arizaana* past the brand new sun and through the cloud of cosmic dust from which it had emerged.

They had flown *Al Arizaana* together since they were married; their sons had been born in the void between stars. They were Cosilai, the pilot race, the people of the ships.

Hanif was waiting for her down on the bridge.

"Are the tourists ready?" Sabra asked.

"Saali is getting them together now." He smiled at her. "I don't think any of them have walked before."

Sabra smiled back. "I'll keep a close eye."

***

"My father spoke to me again before we left," Brevan said to Alya.

They stood in the ready room, pulling on spacesuits with the other tourists under the attentive watch of Half-Captain Sabra. A deckhand called Saali was helping out — probably a relative, if Alya knew anything about Cosilai. Families worked together on the ships.

"What did he want?" Alya asked.

"He wants me to settle down." Brevan laid his hand on hers, darker brown against her golden brown skin. "I think he's right. It's time I start thinking about the family business."

Alya's eyes flickered up to his wild hair. He'd shave that off when he went to work for the company — it was a Delgardia family tradition. You weren't a man until your head was shaved and your backside was behind a desk at Delgardia Cybotics. The business empire needed its stewards.

"You're ready for that now?" she asked.

"I think I am, yes," he said.

Alya frowned as she pulled on her spacesuit, hands working automatically. The delay was partly her doing. If it weren't for her, Brevan would be a bald businessman by now.

Across the room, Sabra fussed over the clueless tourists like a mother *chibrij* bird, her warm, reassuring smile calming nerves as she adjusted fastenings and checked safety lines. She had a maternal face; chocolate brown skin framed by the gold *dupata* firmly wrapped around her head and neck.

Alya thought of her own *dupata*, shoved away in the corner of her luggage like a shameful secret. She put a gloved hand on her hair. But that had been another reminder that she was different — and Brevan didn't like reminders. Especially not public ones.

***

Sabra ushered the tourists into the airlock. There were a lot of anxious grins behind the reinforced helmets, and they held their hand-jets awkwardly. Better to let them practice zero-g a little first.

"All right, we're going to try being weightless," she said. "Hold on tight!" The helmet coms carried her voice into everyone's suits. Voices came back through the speakers as the gravity went off — little gasps and nervous giggles.

One tourist stood out — a young woman who greeted zero-g with stoic, unaffected silence. She hadn't struggled with the spacesuit either. Hanif had been wrong — one of the tourists had clearly walked in space before.

***

The airlock opened, and the ship exhaled atmosphere and tourists. They panicked, predictably, but Half-Captain Sabra was doing a good job of looking after them.

Brevan wasn't one to show fear, and as he drifted out he tried to look as unperturbed as Alya. Apart from a little arm-flailing, he held up well.

Alya left him to it, and pulled herself around until she faced the ship's side, putting her hands and helmet against the metal. She'd been longing to do this ever since she came onboard.

A deep murmur came from within the hull; rising and falling in steady waves, making the helmet vibrate. Alya closed her eyes, feeling the heartbeat of the engines. *Al Arizaana*'s voice came through to her — air rushing through filters, mechanisms ticking over, the tremble of the ship's skin. The ship lived.

Brevan arrived beside her with a crash, careening into the hull. Alya caught him before he could bounce off again.

"I think I'm getting the hang of this!" His face behind the helmet lit up with excitement.

Alya smiled at him. "You're not doing too badly," she said. "Come on, I want to go way out."

She pushed off from the hull and sailed out into the dust cloud, leaving Brevan behind trying to figure out how to push off in the right direction.

Dust particles and rock fragments waltzed past her visor, like water droplets swirling in fog. Tiny crystal structures had fused together out of the rich mineral dust, and they caught the running lights of the ship, glinting as they tumbled over and over. Alya coasted out through the glittering cloud, miniature gems scattering from her helmet and suit. Only the gentle tug of her safety line brought her to a halt.

This part of the cloud was warm with nascent glows of fusion — the opening buds of a new star. The dance of the dust whispered of tiny gravitational pulls. Not strong enough — not yet — but soon. One day the very dust where Alya hung would burn bright in the belly of a star. This point in space would fall within the vast radius of the new sun; these rocks would melt in the furnace. She touched a tumbling crystal with a gloved hand, infinitely small compared to the star that would one day be.

People thought the void of space was empty and dead. But life was hiding out here in the dark.

The chatter on the shared coms dragged her from her contemplations. She pulled the trigger on her hand-jet, spinning herself gently around. The tourists were starting to get the hang of walking, but deep space still terrified them, and they clung to the ship's side like kids on the edge of a swimming pool. Sabra kept trying to encourage them to let go.

Brevan was doing better than the others. He'd conquered his nerves, set his vector and now coasted towards her, brandishing his hand-jet like a gun. She couldn't help grinning at his boyish pride.

"Do you like it?" he asked over the coms. Alya caught him around the waist as his enthusiastic drift threatened to shoot him right past her.

"It's wonderful," she said.

"We can do this whenever you want, you know," he went on. "Any time you like. I'll make it happen."

"Uh . . . Thanks."

It was an odd thing to say, given that she could make this happen on her own at a moment's notice. It wasn't as if Brevan could stop her.

A tiny bud of doubt opened in her mind.

"It's my gift to you," he went on. "I wanted to give you something, because I want to ask you something very important."

Alya blinked. The bud blossomed.

"Father's right. I need to settle down," Brevan said. "And . . . I want you to settle with me. I want you to marry me."

Alya stared at him. Suddenly the helmet felt too small and the airflow wasn't enough. Her mind raced.

"Will you marry me, Alya?" Brevan asked.

The chatter of the tourists stopped. They could all hear Brevan over the coms, and now they were waiting for Alya's answer. She couldn't speak.

She closed her eyes, her hands on her helmet. In the dark her breath rushed through the constricted space. She needed to be calm. She had to say something.

"Brevan," she said, looking up. "You know I love you. And it's been wonderful, being with you."

"What's the matter?" he asked. By the look on his face, he'd been expecting an immediate yes. He thought he'd solved all their differences by throwing a little money at the problem.

"It's just . . . I need to think about it. I'm not saying no! Just . . . it's a big decision, and I'd like some time to consider. Please?"

He stared at her. Hope drained from his face, replaced by hurt.

"But I brought you out here!" he said. "I did this to make you happy! Aren't you happy?"

"Yes, I'm happy, it's just . . ."

"So say yes!" Brevan gripped her arms. "We'll come out here whenever you want, I promise!"

"I just need to think," Alya pleaded. She looked into his dark eyes. "Please. Just let me think about it."

He let go of her arms abruptly.

"Fine. Take all the time you need."

Alya glanced back at the other tourists, now industriously pretending they hadn't heard anything. Brevan was already coasting back towards the ship. She drifted alone in the void.

***

Sabra wound up the feed lines and safety cables and put the helmets back on their shelves. The deep hum of the ship's heartbeat subtly changed as Hanif adjusted course and acceleration. Saali led the tourists away for dinner.

One tourist lingered, gazing wistfully back at the airlock — the young woman. Now there was a girl at home in deep space.

Hanif sat at the helm, bringing <u>Al Arizaana</u> round to put the dust in their wake and the new sun ahead of them once more. The children were playing giant robot space battles on the console.

"One of the tourists is an expert walker," Sabra said, kissing her husband and ruffling her sons' hair. "I think she's lived in space before."

"None of them said anything," Hanif replied.
"Which one?"

"The young woman who came with the Delgardia boy."

"There's an unlikely alliance," Hanif muttered.

Sabra left him on the bridge and headed up to the family rooms to change.

She smiled to herself as she pulled off her work tunic. Hanif wanted another child; a girl this time. She hadn't said anything yet, but she was almost certain she was pregnant. It would be her secret until she was sure.

Right now, the tree in the green-room needed her attention. Sabra walked barefoot through the ship's hallways, running her hands over the walls, the engines rumbling through the soles of her feet, the ship's voice at her fingertips.

***

Alya stood in the green-room and stared up at the tree.

She had come here for the plants, the lively smell of earth, the fresh drip-drip of water in the tanks, the scent of flowers. Being in the green-room always helped her think.

In truth, she had forgotten just how peaceful a green-room could be. Brevan had taken her to parks on El Iymus, and she'd lain on the grass and looked at the sky, but it just wasn't the same. There was something special about the way this tiny patch of life floated through the void of deep space, a flash of vibrant green in the dark.

Brevan. He'd spent two years trying to keep her on the ground.

Alya looked up at the tree. Then she leapt for the lowest branch, caught hold, swung herself up, and began to climb.

She pulled herself upwards through the cloud of fresh green leaves, pink blossoms bursting from the foliage like stars bursting into life. The rough branches grazed her hands and the twigs caught in her hair, but she pushed on, heading for the top. There, she lay panting on the wood, her heart racing. The great window above let in the eternal night of deep space, and she grinned up at the dark.

Life meant so much more on a spaceship. Outside, the vast emptiness of space stretched out for eternity, and even the mightiest sun was a lost speck of light. But here was a stolen patch of life and light and green, drifting defiantly through the dark in a tiny metal eggshell.

She'd done this so many times when she was younger. Lying in the leaves under the void was a cure for any problem. Well — it had been back then.

Alya sighed. She loved Brevan. She really did. And she knew why she was here. It was Brevan's way of saying "Look! I care about you and will spend lavish amounts of money making you happy!" But money couldn't fix the differences between them.

The door opened, and she sat up suddenly, clutching at the branches. Half-Captain Sabra had entered the green-room. She stood by the door, looking up through the cloud of leaves. Their eyes met.

"I'm so sorry," Alya began. "I didn't mean..."

"Stay," Sabra said. "It's all right. I'm not really surprised to see you here."

"You're not?"

"No," Sabra smiled. She wore a pretty, flowing dress, and her *dupata* was draped loosely over her dark hair.

"I'm going to prune the tree," she went on. "Would you like to help?"

Alya hesitated. "All right then," she said.

"I'm switching off the gravity. Hang on."

Weight disappeared suddenly, and Alya let herself float off the branch. Sabra drifted up, two cutters and a waste-basket in her hands.

They worked methodically, drifting through the branches, cutting back the dead twigs and leaves. Alya smiled as she worked, humming to herself as the fragile blossoms opened around her.

When they were through, they sat under the window and looked up at the stars.

"You are Cosilai," Sabra said. She spoke in Coslin, the language only the pilots knew. Alya blinked.

"Was it the spacewalk?" she asked eventually. She answered in Coslin — there didn't seem much point in pretending.

"Among other things," Sabra said. "You were born in space?"

"In the deeps," Alya said. "My parents are Cosilai from the *Arfal*. They still roam there."

"You're a little far from home, aren't you?"

Alya looked into her maternal face. "I stayed world-side for Brevan. People tell me I'm crazy, but I really do love him."

"You love him so much you gave up being Cosilai for him?"

"I haven't given it up," Alya replied. But she would. If she married Brevan, she'd be a world-side wife — no more trips out into the void. A Delgardia wife couldn't run off to pilot spaceships whenever the mood took her.

"Do you think I should marry him?" she blurted. She looked desperately at Sabra.

"How can I tell you that?" the older woman said.

"Please. If I was your daughter, what would you say to me? I have no idea what to do."

Sabra looked at her for a long time, and sighed.

"My mother always told me that no man is worth giving up the sky over," she said kindly. "Could you marry him and live on a ship?"

"No," Alya said dejectedly. "He's Delgardia. His father wants him to settle on El Iymus and work in the business. We'd live on the world."

Sabra's soft hand encircled hers, and Alya looked over into the older woman's face.

"You are Cosilai," Sabra said gently. "We live in the sky. You were born in the deeps. It is who we are."

"I know," Alya said.

"It is who *you* are. And you would give this up to be with him. You must be sure that it's worth it."

Alya stared up at the void. "I honestly don't know if it is," she whispered.

***

Alya found Brevan in the guest cabin, playing idly with his smart phone, his face blank. She announced her presence with a cough.

He glanced at her. "Oh. You're back."

"Uh . . . yes. I've been thinking."

"Well, at least you choose to humiliate me in private this time," Brevan said bitterly. He put down the phone and looked at her properly.

"That's hardly fair," Alya said. "You decided to propose to me in front of everyone. You could've done that privately."

"I didn't expect you to blow me off like that!" Hurt and anger clouded his face.

"Really? You didn't expect it?" Alya asked. "You're asking me to give up a lot, Brevan."

"You'll be Delgardia. What could you possibly want that we couldn't buy for you?"

"This!" Alya gestured around her. "This life! You don't even understand it! You think you can buy me a holiday on a Cosilai cruise ship twice a year and I'll be happy to live on the world with you?"

"Oh, after two years of dating suddenly you don't want to live on the world anymore?"

"It was never permanent before!" Alya took a deep breath, trying to stop her hands from shaking.

Brevan took a step towards her. He gripped her arms, thunder on his face. "Marriage requires compromise," he said. His voice was firm. "I'm risking a lot, bringing an outsider into the family. People are already talking."

"But you're not giving anything up, are you?" Alya pulled away from him. "You'll get everything just the way you want it. But if I marry you, I'll never live in the sky again. Don't you get this?"

"Alya." He stepped towards her again, trying to close the distance that was opening up between them. "I love you. I want to show you a different life. Something better."

She shook her head, brushing off his reaching arms. "Nothing is better than this," she whispered. She met his gaze. "I'm sorry. I can't. I belong here. It was nice while it lasted, but you're not Cosilai." Her voice was stronger now. "You can't give me what I really want."

Brevan watched her above folded arms. "You really have been thinking."

"I'm sorry, Brevan. But it hasn't been right for a long time. Bringing me out here won't fix that."

***

Sabra sat on the floor with her husband and sipped sweet milk tea. The boys played on the wooden floor beneath the window. Stars shone pin sharp in the void.

Sabra smiled at Hanif through the steam rising from her tea mug. Her dark hair hung loose around her shoulders, her *dupata* discarded on the chair.

"*Habib*, I have something to tell you," she said. She touched his cheek with her hand. "I'm pregnant."

Hanif's surprise melted away into a grin of delight.

"A daughter this time?" he asked, hopefully.

She shrugged. "Allah knows best," she said.

Hanif put his arm around her, smiling into her hair.

"Could we take a trip out to the *Arfal*?" Sabra added.

"What for?"

"Just a feeling," Sabra smiled. "We might need to take someone home."

***

In the guest cabin, Brevan sat in front of the mirror and shaved his head. He'd found some clippers, and attacked the dark 'fro without remorse.

Like trimming off the dead wood, Alya thought as she watched from the doorway. She'd been given the cut as well.

Like every Delgardia, Brevan's skull was covered in viso-tattoos. Micro-filament implants lay beneath his dark skin like wire circuitry, white lights constantly moving along intricate lines. It was the mark of the Delgardia family. As the cloud of black hair fell away, the glittering lights emerged from hiding.

Brevan set down the clippers and ran his hands over his bare head. The white lines blinked and rippled. Delgardia's wayward son was ready to come home.

Alya turned her back on him, and wandered away down the corridors of *Al Arizaana*. The steady rumble of the engines vibrated through her bare feet, and made her fingers tingle as she ran her hands along the walls. At least the ship was still talking to her.

She made her way up to the helm, where Saali the deckhand was on duty.

"Sabra said I could come on the bridge," she said. She used Cosilin now, delighting in the way it rolled off her tongue. "My name is Alya de Valundro bint Haji, of the *Arfal* Cosilai."

The deckhand nodded at her. "Take a seat," he offered.

She hesitated behind the co-pilot's chair. Lights flickered on the instrument panels and the heads up display, framing the deep night beyond.

Alya ran her *dupata* through her hands, the soft fabric flowing like water through her fingers. The stars of the void winked at her, and she smiled back. She wound the *dupata* tight around her head and tucked it firmly in place, and sat down in the co-pilot's seat.

The void's wayward daughter was ready to come home.

PART 2
EXPLORATION

From Antardigus-7

By Timothy Power

From: Antardigus-7
To: Earth dwellers
Subject: Rift in s/t continuum

Sorry, all. A construction project on our end accidentally caused a rift in the space/time continuum on Earth at 8:765:045.5 Antardigus-7 time, which the best person we've got on the job says was either 3:15 or 12:45 am or 2:27 am/pm your EST. No one in the Antardigus-7 scientific community seems to know for sure. If you would be so good as to get back to us on that, we'd be grateful. We're writing a report, and we want to get it right.

We are delighted with your magical creatures that float on infinitesimally thin panes of colored light. They're coming through the rift on our end and we just can't get enough of them. What is your name for those, in your world? Let us know that, too.

***

From: Antardigus-7
To: Earth dwellers
Subject: Re: PLEASE ADVISE!!!

If it's any consolation, you're not alone on this one. Seven planetary systems have already had their ups and downs with the Zejikatic laser octopi. We weren't surprised to hear they were the first to take advantage of a fresh hunting ground. The news on the grapevine is that you were surprised, however, and for that we're truly sorry. We'd like to invite any survivors from the American Eastern Seaboard to accept a discount coupon for our fine holographic entertainment products, including the newly released X-Taticum Spreel!, which is a big favorite here. The individual game player requires seven thumbs. How many thumbs does the average human have? If you could get back to us about that as well, that would be great.

The shimmering creatures that float on colored light continue to delight. What a lovely planet Earth must be!

FROM ANTARDIGUS-7 BY TIMOTHY POWER

***

From: Antardigus-7
To: Earth dwellers
Subject: Re: FIX THIS!!!

Unfortunately, there's no tried-and-true solution to closing the rift. It's a case of theoretical versus practical methodology. But we feel we're getting closer. How are things on your end? A little less dire, we hope. Let us know. And don't forget about the coupons for our complimentary holographic entertainment products. Judging by the enthusiastic reaction it's getting around here, X-Taticum Spreel! is like no other seven-thumb sensory overload adventure you've ever experienced. It's enhanced with Betaloxic nitroid-D injection. Fun!

We'd still like to know what you call those shimmering creatures that float on colored light. They've got quite a few fans around here.

***

From: Antardigus-7
To: Earth dwellers
Subject: Re: Re: FIX THIS!!!

Well, this is embarrassing. Thirty or forty relentless predators with hypodermic fangs and an insatiable thirst for fresh blood just got through the rift. Our name for them is Swaqil. To be completely fair, they need the blood to nourish the eggs in the enormous hanging sacs they build from ultra-corrosive acids. We're sending a shipment of pesticide canisters your way. A few squirts should eradicate the typical nest. Just be sure to allow two hundred or so Earth "years" for the radiation to cool off before you come within fifty or so "miles" of the treatment site after every application.

Thanks for the Google URL. We're catching up on all things Earth. What an interesting name — "butterflies." We've identified seven species that have come through the rift over here. Our favorites so far are the Spicebush Swallowtail and the Baltimore Checkerspot. This just in! There is an unconfirmed sighting of a Queen Victoria Birdwing!

***

From: Antardigus-7
To: Earth dwellers
Subject: Re: CANISTER INSTRUCTIONS!!!

We cannot emphasize strongly enough that closing the rift is our number-one priority. However, we're going to be offline for a mega-tic or two. The Krylon command on Stubchoze-Ar-El-Mit-67 has challenged us to an intergalactic game of X-Taticum Spreel! and we're going to go all black-hole on their astronomy.

Butterflies are quite the rage here. There's talk of developing a new sensory overload program about them enhanced with Betaloxic nitroid-D injection. We'll keep you posted.

Sending you the manual for the pesticide canisters in an rtf file. It should really help out in your tactical assaults against the Swaqil. We'll get back to you just as soon as we've kicked some Stubchoze-Ar-El-Mit-67 butt.

***

From: Antardigus-7
To: Earth dwellers
Subject: Good news!

You're probably dying to know, but is there really any question about it? Antardigus-7 totally owns Stubchoze-Ar-El-Mit-67. The final score wasn't even close.

Also, we've fixed the rift! Yay! Although the chance of never seeing another variety of Swallowtail breaks our hearts. The Queen Victoria Birdwing turned out to be another Spicebush.

***

From: Antardigus-7
To: Earth dwellers

Subject: Correction

The good news is our wishes have been answered. Giant Swallowtails have been coming through the rift here in droves. The bad news is it's back to the drawing board for us. The rift didn't stay shut. Keep a lookout for colossal creatures that resemble a cross between your "praying mantis" and "dinosaur" because a few of them just slipped past us. We call them Umdux. One appeared ready to lay a clutch of eggs. Don't worry, not all of them hatch. But you can expect another five or six thousand of them in a couple of days or so.

Do you have any pesticide canisters left? You might want to try using it on these things too. Keep in mind they've got pretty short tempers, hence their scientific name here: Okkituli Quatarumdux. They communicate with powerful pheromones and any show of hostility on your part will likely send them into a destructive group frenzy. Their two-ton pincers can cause a bit of damage. So whatever you do, be careful.

Do you like frozen regyet? Our products division has come up with some wonderful new flavors. We're sending an assortment through the rift. It's the least we can do, considering that the Umdux wouldn't have gotten through if we had really been on the ball.

***

From: Antardigus-7
To: Earth dwellers
Subject: Pollen

As you doubtless know, longwing butterflies such as the Zebra butterfly are able to collect pollen from certain flowers with their proboscis and to break it down and absorb amino acids that contribute to their ability to survive, mate, and lay eggs.

We don't have a lot of blooming plants here in the Antardigus-7 system. In fact, none. If you could send ten or twenty tons of pollen-bearing flowers through the rift to us in appropriate garden containers, we'd be grateful. And our butterfly friends will thank you, too.

P.S. More pesticide containers are on the way. Sorry about the manual. The correct file is attached.

***

From: Antardigus-7
To: Earth dwellers

Subject: Re: Re: Pollen

Of course we understand. Please take our word for it. We had no idea Swaqil venom was so deadly to chlorophyll producers. Lesson learned. Fortunately for our butterfly friends we've already managed to synthesize a variety of pollen-bearing plants. Hopefully these will meet their dietary needs.

***

From: Antardigus-7
To: Earth dwellers

Subject: Good news (again!)

Our top guys on the job are 87.753% positive that the rift will heal itself in time, like all wounds, ha-ha! Fingers crossed. If their calculations are correct, expect total rift closure in 2500 or so Earth years, tops. Not long considering the big picture, galactic-wise. Could be worse.

Butterfly Spreel! is out. Is it unreasonable to hope human evolution leads to six more thumbs for you anytime soon?

***

From: Antardigus-7
To: Earth dwellers
Subject: Re. WTFWTFWTF?????

We realize the problem with the rift has been an inconvenience for you, to say the least, and we hope you accept our apology along with fifty more cases of frozen regyet. But "it's an ill wind that blows no good," as you put it. While your planet faces a few eons of existence as a sterile desert wasteland, lush, luxuriant gardens are sprouting up all over Antardigus-7. The latest is fifteen times bigger in size than your "Central Park" and features 5800 varieties of "roses." Breathtaking sights of natural beauty are a real treat for us.

Our butterflies are thriving. We've now added Brush-foots and Hairstreaks to our list of confirmed sightings (including Banded Peacocks and California Tortoiseshells) and eagerly await our first Metalmarks.

It's too bad it took an accident of catastrophic proportion to bring our two worlds closer together, but we couldn't be more thrilled about it. Let's stay in touch.

"Kiss of the Jade Fox" illustrated by Puss in Boots

Kiss of the Jade Fox

By K.L. Townsend

On the west winds Mei flew, dancing not on slippers of silk but with the worn boots belonging to her brother, Song. Any other day the ability to soar with the cranes would have filled her with the taste of freedom and promise, but today the wind spirit held back, cold and abrupt, matching the chill from her own heart.

Tonight everyone would remember her name. Tonight her brother would open his eyes and be human again. Tonight the Jade Fox kissed her last kiss.

Mei's breath caught in her throat as she glided over the forest canopies. She drifted until her feet brushed against the soft dirt at the base of Zhen Mountain. Once the spell broke, she gave thanks to the wind spirit and promised him a worthy sacrifice if she returned to her ancestral home. He gave a somber goodbye, though one filled with gratitude, before the air became still and quiet.

Mei surveyed Zhen Mountain. Aged and withered, the mountain buckled between its two brothers like an old man with a broken back. She hoped the mountain spirit slept. Mei had already charmed the wind spirits and didn't need to fight with the stubborn mountains as well.

She dusted off her hands and sighed. While thick leaves and branches obscured most of the mountainside, Mei discovered a long, vertical gap between the folds of rock. The mouth of the cave yawned into a lazy stretch, an invitation to enter.

She knew better than to sneak inside without testing the spirit.

Mei sucked in the crisp air. "I'm here!"

"Shh. They will hear you!"

Mei pressed her hand against the metal medallion. "Ow."

"Hush, Qiao. That is the point."

"Mad. You are mad. I should have stayed home."

Mei sighed. "It would have been a more peaceful trip."

"You're cruel. Very cruel."

Qiao would learn to deal with it. She always did.

After a three-month journey, Mei refused to go back because her adopted guardian spirit was lazy. She had traveled across the Seven Hills and the Ying Sea to reach the Zhen. She had promised both her mother and father she would save Song.

Mei took a deep breath as she unsheathed the Shanzhou, her brother's battle sword from his days in the Ling army. Blessed by each ancestor who had wielded the blade, the centuries old sword contained the collective power of their souls. Intricate calligraphy, including its owners' names, decorated the blade and hilt. The Shanzhou was Song's most treasured item.

She tested its weight. Despite carrying it for months, each day it grew heavier.

Shanzhou had never been meant for her. The sword was never meant to fit her hands, never meant to channel her will, never meant to carry her name.

Mei would save her brother no matter the price, even if she died nameless and without honor.

"Chen Mei?"

Mei straightened at the sound of her full name. "It's nothing, Qiao. Let's go."

She took measured steps toward the cave. One tap, two taps. The sword hummed as it hit the rock, but the mountain didn't awaken.

Thank the spirits.

"Are you ready?" Mei asked.

"No."

"We're going."

Taking a deep breath, Mei squeezed through the gaps in the rock.

Darkness blanketed the cave. As she crept inside, the black swallowed her whole until she couldn't tell right from left.

Steady. She had to stay steady. She had made it this far.

The distinct drip-drip of water startled the dark from its silence, while bats chittered near the ceiling. Her eyes watered. Mei covered her face as her nose started to burn.

"It smells," Qiao said. "Smells like bad eggs."

"I know."

Mei scooted closer to the wall. It ran to her left, wet and slick, but offered enough support.

"The cave is dark."

"Yes, Qiao. Caves tend to be dark."

"I hate the dark. It is always dark. I want to touch the sun again."

Mei shook her head. While she felt bad Qiao was trapped in a tiny prison, Mei had made a promise to her family first. She would save Song from the fox spirit before it consumed his entire soul. Once she saved him, she would help Qiao, as promised, even if it meant her own death.

"We're almost done," Mei said. "Maybe some light would help?"

A flutter rippled across Mei's breast as Qiao sighed. "Want. You only want from me."

Despite the protest, a pocket of warmth began to expand against her skin. Mei reached under her robes and pulled out the medallion. Its faint light grew, scattering the shadows to the cave's far corners. With the darkness muted, Mei examined the cavern.

The chamber was large and littered with stone ribbons. Some hung above, while others jutted from the floor, stretching toward the ceiling in long spirals. Beautiful and lethal.

Just like the Jade Fox.

"Song would have loved to explore this cave," Mei whispered. "He was always the adventurous one."

"You'll see him again. The Keepers of the East tell me so."

Mei bit her lip. Much could be inferred from the words of a fire spirit. Mei would see her brother again, but in what state? The last time she'd seen Song, he had been slinking around the village temple floor, growling, covered in his own filth. Maybe the fox spirits found it funny to toy with people, but Mei couldn't watch anymore. She couldn't go back to her brother if she failed.

Holding the medallion steady, Mei headed down the narrow path from the chamber. Each step crackled like broken glass. She fought the urge to sheath the sword to grab the walls. With the Jade Fox's lair within reach,

Mei didn't want to be caught unprepared. She had to push forward.

"This is bad," Qiao said. "I don't like it here."

"I don't like it, either."

"Then, let's go. Let's leave. Fly away."

Mei shook her head. "I'm going to save him."

"I know, I know. But I'm afraid for you."

Hearing Qiao's words helped ease some of Mei's anxiety, but not all. The Jade Fox's powers eclipsed the spells of her lesser kin. Her charm and intelligence outweighed Qiao's loyalty and her temporary companionship. Qiao's protective words wouldn't mean anything once Mei destroyed the Jade Fox. Not that it mattered. One day Qiao would leave. Mei was doing them both a favor.

"You miss home. I miss home. Home was nice," Qiao muttered as they pressed deeper down the winding path. "The East Sun always said hello. He gave me a stream."

"I'm happy for you."

"You don't sound happy. It was a nice stream, you know. I had my own fish."

Mei rolled her eyes. The fish story again.

"I had a village. I loved them. I always flew after the rains came. The elders would decorate shrines with my feathers."

"It must have been lovely."

"It was. One day I will show you."

"Hmm."

"I'm with you until the end, Chen Mei. To the end."

Mei said nothing. She tucked away Qiao's promise and stepped off the final stone.

The lower chamber was smaller than the first, but just as impressive. A white cedar stretched toward a hole in the ceiling, the room's only light source, while its roots dug into the rock. Rays of sunlight filtered through the branches that crisscrossed the opening, yet each beam seemed to find its way to the center.

The Jade Fox waited on her throne of dead leaves. She was beautiful, tall yet curvy, the same as all the other Lady Foxes, with centuries' old grace.

Mei shivered, the drops of sweat cooling her neck and back. The cold light gave no warmth, not even to the fox spirit. Mei stifled the urge to rub her arms.

"You've come for me."

Mei clenched her teeth. She had to remain strong.

"Have you come to kill me, little girl?" Her eyes twinkled under the light. "Perhaps a suicide mission?"

Qiao jerked. "Suicide? Chen Mei…"

"There is no honor in such a death," the Jade Fox said. "Foolish girl. I shall crush you."

"I have a proposition for you," Mei said. When the Jade Fox's gaze flitted to her chest, Mei grabbed the medallion and shoved it under her robes.

The Jade Fox tilted her head. "You've come to bargain with me? What could you have that I would want?"

"Anything you ask. Anything to save my brother."

The Jade Fox slid off her throne and glided across the cave floor. "I find desperation unappealing."

"Me too," whispered Qiao. "This wasn't part of the plan."

Mei ignored the faint whisper from the medallion and stayed focused on the Jade Fox. "It's a good deal, coming from me. You know I can always go deal with someone else." She started to retreat.

"Wait," came the fox's cool voice. "I have a deal for you."

"Chen Mei, this is bad," Qiao whispered. "Never deal with a fox."

Mei knew she was playing a dangerous game. As a child, her mother had warned about the wood spirits who claimed the weak, the reckless, and the young. Fox spirits, her mother had said, were the worst. Brilliant, cunning, and vindictive, they ravished people until nothing remained. Mei had learned about their false promises, their empty gifts, and their high price: a corrupted soul.

Not even escape through death awaited its victims.

"What are you offering?"

"I'll give you your brother back." The Jade Fox smiled and stroked Mei's cheek. "But I want you in exchange."

Mei shuttered at the Jade Fox's caress. Cold, but calming, it eased some of Mei's fears. New feelings awakened, including an urgent desire to be with the fox. Her touch held the promise of freedom. No more working in the rice fields. No longer would she be bound to the house. No longer would the villagers ignore her. Mei could be someone special.

Her chest shook as Qiao protested.

"Yes," whispered the Jade Fox. "Give to me. We'll be happy together."

Her mother's warnings faded. If Mei's name couldn't be on a single sword, it would be on a hundred temples. People would utter her name out of fear and respect. She wouldn't be a nameless face. She would never be forgotten.

She would be the Jade Fox.

A threaded breath escaped Mei's lips. "I — "

The medallion hummed, sending a warm ripple through her body. Rolling hills flashed appeared in her mind, undercut with the trickle from a lazy stream. Mei blinked. Qiao.

The medallion's hum morphed into a beat, strong and urgent.

Mei's mind snapped into focus.

"Well?" The Jade Fox stroked Mei's cheekbone once more before she withdrew.

A stab of longing struck Mei as the Jade Fox denied her touch. The beating from the medallion quickened, manic and fearful. Shanzhou grew heavier in hand.

Mei bowed her head and sighed. "Take me, Lady Fox. Call your sister from my brother and take me."

The Jade Fox licked her blood-red lips. "You take me willingly?"

Mei stared at the face the Jade Fox wore and wondered where she had lived, if she had ever been happy. Had she wanted a new life? Had she been tricked into giving away her soul? Had she sacrificed for someone she loved? Mei would never know the answers. The girl had long lost her light. For the new victims, including her brother, maybe there was hope. Mei had no future. Song did.

Mei glanced down at the sword that shouldn't be hers. There would be a heavy price, but Mei knew what she had to do.

"Yes."

"No!" Qiao cried. "Chen Mei!"

Her muffled pleas never escaped Mei's robes. The Jade Fox smiled, the promise of fresh blood pooling in her eyes. "I release your brother."

"Prove it to me."

The Jade Fox arched her eyebrows, but made no move. Mei tightened her grip on the Shanzhou. What if the Jade Fox didn't accept her terms? Mei would be a failure even in her final act.

Silence hung between them. Mei never took her gaze off the fox spirit. Qiao continued to protest, and while Mei appreciated her guardian's concern, this was something she had to do on her own.

The silence broke when the Jade Fox let out a curt laugh, which echoed through the chamber. "All right, young one. I'll give you what you want."

The Jade Fox licked her nail and dug the pointed tip into her arm. Crimson contrasted against her pale skin as the blood traveled in rivets down her wrist and fingers. Droplets spattered on the rocks beside her slippers.

As she kneeled before the spilled blood, the Jade Fox uttered a low, whispery chant into the pool. An image of a fox spirit rippled in the blood. Within it flickered a man's silhouette.

Song.

The silhouette twisted from a man to a fox to a man again. Around him danced his fox spirit, painted with a wicked grin. Both swirled together, red and black, as they struggled to stay together, to stay apart.

Mei reached for the blood. "Song."

A stream of vapor hissed from the pool. Mei jerked back as the fox spirit inside broke from her brother and evaporated into nothing. She bit back tears as Song's silhouette faded into the rocks.

"It's done."

"It could be a lie," Mei said, unable to shake the sense of dread over Song's fading image. Her mother's voice echoed in her mind: Never trust a fox spirit. Never.

"I cannot lie against my own blood. Your brother is free."

Mei narrowed her eyes. Spells sealed with blood were bound by truth. Not even a fox spirit could lie to its own essence. Still, Mei didn't trust the Jade Fox. She needed to take the risk.

She relaxed the grip on the sword and ignored the medallion burning under her robes. Qiao would understand soon enough. They all would understand, and she, the girl with the name no one would remember, would finally have done something important.

"Then take me as promised," Mei said.

The fox spirit slipped closer, her eyes dark. Mei's heart thundered. The fox would consume her soul and she would fall into madness. One kiss on the forehead to mark her. One kiss to seal the deal.

Mei bowed her head. The golden medallion slipped from her robes, dangling between them, as it should be.

The salt from her own sweat tasted bitter.

Come and take me, Mei thought as she stared at the ground. The Jade Fox's silk robes brushed against the medallion. *Come let us journey to the netherworld together.*

Qiao quivered. "I understand, Chen Mei. I understand. How sad you do not. I am here until the end."

Mei shook off Qiao's final words and squeezed her eyes shut as she accepted her fate, her final act. She tightened her grip around the Shanzhou. Neither of them would see the rising sun again.

The spirit's breath tickled her skin. Mei pulled the heavy sword back, the pointed tip angled at her hip. The sword bit at her hands, a warning not to use its power. She stood firm even as her fingers bled.

The Jade Fox planted cold lips on her forehead.

The gold medallion jerked forward and rammed itself against the fox spirit's chest.

"No! Qiao!"

The Jade Fox stumbled back and let out a wail that shook the chamber. Her porcelain face shattered as ribbons of light from the medallion streamed through her body. The more Qiao's fire mingled with the Jade Fox's icy skin, the more tormented her scream.

Mei stared, resisting the urge to drop her brother's sword to cover her ears. As the fox spirit's shriek persisted, Mei rose on shaky limbs and ripped the cord from her neck.

The medallion continued to burrow into the Jade Fox's chest until the light started to burn through the fox's borrowed body. The light cleaved her in two; the fox spirit erupted from its dried out husk. As the Jade Fox rose to the sky, she left behind the medallion in a pile of chalky ash.

Blood pounded at Mei's temples. She'd missed her chance to end this forever, but maybe she could at least keep her promise to Qiao. Biting back the pain that ripped through her arm from both the Shanzhou's weight and magic, she jammed the blade deep into its now softened center.

A jolt shot up Mei's right arm as the mixed magic from the medallion and sword attacked. Her skin bubbled and darkened. Her grip grew weak. She didn't care.

Mei held steady. The medallion split in four.

Qiao did not cry.

She buzzed with joy.

Through the split in the medallion came a reddish glow. Ruddy smoke chased the fox spirit in whorls. Mei scrambled away and pressed against the wall as Qiao escaped the medallion and took her rightful shape.

The fenghuang unfurled itself, a morning rose peeling open at first dawn. Each feather glistened, red and golden, chasing shadows from the deepest parts of the cave. The phoenix had risen.

The Jade Fox leapt toward the opening in the sky, her sleek black spirit no match for the fenghuang. In one swoop, Qiao blazed through the fox spirit and ripped her into charred black dust, which rained down on Mei and the cave floor.

Mei collapsed and dropped the Shanzhou, her right arm dead. The Jade Fox was defeated. No one would ever be taken by her kiss of death again. Once her sisters fled, Mei prayed their victims would shake off the madness and be free.

They were all free.

"Thank you." Qiao's voice boomed throughout the cave. She hovered in the middle of the chamber, her smoldering wings and tail feathers crowding the small room. Mei looked away for fear she would burn as well.

"I made a promise, both to you and my brother. I keep my promises." Mei swallowed hard, afraid to speak further.

"Ask it," Qiao said.

"Why?"

"Why not? Have you not learned, Chen Mei?"

"I was to free you, but not like this. When we died, you would be free."

"And you still do not listen?"

Mei stared at her useless arm.

"I am with you until the end. We travel the way together, not alone."

"I know. I just wanted to be — "

"Remembered. You do not need to die to be remembered. I will always remember you in my heart. Is that not enough?"

Mei started to think maybe it was.

"My brother?"

Qiao's wings flickered. "Shall we go see?"

Mei straightened, daring a glance at the fenghuang. "You will take me to see him?"

Qiao bowed her small head.

Mei's stomach fluttered with excitement. After searching for three long months, fighting water demons, dodging sky people, and bargaining with the winds and seas, she could return to her family and brother.

She didn't know whether Song had been healed or if it had been a trick. She didn't know if her parents would be angry or proud. None of it mattered. Mei wanted to go home.

Having her name engraved on the sword no longer meant anything. She jumped to her feet and used her good hand to slide the Shanzhou into its sheath. Time for the sword to return to its rightful owner. Her hunting days were over.

Using fabric torn from her robes, Mei made a makeshift sling and approached her guardian spirit. The red and white flames licked at Qiao's glowing center, and Mei hesitated.

She wouldn't be afraid.

Mei pushed her hand through the fire. The flames licked at her fingers, light and warm. She grabbed the fenghuang's thick talons and Qiao lifted her with ease, carrying her up towards the hole in the ceiling. The fire-lit feathers burned through the branches that blocked the opening, but remained a warm, comforting glow to Mei.

Qiao would always be her guardian spirit. Now and forever, wherever she may fly. Yes, Mei knew that now.

As they rose into the late afternoon sky, Qiao's voice echoed over Zhen Mountain. "You will never be forgotten. Your name might never grace a sword. It might never line a temple. But today, Chen Mei, I promise you will always be remembered."

In the morning song chanted by the fenghuang for centuries to come, she was.

Lipspeak

By Dedria A. Humphries Barker

The line outside the club stretched a city block or more, all the way back to where the Rasta guy banged on a set of newer looking drums. The percussive dented the late summer night. He swung his head on beat, sweeping his long thick locks across his shoulders. Waving a stick, he hailed the young women: the ones in mini dresses and thigh-high boots and the one in jeans and stilettos. The ones in the plunging sequined tops, leggings and booties. They all ignored him, contempt oozing for men they knew lusted to disrupt these careful presentations.

Yet, at the door of the club, the babes flirted with the two beefy bouncers, in case, under inspection, their IDs did not uphold the brag of their raccoon eyeliner. The

118

doormen admitted one after the one, up to the limit set by the fire marshal.

"And one more," the bigger of the two doormen muttered as he waved into the flashing strobe light five honeys begging to step across the threshold out of the mist blowing off the Detroit River.

The sparkles on their bare-naked flesh winked appreciation, but not seductively enough to capture Jeff's attention. Instead, he cocked his head to the open door of the Club. He seemed to be listening to a far-off cry. His hazel eyes narrowed in puzzlement.

"Hey, man, get over here," Jeff called to the third bouncer.

A slender man leaning on the edge of the building flicked his lit cigarette in the gutter.

Jeff continued, "I gotta round the inside."

***

From under the round crown of her black bowler hat Betina Smith checked herself out in the mirror. The curve of the brim echoed her perfect tru-black eyes, its crown concealing the nubs of her young dreadlocks. Dorothy Dandridge and Marilyn Monroe pouted in postcards stuck to corners of the mirror. Candy and eye shadow and other nightclub goodies in the African weave basket on the counter teased women through clear plastic baggies.

Music from the dance floor roared down the hall past the open rest room door, notes peeling off into the restroom like a locomotive onto a side rail. It was background noise to Bettina. She leaned over the sink, peering in the mirror, checking her lipstick. Perfume of the lavender and peppermint hand soap and scent-matching hand lotion wafting up from the counter tickled her nose. Certain lipstick colors — the ones Bettina always seemed to pick — darkened the soft fuzz above her upper lip. This soft mustache had irritated her older sister, impeccably-groomed Reynolds. She had given Bettina the flattering lipstick she wore tonight.

"Here girl," Reynolds had thrust a gleaming white tube toward Bettina, who turned it upside down to check the color name. Finding a date of expiration long past, she held it out for her sister to take back.

"Don't worry bout that," Reynolds had said, refusing. "It's still good."

The color name was scratched out, but when Bettina rolled the lipstick up it was a glittery gold, sparkling like Cristal champagne. It was pretty against her mocha skin, besides Bettina didn't like to cross Reynolds. It was just the two of them now.

Over the next few days Bettina had watched for chapping or other effects of expired chemicals on her lips, but there was none that she could see. Except her lip hair was no longer the focal point of her face. That had saddened Bettina. The shadow was sort of a family trademark. Reynolds didn't have one, but their mom had never disguised or eliminated hers.

Watching herself in the restroom mirror, Betina absently pulled the Cristal lipstick from her jacket pocket, uncapped and swiveled it up from the tube, dragged it over her lips. Betina pushed out her thickly coated, glittering bottom lip, dipping her head from side to side.

"Oh yeah," she cooed to herself. She was feeling pretty good; had quit beating herself up, and was more adjusted to her new job.

In the mirror another person entered the restroom. Bettina sharply shifted her focus.

"Oh god," she thought, "anybody but her."

Behind her Keisha scooted over the threshold of the bathroom on silver ankle-strap platforms. Darting straight for the john, she waved a hand with blue fingernails. Bettina nodded. She smoothed the baby fine hair at the edge of the bowler and once again wished she and her former running buddies frequented different clubs. It was like they had broke up but nobody wanted to move their shit out of the apartment. They all loved the Club and nobody wanted to give it up. It was the favorite hang-out except Bettina was hanging in the

Women's. With a pang, she wondered, again, how had she become the Club's restroom attendant?

She pulled on the bottom of her bomber jacket and squared her shoulders. The mirror caught the flash of pain disheveling her face in a wince. God damnit, that mugger had hurt her, and the cops never nabbed him. Her mother would have hunted that sucker down in the streets, that's how great a mom she was and how good a cop. But her mother was gone.

Done in the stall, Keisha slid up to the sink. "Hey B."

Bettina hated the shortening of her name, which didn't even start with the sharp "b" sound, but with the softer "bet." Keisha was one of her oldest and most infuriating frienemies.

Women in the bathroom came in two groups, Bettina found. Cleanies, like Keisha, hooked the quick turn to the sink where Bettina waited. The McNasties fled the stall, sidestepped Bettina and the sink, and headed straight to the wall mirror to pat their hair with dirty hands before jetting back to the dance floor. In idle moments Bettina wondered about the women who carried their drinks into the rest room and further, into the stall.

Over the sink, Keisha displayed the palm of her hand. Her lifeline creased dark. The bottle of liquid soap already in her hand, Bettina's greeting was to draw down the trigger to squirt a jet of lavender, but Keisha moved her hand. The violet stream splashed down on the white porcelain.

"I'm feeling the peppermint tonight. Pepper; you know 'hot.' "

Keisha did look hot as she shook her long weave. It rippled like mink.

Bettina noted that the lavender waste was out of reach of water rushing from the faucet. She'd have to wipe it up. She got the pink bottle, squirted Keisha; wanted to shoot it in her eye.

"That's a cute hat, B. Got another one?"

If Bettina had one of a thing in the restroom, she had two. One for her, one for sale.

Bettina stooped over and bent under the counter to get to her valise. When she came up from under the sink Keisha was frowning at herself in the mirror and using both manicured hands to smooth her Beyonce weave. "It's a damn shame you had to get rid of your hair," she said.

Bettina shrugged, held the hat out. Keisha lowered her hands to let Bettina place the bowler lightly on top of her head. It was cute, but cheap. Keisha's eyes wandered in the mirror to look behind them. A dark Asian woman had crossed the threshold.

"Ump," Keisha grunted.

Bettina didn't want trouble. She ignored as much of Keisha's bullshit as she could.

"That hat looks damn skippy on you," Bettina said.

The words pulled Keisha's eyes back to her image in the mirror, but she mumbled, "We can't have nothing for ourselves."

"What's your problem?"

"Damn Indian bitch in the Club."

Bettina knew what she meant. The Club was pulling in all sorts of people. Becoming more diverse. It sat down on Atwater Street, under Jefferson Avenue. Blacks, yeah; whites, OK; and now, apparently, East Indians. Unusual. Where were they coming from? The new lofts?

Keisha fiddled with the hat, her gleaming blue fingernails tiny ocean waves washing against the brim of the black hat. She turned her head this way and that, her dangling gold hoop earrings shaking.

The stall door slammed. The Indian babe was behind them. Keisha stopped looking at herself, tracked the woman in the mirror to the sink on Bettina's far side.

"Can't have nothin' to ourselves." Her voice was loud. The words ricocheted in the mirror. She exploded. "Yeah, I'm talking to you, Mother Teresa!"

"Keisha!" Bettina gasped. "I'm trying to make a living here."

The restroom was Bettina's only job.

Bettina turned to the client on her other side. "You have to excuse her. She's crazy."

The East Indian chick coolly extended her palm for her squirt of soap. That igged Bettina, but she shot the peppermint into the woman's left palm, glancing and then pausing at what she saw in the woman's palm. Keisha broke into her thoughts.

"Just here to get our men."

"You mean Toby?" the East Indian woman said. She hung her right hand in the mirror. A giant ruby red as arterial blood glowed on her index finger. "Got him."

Keisha pushed Bettina off-kilter as she reached both arms around Bettina straining for the East Indian intruder. Bettina's heart raced as she regained her balance and pushed Keisha back.

"What are you doing?" she demanded.

"You don't remember her from Cadieux Street? Father owned the gas station. They moved when she got some little titties, but her father kept the station and the stale-ass candy shelf open. Get outta my way!"

Bettina held Keisha against the john wall.

"Quit it, will you? Get out of here, Keisha. Take that shit somewhere else."

She knew Jeff wouldn't allow no mess like this in the Club and she resented Keisha trying to start something on her turf. She turned and pushed Keisha toward the door. Keisha stumbled, balanced herself.

"Uncle Tom," she spat at Bettina.

"I'm a woman."

"Don't matter."

Keisha turned her back in a huff, the hat still riding her head.

"Twenty bucks," Bettina called the price of the hat to the curtain of fake hair.

"Whatever," Keisha threw back over her shoulder.

The East Indian woman was lathering up. Peppermint stung the air.

"Friend of yours?" she asked.

"Sometime," Bettina said. She asked about what she saw in the woman's palm. "You been somewhere special?"

"Oh, this?" The woman opened her hand.

Henna was no news to Bettina. She learned about the beautification rite in college. What gave her pause was, smack in the middle of this woman's palm, a hennaed Star of David. It had wide borders, crossed with lines. Its middle covered with a checkerboard.

"You Jewish?" Bettina asked in confusion. She glanced up from the woman's palm to her face. She looked like a Hatha goddess. Her olive skin clear, fresh; her dark hair long, her eyes a soft dove gray.

"No," the woman said. Tendrils of sorghum-colored hair fell down across the Indian woman's eye as she shook her head. "Where you see a Star of David, I just see a star. It's interlocking triangles." She added, "My sister got married, arranged."

"Elaborate," Bettina said. "I learned about henna designs in college in my global feminist diversity class. The subjectiveness of beauty . . . . Every people on the face of the earth does something, some of it very strange."

Bettina didn't add that this was the first time that class had come in handy or that until this moment, college, in her estimation, had been a big waste of money.

"We call henna, *mehndi*," the woman said. "*Mehndi* gives color only when ground on stone with pestle."

Bettina's smile was again confusion.

"That means, 'experience comes only after hardship.'"

Bettina had enough of that, and it was making her hard, just like her mama. She didn't rely on help. Relished her independence, just like her mama. Bettina had heard people mutter at her mom's family hour, "It was just silly Tina refused a patrol partner when all the other female officers had one." Maybe it was silly, Bettina thought, but that's how it was.

Bettina's silliness was this job. At the sink she rattled on trying to close the gap between the tip jar's bottom and its wide yawning mouth.

It was bad enough that the private investor had swindled the charity that ran the community center where she had supervised the jobs club, but then the whole fricking economy crashed. And there were no jobs. So here she was standing at the sink. A bathroom maid.

Clenching her teeth, she shifted her eyes from the woman to focus in the mirror. Behind her at the door was a man. He wore a dark Italian suit.

"Hold on," Bettina murmured to her guest. She spoke loudly to the man.

"Hey, don't do that."

He was kicking at the doorstop with the toe of a dark cowboy boot.

The East Indian woman now looked in the mirror backwards over her shoulder.

The doorstop came loose with a clatter.

"What makes you think we want to see into the woman's john?" the man bellowed. His hand gripped the edge of the door. "You're blowing my buzz."

Bettina kept the women's door open to keep the air circulating and stop the women from congregating in the restroom in front of the long mirror.

If she didn't handle this guy – the first bozo of the evening — he might annoy her all night. Bettina hurried to the door on ankles wobbly in high-heeled oxfords.

"Don't." Bettina pushed the door back against the wall. She stood with her hand on the door. Where was Jeff?

She faced the man, and he blurted out, "Juicy Fruit."

She ignored the reference to her glowing lips. "Jeff will be around here."

She just wanted this guy to go away. Everyone knew the big bouncer. Just uttering his name should do it.

Bettina needed to get back to the sink and earn her tip. She aimed the toe of her shoe at the brown rubber stopper in the middle of the doorway, and nudged it under the door bottom again.

Strobe light flashed at the end of the hall. She felt pulled to be out there in a sequined top clubbing with her girls. Certainly, she'd rather be dancing away from a drunk man than standing up to one.

"You do not want to be loitering outside the women's restroom," Bettina admonished the man. "Here by the women's rest room is no place to make trouble."

The East Indian chick, for all her braggadocio with Keisha, had backed up hard against the sink. She held a bottle of soap in front of her like it was a can of pepper spray. Her face looked apprehensive. Bettina tore her eyes from the woman. Turned again to the man. His hard gaze fixed on her dazzling lips.

More than just being a bozo, this guy creeped her out. She'd been robbed when she first began working at The Club, in the parking lot. Knocked to the asphalt by a ghoul in a brown zipper sweatshirt, the hood shrouding his face. Bettina tried to climb to her feet as he yanked on her purse strap, and he ended up pulling her to her feet. He wrenched her shoulder, but the hardware held. Who said no purse was worth twelve hundred dollars? She only wished she hadn't told anyone. Now Jeff walked Bettina to her car each night.

At the restroom door, she threw back her shoulders, igniting the pain in her left shoulder. "Beat it." She hoped it sounded like a growl.

The Italian cowboy met her menacing eye until behind him the silence was broken by a tough tone.

"The party's out there."

Finally, Jeff. He approached through the open doorway at the end of the long back hall. Moving out of the strobe into plain light, the bouncer lumbered in slow motion, each step careening him from one wall to the other.

"That's the women's," Jeff yelled. "Just take a look down and you'll see you're a man. Move along." Jeff jerked a thumb over his shoulder.

The man walked off. Passing Jeff, he muttered, "muthafucker."

Jeff let it go, preferring to survey Bettina from her slim ankles to her hat, zeroing in on her luscious lips. Stepping close to Bettina in the open door, together they watched the cowboy amble down the hall. His stacked heels clicked.

"Nice lipstick," Jeff said off-hand, and then he got serious. "I'm glad you yelled for me. We don't need nobody else accosting you."

Bettina relaxed against the door, felt his forearm across the small of her back. "You heard me?"

"Not so loud or so clear," Jeff said. He gazed closely at her. "But I figured if I could hear you all the way out at the front entrance, you must've been yelling. I left 'em flat with a line back to the Rasta man." Jeff sang Marley "Positive vibrations, yea, pos-it-tive," and tipped from side to side on his toes. He smiled at her with perfect teeth.

Bettina smiled. He was handsome, brawny.

"Well, I 'ppreciate your attention."

"You should," Jeff said. "I got plenty others wanting it.

A little cough came from over by the sink.

Bettina flashed a smile at Jeff, put her hand on his rock hard thigh to push him away, and turning, she hurried to the sink. A slinky white-blond wafted into the restroom.

"This ain't no easy gig, is it? The East Indian babe said. "You stop chicks from mixing it up. Pander at the sink. Run off drunk men."

Bettina's shoulders rose indignantly. The low grumble seeping through her lips were actual words. "Fat lotta help you were."

The Indian woman's armor softened a bit.

"Look," she said. "My name is Guro."

She was quiet a few moments. A stall door clanged shut behind Her Blond Slinkiness.

Guro said, "Life is so much easier in a female society; but the world," she waved her hand around and toward the door, "reeks with danger. That's why I don't mind this."

She held up her palm up to the mirror. The star seemed to plaster itself onto the silver surface. "It brings God's protection."

I could use it, Bettina thought. My mother needed it. Bettina reached into her pocket and withdrew her lipstick. Guro dropped a crisp bill into the tip jar, but the tube caught her eye. "Do you have another?"

"Uh, no," Bettina apologized. "My sister gave it to me."

Glad her tip was not held responsible for Keisha, or the frightening man, Bettina held up her index finger to motion, 'just a minute.' She plucked a plastic lipstick applicator from a dish of little things in the corner of the counter, and held it out with the lipstick. Guro, however, reached only for the lipstick. She took it with her blessed hand. Like a gambler eyeing his dice, she rolled the lipstick tube in her palm across the star. "Nice case."

Guro swiveled the lipstick up out of the tube.

"Pretty," she said, looking at the gleaming wax. "But not my color. Looks great on you though."

With a smile, she rolled the lipstick down, recapped the tube. The case was now blemished with a dot of henna/*mehndi*.

132

"They put it on thick for the wedding," Guro said.

She wiped at the scrap of red henna/*mehndi* and it smeared the white plastic tube. She grimaced, handing the tube back. "Sorry."

Bettina hiked a high smile, trying to stay agreeable. Failed. When Reynolds sees that, Bettina worried, she'll pitch one.

Guro leaned into Bettina's personal space.

"Help arrives at your beck and call," she whispered, and then she floated toward the door.

"Huh?" Bettina wondered. And then she followed, oddly compliant.

Jeff was still on guard in the doorway. The East Asian turned sideways, and passing him, brushed the tips of her breasts against his chest. Seeing that, Bettina stopped stock still, 'cause in the next step she would have finished up what Keisha started. Instead, she licked her lips to moisten the lipstick. They glittered when she smiled at Jeff.

"It's busy tonight," he said.

"Money, money, money," Bettina sang. She balled her hand in a loose fist and pumped it in glee.

Jeff leaned closer, holding her eye. The space them between collapsed to a tight dark hole. She felt his arm slide along her back. She leaned away, teasing.

At the sink the thin woman finished up. By-passing the tip jar, she crossed the short distance to stand in front of the wall mirror to shake her platinum hair. She combed it with crescent-shaped fingertips. In four steps this Cleanie was gliding to the door, and drifting between Jeff and Bettina, she smooshed her boobs into Jeff's chest. He put his big hands on the woman's shoulders and moved her into the hall. Bettina shook her head, and laughed. He was desire, personified. When Bettina pirouetted on the tips of her oxfords back into the restroom, she felt Jeff's admiring eyes on her backside.

"If I don't see you during the night," he called. "I'll meet you at the bar at closing."

***

It was a great night at The Club. The dance floor was jam-packed. Liquor flowed with the money. In the restroom, Bettina emptied her tip jar twice. And again it sprouted dollar bills out the top as she complimented women and helped them freshen up.

***

Later that evening, Bettina's used-to-be running buddy Cynthia was casually looking over Bettina's stuff and chatting when Bettina said she was thirsty. All that talking and being solicitous caused dry mouth. The lipstick kept her lips moist, but her mouth was like a cotton ball.

"But I can't just slurp from the face bowl, can I?"

"I'll keep watch while you go for a drink," Cynthia said.

Bettina shook her head. Her response to offers of help was always no.

"I wish Sheila delivered."

Cynthia shrugged her shoulders. "Suit yourself. It's hot out there and my hair is fried," she said. "Say B, when you gonna come take that job?"

Bettina snorted. Cynthia's brother's fast-food restaurant always needed people. Cynthia rolled her eyes at Bettina.

"Don't ever say I didn't try to help you out," she said. Cynthia massaged her scalp and made her 'do leap.

That was the thing with people, Bettina thought, they wanted to be able to say they helped you out. Cynthia blew herself a kiss in the mirror and waggled two fingers goodbye. A few minutes later, Sheila arrived with a drink in hand. Bettina was waiting on a guest, and she avoided Sheila's eyes in the mirror. Her mouth watered for the grenadine and club soda, but with the taste of annoyance also. "That Cynthia," she said.

"Cynthia?" Sheila's hand cradled the glass with the wedge of lime stuck to the rim, as she waited for the guest to move to the wall mirror.

"She told you, I was thirsty."

"Have I seen Cynthia tonight? Shit, I don't know; it's a fierce clang-chang in The Club. It's a lot of babes out there. Thing is, it just came to me, like an echo in my head, to bring your drink. So I took a break to help you out."

"Came into your head?"

"They're drinking wit' both hands and feet out there." Sheila chuckled, and added, "Yeah, it was like we was talking. You said 'I wish Sheila delivered.' I don't know, must be my inner chit-chat, imaginariness. But, hey, no problem; I'm glad to do it."

She laughed, looked approvingly at the tip jar. "Looks like you keeping pace with the floor. It's a good night."

"But, but, Jeff heard me too."

"No kidding," Sheila said. "Hey look, I'll talk to you at closing. Got to go."

***

Closing time. The rest room was empty. Over the dance floor, the air settled but the music still boomed. It was a courtesy to keep it cranked until people finished their last drink. Bettina idly wondered about Jeff and Sheila hearing her voice as she packed her goods into the suitcase. After just one year working at the club, she felt her co-workers were like family. Sometimes people who were close were prescient, sort of like how women spending a lot of time together came on their period together. She sighed. She hoped one day soon to be closer to Jeff than "like family."

Straightening up from zipping the suitcase, Bettina glanced at her tip jar. She liked to look at it sitting there. It was as quiet as the music was loud. She took out her lipstick and glossed her lips. She regarded the lipstick remembering what she learned about this cosmetic: the world over since ancient history, lipstick had been the siren call for sex because its scarlet color reminded men of fertile women. She admired her lips in the mirror, and then stared incredulously behind her.

Again? What da hell?

The Italian suit, cowboy boots guy was closing the door shut behind him. Cool metal fear flowed into Bettina's mouth.

"Get the hell. . . . ," she yelled, but she need not. The man moved so quick he stood right behind her. He eyed the tip jar. Her rent money, her cell phone.

"Take it," she cut each word with precision, "and get the fuck out."

He shifted his gaze from the jar to the mirror. "Oh there's more than that, I know, and more than money."

His gravel voice curled the baby hair at Bettina's temple.

"I've been thinking of you all night." His breath reached out and grabbed her with its stank.

Bettina pulled on the bottom of her bomber jacket and pushed her shoulders back, pushing down the pain of squaring them. Her knife was in her purse. His eyes were blood shot drunk.

"What juicy lips you have, my dear,"

"Back off."

Women loitered in the club, some still batting their eyelashes and thinking to freshen up before leaving with their love of that night. In just a moment the restroom door would swing open, and music and a good person would rush in, Bettina hoped. She searched the door from top to bottom for even the faintest motion.

At the bottom of the door she saw the brown stopper. It was on the floor, wedged under the door from the inside. She could throw this guy off, but then she'd have to stop, bend over and dislodge it. They were barricaded in the restroom together.

Bettina slid her hand in her pocket. She wished for her knife, but she felt her lipstick. She wondered why her mother had not shot first and later asked questions, questions she had never got a chance to ask. Bettina pulled her lipstick from her pocket. The man was not concerned about Bettina's weapon of choice.

She applied the lipstick, coolly, watching him in the mirror, willing herself to look as unconcerned as he at their situation.

She recapped the lipstick. In her head she heard the eye-hand woman say, "Help arrives at your beck and call." She remembered how her mother announced being home for lunch with a short burst of the squad car siren. And how she swaggered up the walk, every other step throwing the hip carrying her holstered service revolver. Tina Smith had believed in the power of her badge, her uniform and her firearm. But in the final moments of her mother's life, had she regretted for one second being alone on patrol, and for that matter, rendering her life an island? For the first time in her grown-up life, Bettina felt the burden of being alone. She thought that community, friends and lovers, their help and their prying, was a gift. In despair, a whimper escaped her lips. It sounded like defeat, but was new life.

"Jeff."

The man in the rest room with her turned slowly to look at the barricaded door. He turned back to her and smiled. His teeth gleamed. Music was the only thing bumping against the door.

"Jeff."

The second uttering flowed from her heart, thought her voice echoed off the cold porcelain fixtures.

"He walks me to my car after work every night. He'll be here in a minute. "

The man was in no hurry to subdue her. As he pulled his arms up from the long sides of his body, he noticed dirt under his right pinky nail and with nonchalance picked at it. She whirled around, shoved him, as she wished her mother had shoved the man against the squad car that night. The rest room stranger stumbled, but did not fall. He sneered.

"Just keep that sweet mouth open."

He heaved Bettina against the counter. Her head whipped back into the mirror, striking it, fracturing it, but the pieces did not fall. Her head imploded and she lay still while the shape of her consciousness reformed to match the O her mouth fell into. Her heart darkened to the blue of her mother's uniform, like a soft night, the north star of her badge shining, her arms flailing, her body falling, her head striking against the concrete curb, and her laying still while he ran off.

"Oh, I like that," the bathroom creep said, grinning at Bettina. His open mouth showed a thrashing pink serpent tongue. He straddled her. Then laid down, dead weight on her. She felt his hand fumbling down there. Bettina's chest heaved. Desperate, she thrust her knee to the soft V between his legs.

The pervert flew back and crashed to the floor. His body slid along the floor. His arms and legs scrambled in the air like a bug on its back. Bettina was amazed at her power, but there standing over the man, raising his foot, Jeff. Behind him, the door was broken down. He kicked the pervert in the ribs, cursed and planted his foot hard on the man's chest.

"Get the hell down here," Jeff yelled out the open doorway. "Call the fuckin' cops."

Turning to her, he shouted, "Get out from under that mirror!"

Bettina stumbled up from the counter. Behind her the mirror crashed from the wall into pieces.

***

Lights up in The Club showed it was an empty barn. At the bar, Bettina leaned against Jeff. Shelia leaned over the bar making their group a triangle. Coming toward them, two uniforms, one clearing the way in front and the other on the far side, leading the Italian cowboy, his hands handcuffed behind. When he passed Bettina stuck out her left oxford and tripped him. He fell to the floor, causing the young officer escorting him to stumble. Bettina raised her foot and kicked the Italian in the ass. The younger cop turned back.

"B," he chided her, but the older police officer gave her a discrete thumbs up.

Sheila hanging over the bar, laughed. "Son of a bitch," she said.

They watched the trio move to the door. Jeff told amazed cocktail servers and Silas, the appreciative manager, the story he had told the cops.

"I heard her. Over the music, loud. I heard you in my head, screaming my name."

"Me too," Sheila put in. "B seemed surprised when I showed up with her drink, but I heard her order it."

Jeff continued. "I was out here, chewing on ice, just waiting to walk her to her car. Then just like earlier in the evening, I heard her call my name. Only this time she was screaming, drowning out the music," he regarded Bettina with admiration. "That's some mouth you got on you, girl."

Sheila nodded, her silky hair shaking. "Sho do."

Jeff grinned, turned to face the damsel he had rescued. Noses just inches apart, their warm breaths mixed. Jeff said, huskily, "But frankly, I think it's the lipstick."

Bettina laid her fingertips on her pockets to sooth the butterflies flitting through her body. Through the fabric she felt the lipstick tube. She whispered, "Me too."

Jeff touched his lips to hers.

Money for Nothing

By Katherine Tomlinson

When her supervisor summoned Andrea to his office before she even clocked in, she knew it wouldn't be good news. She was prepared to hear that he was cutting her hours or taking away her weekday shifts and putting her on weekend nights. She was not prepared for him to tell her she was being laid off.

Starting immediately.

He'd handed her a check for one day's pay ($43.38) and offered her a farewell handshake before she'd processed the many degrees of terrible this turn of events represented.

At first the only coherent thought she had was that if he'd called her at home to fire her, it would have saved her $3 in bus fare. That thought produced a little flare of anger that kept the larger, darker thoughts at bay long enough for her to turn in her employee smock, steal a candy bar from the break room, and grab her purse from the locked wire baskets where the employees kept their personal items.

By the time she got to the bus stop the anger had worn off and the dread was surfacing.

It was a very cold day with a flensing wind that cut right through the layers of clothing she was wearing. Andrea couldn't button her coat because it was a size 10 and she had a size 16 belly.

She hated being fat, knew it made her just that much less employable, but she and the kids had been living on cheap carbs for nearly a year and it was taking its toll. Fortunately Dan and Tina qualified for free hot meals at school, so they were getting some vegetables in their diet and some quality protein.

They hardly ever complained about the endless dinners of fried potatoes and eggs or the weekend lunches of peanut butter and jelly sandwiches. It broke Andrea's heart.

They were such good kids. It wasn't their fault that their daddy had been killed by a mugger who made off with his wallet and a pack of cigarettes. It wasn't their fault there was no life insurance.

Dan senior had only been 34 and their budget had already been so stressed that paying for life insurance seemed like a luxury; something they could put off until he turned 40 at least.

They hadn't had much of a safety net before Dan's death but after? There was no cushion at all. The only thing between the family and utter disaster had been Andrea's job and now that was gone.

She'd sold Dan's beater car. She'd cancelled the phone and bought a pay-as-you-go cell for emergencies.

A month ago she'd begged a coworker to adopt the family cat because she could no longer afford to buy kibble and litter.

Giving away Sweet Pea had just about killed Andrea and her kids had been devastated.

What am I going to do? she asked herself, what am I going to do?

She pulled out the candy bar she'd stolen and gobbled it in two bites. The sugar hit her system like a gut-punch, instantly triggering a feeling of almost overwhelming guilt. She'd intended to bring the candy home to the kids. It was big enough for them to share but she'd greedily stuffed it down her own gullet.

I am such a bad mother, she thought. And even though she knew it wasn't true, a wave of despair engulfed her; a physical pain that bent her double and took her breath away.

What am I going to do? she asked herself again.

And then she saw the gleam of the coin on the sidewalk, reflecting the pale winter light

It was about half again the size of a quarter and a bronze color that made her think it might be a foreign coin, a Euro maybe, or a Mexican peso. She'd never seen a Mexican peso but there were lots of Hispanics in the area. It wasn't outside the realm of possibility that someone had dropped it at the bus stop while fumbling for their fare.

Andrea picked it up off the ground and was surprised that it was warm to the touch despite the cold.

There was a strange inscription engraved on the face of the coin, an intricate calligraphy that meant nothing to her. On the back of the coin was the image of a butterfly. It was pretty.

For some reason, holding the object in her hand made Andrea feel good and she pocketed it on impulse, thinking she would give it to Tina as a good luck charm.

That night, when Andrea took off her pants, she heard jingling in the pockets. She emptied them out and found a handful of dollar coins. She counted them up and discovered she had $30 in change and the strange bronze coin.

Not sure what to make of her sudden windfall but not one to question her good luck, Andrea used the emergencies-only cell phone to order a feast from the nearest Chinese restaurant.

Money for Nothing By Katherine Tomlinson

And even though all three of them chowed down on egg rolls and moo goo gai pan, and fortune cookies, there was food left over.

That night she put the bronze coin on her night table, right next to the framed picture of her and Dan on their honeymoon in Yosemite.

The next morning, she woke to find a pile of dollar coins scattered across the table and spilling onto the bedroom floor.

As soon as the kids were off to school, Andrea took a bus to the nearest mall where she transformed the coins into a cash voucher using the Coinstar machine in the grocery store. Even with Coinstar's bite, it came to more than $300 and she used almost all of it to buy groceries and toiletries. (They'd been brushing their teeth with baking soda.)

Andrea had enough left to take a taxi home with all her bags. The driver helped her bring the bags into the apartment.

She gave him a nice tip.

That night Andrea put the bronze coin in the drawer of her bedside table and in the morning the whole drawer was filled with coins. This time she took them to her bank and deposited them into her checking account, which had $8.19 in it.

The bored teenage teller hadn't even raised her eyebrows as Andrea handed over a couple of bulging plastic Ziplok bags filled with coins but Andrea had blurted out, "Yard sale," just to be sure.

From then on, the deposits became a regular thing. Andrea paid all her bills and got caught up on her past rent. Her landlord, who'd been about to evict her, asked her where the money came from. "A bonus at work," she told him and he didn't question it.

She bought a used car for cash, which made it a lot easier to get around.

Instead of borrowing dvds from the library, Andrea began treating her kids to first-run movies in 3-D.

She wanted to spoil them to death but she was careful. She knew she'd been the recipient of some sort of cosmic grace and she did not want to be greedy.

She told no one about the coin, afraid that something would happen if she spoke about it.

And morning after morning, the drawer in her bedside table was filled to the brim with coins.

Andrea was profoundly grateful.

She lost weight. She got a haircut. She updated her resume.

When she went out on job interviews, employers saw an attractive young woman with a lot to offer instead of a desperate, overweight loser groveling for a job, any job.

She took a part-time position managing an art gallery, arranging her hours so she could be home when her children got out of school.

She'd moved them all into a bigger apartment so the kids could have their own rooms, but she still lived modestly, banking most of the midnight money, building a nest egg for the future.

When one of the artists whose paintings hung at the gallery asked her out to dinner, she was delighted.

It had been several years since she was widowed and she was ready to begin dating again.

George was older than she was, a handsome man in his mid-40s. He'd worked at Lehman Brothers, cashing out in 2007 before they declared bankruptcy. He was unabashedly unapologetic for walking away with millions.

"Being rich allows me time to paint," he'd said to her over rare steaks and a very good red wine. Andrea had smiled at him and taken another sip of the wine.

He'd gone on to talk about a trip he'd made to the South of France and regaled her with gossip about fellow painters, and by the time they split a dessert of crème brûlée, Andrea was feeling no pain.

They'd parked on the street because the restaurant lot was full and as they approached his car, Andrea noticed a woman crouched in a doorway with her belongings in heaps at her feet.

Oh the poor woman, she thought.

"That's just disgusting," George said.

"I know," Anna said, "Nobody should have to live on the street."

He looked at her as if she'd just grown a second head as she rummaged in her purse for a twenty dollar bill.

"Are you serious?" he asked, taking the money from her hand. "If you pay taxes, you've done your bit to contribute to her welfare."

George was already leading Andrea to his Lexus. "Don't tell me you're one of those people who thinks that it's the system's fault people are homeless."

"I . . . " Andrea began but he cut her off.

"People like that disgust me," he said and waited for her response.

"Me too," she said meekly, hoping her agreement would cut his diatribe short.

When George moved in to kiss her as they pulled up to her apartment, Andrea slid out of his embrace smoothly, a skill she'd learned in high school and hadn't lost.

"Good night," she said.

"I'll call you," George said, not really meaning it because he was miffed at spending $60 on a meal without getting anything in return.

Don't, Andrea thought, and meant it.

In the morning, when Andrea opened the drawer in her bedside table, it was empty.

Not only was there no pile of shiny dollar coins inside, the magic bronze coin was gone as well.

MONEY FOR NOTHING BY KATHERINE TOMLINSON

In her heart, Andrea knew the reason — that split-second of agreement with George's cold-hearted philosophy the night before.

"I didn't mean it," she whispered to the empty bedroom air.

There was no answer.

***

By noon the same day, somewhere else in the city, another woman had spied the bronze coin in the middle of a pedestrian crosswalk on a busy street. She scooped it up before anyone else could claim it and felt, for the first time in many weeks, a sense of hope surging inside her.

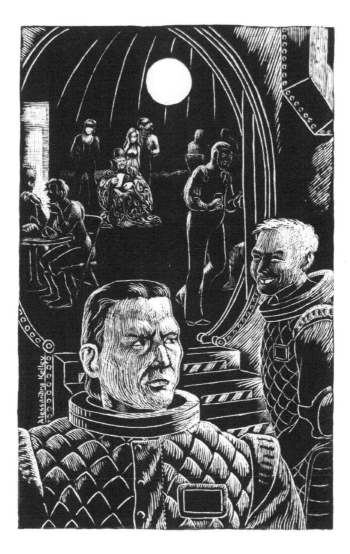

"Mandrake's Folly" illustrated by Alessandra Kelley

Mandrake's Folly

By Suzanne Palmer

The game had begun four years earlier when Onni's cousin Orph got him a job as a hauler on the *Mandrake's Folly*, one of the old skips doing the three-week Tanduou-Beenjai run. Each round started with a new complement of passengers picked up at one end of the run, and the first innocuous item stolen like an earring or a datapad stylus. Passengers came and went in ones and threes along the way, at stations and enclaves and rockcrapper clings as the *Folly* passed them, and with each stop and exchange the oneupmanship escalated, until at last at the far end of the run the round was called as the final set of passengers, bereft of a random assortment of possessions, some big and some small, some missed and some not, walked back down off the ship's ramp and on to the rest

153

of their anonymous lives. The game ended, finally and unexpectedly, as Onni was walking through the ship's service corridors, winning in his thoughts and pride of mischief in his heart, when he found his eye drawn towards something floating outside a small porthole where nothing but stars should be. It was Orph's severed head.

He shouted, every swear and foul turn of phrase he knew, and he pounded on the gunmetal gray hull until his fists were bloody and Gunny, Fin-Fin, and Assface came pounding down the corridor looking for the source of the noise. When he was finally able to say what the matter was the three men crowded around the porthole to look, but what was left of Orph was now, and forever, long gone.

"Bastard owed me ten," Assface said, and Onni added one more blow to the collection of abuses to his hands.

After that, Gunny and Fin-Fin dragged him down to the far end of cargo six, where they pressed a bottle of knockdown into his hands and sat beside him until all the fight had been drowned out of him.

"Musta stole the wrong thing this time," Gunny said, not unkindly.

"We was raised honest," Onni protested, and that was true as far as it went, if no further. Nobody called him on it, and eventually Assface joined them again with a pair of icepacks, one for Onni's hands, the other for his own swollen eye.

Assface sat down on a crate. "We're away," he said, and sure enough now that he said it Onni could feel the hum of the engines through the floor. He hadn't even heard the jump alarms. "No one got on or off at Innich," Assface added.

It took a few minutes for Onni to pull the words through the haze of grief to where he could hear them. "What?"

"Straight mail hand-off, postmaster to station-hand and quick. None a'us even near the main lock, not Orph neither. Means whoever did for Orph gotta still be on the ship."

"Yeh?"

"Yeh. Time for fair justice, afore we reach Tanduou."

"There won't be no justice," Onni said. He stood up, the ice pack curled between his hands. "Nobody's gonna care if something happens to one of us, 'specially not when they say he was stealing. He was my cousin and my best friend and I'm going to be the one to have to tell my aunt and my ma when we get to dock, and they are never gonna get over it, and where can there be fair justice in that?"

Fin-Fin put down the now-empty bottle and kicked it over with one boot. They all watched it roll into a corner of the hold and stop, with a sharp clang, somewhere in the dark. "Go rest, Onn. I'll take your shift tonight," he said.

"No, thanks, Fin. Rather be busy," Onni said. Which was true, but it was also true that he knew most of the places where Orph hid stuff he'd taken, and he wanted to go look for it with no one else around to see. There was no way he was willing to face his aunt and ma without being able to say he made things even, and he figured that if he found what Orph had stolen that got him killed, he'd just as likely find who did it.

***

Problem was, he *was* busy. Less than a day out from Innich Station the skrunge had come back in cargo nine and the whole work-crew was double-timing it. In full suits, they scraped at the walls with long-handled poles trying to knock the reddish-purple goo free so they could vent it out to space. Junior had come down from the bridge himself to make the cargo hands help out the grunts, and no one was happy about it.

"It's never gonna work," Fin-Fin complained, his voice tinny through his faceplate. He'd been willing to give up his free night for Onni, but he had no such love for the owners and crew of the *Folly*. "Waste of our time down here, poking away at this toxic crap yet again, when they ought to just drop the entire bay and get a new one. Not like they can't afford it, with all the cred they save by paying us frotting shit-all."

"An' with us short-handed, what with your stupid cousin gettin' hisself dead," Dougee spoke up from Onni's right.

With one smooth movement Onni brought his scrubber pole around and slammed Dougee against the wall. The man let out a shriek and scrabbled away, flailing at the gobs of skrunge already clinging to his suit. "You fucking assvalve of a Sfazili ground-toad!" the man shouted. "You could have killed me! What if I had a hole in my suit?"

"Then we'd still be short-handed," Onni said, and turned back to scrubbing. Dougee stood there, towering over him, fists clenching and unclenching at his side in impotent rage. Onni wasn't tall — childhood under the heavy gravity of Guratahan Sfazil had seen to that — but his body was a compact mass of muscle head to toe, and he'd been in enough brawls and riots on Tanduou after leaving home to know how to use it well.

Finally Dougee walked back towards the other cargo hands, muttering something as he went. Onni couldn't make it out, which was just as well.

"You don't think it coulda been them cudders?" Fin-Fin asked, nodding his head towards where Dougee had retreated.

"Naw."

"Why?"

"'Cause they'd never make more work for themselves," Onni said. "And if Dougee was gonna try for one of us — assuming he grew himself some beans first — he'd have gone for me."

"Oh yeah," Fin-Fin said. "I forgot about that time you beat him 'til he peed his suit."

"Assvalve said shit 'bout my mother," Onni said. "We have an understanding now."

A bob sailed overhead. The fist-sized metal sphere trained its spotlight on an area where a few small flecks of skrunge had escaped scrubbing, and Onni dipped his brush in the dissolvent bucket and moved over to catch it. Cursing broke out on the far side of the hold, and he turned to look. Gunny was flailing and jumping up and down like a dog trying to shed water, a giant glob of skrunge spreading itself out across his faceplate. "It just fell off the ceiling right onto me!" he shouted.

Junior was standing in the bay doorway again, and pointed at Assface. "You, Erle — go help him. Careful you don't let any of that crap get out of here. The rest of you, quick it up, eh?"

"Yes, sir!" Dougee said, saluting the first mate; Junior just shook his head and walked out.

Onni started in again on a writhing patch of skrunge. "You know we wouldn't never steal," he said to

Fin-Fin when his friend was close again. "Stealing's about profit, right? But we had a game — just that, Orph and me. And I figure it's gotta be one of the passengers updeck who done him for it."

"Part of me hopes you're wrong," Fin-Fin said. "'Cause you know how that goes — you never get just one troublemaker on a ship at a time. They always travel in groups, whether they plan it that way or not."

"Too true," Onni said, as the bob highlighted another missed patch. "Whatever we got, we got no say in it 'cept to keep sailing through."

***

Six grueling hours of scrubbing later, and an hour of decon once they'd peeled their suits, all the grunts went back to the crew-hole for a rest. As Gunny and Assface broke out the cards and counters for a game of Bungknuckle, Onni changed his clothes, combed his hair, and headed for the door.

"Where you off to?" Gunny looked up from counting out pieces.

"Thought maybe I'd go send a letter," he said. Gunny grunted, nodding, and when no one else seemed to have anything to say on the matter Onni slipped out.

The buckled and dirty floor-plates of the downdeck gave way, one floor up, to smooth carpeting and fresh air. He breathed deep as he walked into the ship's common area. Serious Ned sat behind his small desk in the corner, stool tipped onto two legs so he could lean his thin frame more fully against the wall. "Well," he said. "Mr. Onomatopoeia Smith. To what do we owe the pleasure?"

"Was thinking about sending a letter," Onni told the ship's postmaster. "Not sure, though."

"Who do you want to send it to?"

"Not sure."

"What is it about?"

"Not sure." Onni made a point of looking over the room. "Don't get up here too often," he said. "You heard about Orph?"

"Mr. Finley said he'd been killed," Serious Ned answered. "Is that so?"

"Saw him floating outside the porthole, just as we was leaving Innich Station," Orph said. "Seems pretty killed to me."

"I'm sorry to hear it," Ned said, and, as always, sounded entirely serious. "I'm sure Mr. Rosemark will put every effort into finding out what happened."

Onni had his doubts. When did anyone care about grunts?

The *Mandrake's Folly* had six passenger cabins; one was a suite, three regular rooms, and two that were barely more than bunks and walls. Looking around the room it wasn't hard to guess who was where. A large man in blue brocade robes had taken up one entire end of the room, with two toughs to either side and a woman beside him with the look in her eyes of a small, frightened animal. Onni figured he had to be the suite occupant. "He must be somebody," he said.

Ned made a disgusted face. "That's Mr. Pauls, a Basellan *Family Assets Merchant* — you know what that means?"

"Yeh, I heard of that," Onni said. "Means he sells wives."

"I'd suggest avoiding him. Like most people who justify a lifetime of disreputable behavior with the rhetoric of religious fervor, the rot goes right to his core. Also, those two thugs of his together would be enough to take down anybody, even you."

"Or Orph?"

"Orph would have known to stay away from him," Ned said, and Onni figured that was likely true.

Also in the common area was an old man slumped in a chair, snoring lightly with a newspad in his lap and a cane on the floor beside him. Four miners from Traprock were arguing over cups of coffee, a man and a woman sat in chairs at a small table talking quietly, and a young girl sat by one of the few portholes. She had the shade up, and was watching the bendy blackness of jump-space outside. "And them? What's their story?"

"The old man's on his way to Coralla to scatter his dead wife's ashes on the beach where they had their honeymoon fifty-three years ago," Ned said. "Couple I don't know anything about, except they're quiet and polite. Miners are miners."

"And the girl?"

Serious Ned shrugged. "I have no idea. Not everyone talks to me."

"But most everyone."

"But not everyone everyone. Mind you, that doesn't keep me from guessing. She's anxious, moves furtively, avoids the other passengers. I'd say she's running from something. And of course that Basellan's been eyeing her like something shiny he just spotted in a store window. Now, Onni, are you going to send a letter or not?"

"Still don't know what to say," Onni said. "Maybe I'll send it tomorrow after I think about it more, if you don't mind."

"Whatever you need," Ned said.

"So, uh," Onni said, trying to do the math in his head. "We got an empty cabin, then?"

"Miners took the last one; it's a full house this run," Ned said. "Cabin two's another elderly man and what looks like his bodyguard. They've been keeping to themselves in their cabin." He tipped the stool back upright and turning to face Onni. "Look, Onni, I really am sorry about your cousin, but leave the passengers alone, okay? Let Rosemark do his job. There's time. We ought to be dropping out of jump any minute now for the approach to Stinkhole, and nobody's going to be getting off there; it's just a mail call — Ah. See? The engine pitch just changed. We're in normal space again."

The girl by the window suddenly jumped up out of her seat and left the common area. "I wonder — " Onni started to say, just as the general alarm went off. He went to the window and peered out. "Ship out there," he said. "Must've been waiting for us."

There were sounds of boots in the hallway, and then Rosemark and Junior ran through the room and out the far door, heading for the bridge. Stinkin' Steve, Rosemark's deputy, stumbled through a few moments later looking like he'd just got out of bed. Ned stopped him. "What's going on?" he asked.

"Ambush, looks like," Stinkin' Steve said, trying to keep his voice low. "Pirates, maybe. Raiders. Captain's trying to raise 'em, talk 'em off, but you know how these people on the edge live." There was a reason so many of their passengers traveled with bodyguards.

Onni was still at the window. As the other ship neared it banked, and he caught sight of the markings painted on the side. "It's Aurora Enclave," he said.

"Out here? This is way out of their way," Ned said. Aurora Enclave wasn't on their route; the heavily-fortified settlement lay deep within the Sfazili Barrens, where the *Folly* only skirted the edge. "They've never made trouble for us before."

"No, but they make trouble for plenty of others. Maybe it's just our turn," Stinkin' Steve said. With that, he pushed past Ned and pelted after his bosses.

"They gotta be after something particular," Onni said. "We have consignment cargo this run?"

"Lots, but nothing valuable. Agro supplies, mostly."

"Are they going to attack us?" The old man spoke up. As if in answer, the ship shuddered as if struck by a giant hand and the pitch of the engines rose.

"Momentum dampeners," Ned said. "They're serious."

The miners got up from their seats and headed back towards their cabin, though what good that would do them if they were boarded Onni couldn't say. As he watched them go, a flicker of movement caught his eye, and he turned to see the woman of the couple with a small device in her hand. She pressed a button, and a light turned green. One corner of her mouth quirked up momentarily — more satisfaction than amusement — as she slipped it away again.

The feeling of drag on the ship immediately ceased.

Ned was now at the window beside him. "They're backing off," he said. "That doesn't make sense."

"It might," Onni said, glancing over towards the couple, and met the woman's eyes looking steadily at him. He quickly turned away. "None of my business anyway," he said, probably too loud. *And it isn't*, he told himself.

Rosemark and Stinkin' Steve came back through the room, arguing in low, sharp voices. Feeling the woman's eyes still on him, Onni slipped into the *Folly's* small kitchenette and poured himself a cup of coffee. He held it, warm in his hands, and lingered there to see if anyone was going to follow him.

Captain Lautterson stomped through with Junior on his heels, poured his own coffee without even looking at Onni. ". . . Fell in behind us and is just following," he was saying. "Do we have any idea what happened?"

"Not a clue, but something scared them off," Junior said. "Reiborn is checking the comm logs, see if there's any traffic there that might dot some dots for us."

The Captain turned, looking straight at Onni. "I'm sorry about your brother," he said.

"Thank you," Onni replied, too startled to correct him.

"I want a full report as soon as possible, including an inventory of exactly what we're carrying that might have attracted their attention." The Captain was already walking away, heading back to the bridge with Junior right behind him. "And I want security on the bridge at all times until either the Aurorans leave or we've safely arrived at Tanduou. Have Rosemark . . ."

And then they were out of earshot again. Onni topped up his cup. When he was sure no one was near he slid an old tin with a peeling ration crackers label out from the top shelf, and carefully pried the lid open. The tin was one of Orph's favorite hiding spots.

So far Onni had only collected two items, though he was very proud of one and less proud of the other after talking to Serious Ned. The tin also held two things — a small pocket knife and a cord with a religious symbol of some sort.

"What're you doing up here?" The voice startled him and he jumped, nearly dropping the tin. It was one of Dougee's crew.

"None'a your business, Beersmooches." He palmed the items from Orph's stash, and then slipped them into his pocket as he put the empty tin back on the shelf.

"The name's Franick," the man snarled. He reached past Onni and grabbed the tin. "You weren't thinking of eating this crap, were you? We don't need another dead grunt leaving us his work to do."

"I was, but it's empty."

Beersmooches popped the lid off, peered inside, then threw both lid and tin into the flash recycler. "Want my advice?"

"No."

"Too bad. You and your cousin were always making trouble, and it's no surprise that trouble found you back.

If I were you, I'd go back downdeck before you scare the passengers with your stink, keep your head down and your fat toad mouth shut, and hope trouble's feeling satisfied."

"You know anything about what happened to Orph, Smooches?"

"I don't know nothing 'cept that I wouldn't've minded being there to see it happen."

Onni considered. "If you want to see someone die horrible all close up, I can arrange that for you right now," he said. "If not, I'd shut yer facehole and think about what it might just sound like to have someone crush your head with their bare hands. Lotsa poppin' and squickin' sounds, I bet. Wanna find out right now?"

"You really think you could?"

"Don't have to think," Onni said. He cracked his meaty knuckles, and then flexed his fingers. "It'd be that easy."

"I sure hope you get yourself killed next," Beersmooches said, and then turned and quickly left the kitchenette.

He considered following the guy, cracking his knuckles some more as he walked behind him just to see if he could make the man break into a run, but as he turned from the kitchenette he found himself face to face with the woman from the common room. "You have poor luck in choosing when to be observant," the woman said, leaning against the doorframe blocking his way. She was tall and thin, middle-aged, her hair a short, frizzled brown flecked with gray, and the way she moved as she suggested that she wasn't at all intimidated by Onni's bulk.

"You're from Kōrogi Enclave," he guessed. "Nobody else Aurora'd be afraid of."

She nodded. "I would rather not have this conversation with your Captain or your security officers," she said. "The Aurorans will leave this ship alone until my partner and I have disembarked, which we intend to do at Tanduou. Then you're on your own. I would be unhappy if any awkward questions arose in the meantime. Unhappy with you, if you understand me."

"I understand," Onni said. "I have to ask — did you kill my cousin Orph?"

"We did not. We aren't here on business."

"Then I don't see we have any reason to be making trouble for each other."

"I'm glad we understand each other so well," she said. She turned and was gone from the doorway without another word.

Onni put a hand in his pocket, around the small collection of objects there, and headed back downdeck. If he was lucky, he'd get five hours of decent sleep before next shift, and maybe waking would bring some fresh ideas with it.

***

"I hate to break it to you, Onni," Fin-Fin said as they were getting their heavy boots on for a muck-out of the garbage drays, "but you're not exactly a giant bucket of smarts. How do you think you're gonna figure this out on your own?"

"By tryin'," Onni said, "something nobody else ain't." He pulled up his plastisuit, and just before he pulled the hood over his face he added, "I got a plan." Then he zipped the hood shut and didn't have to worry about Fin-Fin asking him for particulars.

The ship's flash recyclers were able to render down most materials, but some metals and alloys were made of tough stuff. It all ended up down here in sleds, where some lucky grunt got to pull the metal out for later scrapping before what was left got ejected into space. Onni poked through the sticky, smelly ash and rubble with his pole, turning up nothing unexpected.

There was a click and a hiss, and both of them instinctively ducked as a cloud of ash and lumpish drops fell from the ceiling vents. "I hate this job," Fin-Fin said, wiping the remains of a direct hit from his hood lamp. Bobs were too vulnerable to use in here, so their own lamps were all they had to see by. It made the chore harder, but this one time it was about to make Onni's life a little easier.

He waited until Fin-Fin was turned the other way, then dropped the knife and the religious symbol from Orph's stash down onto the floor He pushed it around in the muck a bit, and when it was good and dirty he called out. "Hey, Fin! Got something here, come see!"

Fin trudged over and stood there while Onni uncovered the two things with his pole, then bent down and picked them up. "Huh," he said. "Bet someone threw those out by accident. I better take them up to the passenger level and see if I can find who lost 'em."

Fin-Fin reached out with one gloved hand and pulled the items out of Onni's. "Huh is right," he said. "That's your plan, Onni? No one's gonna believe these were flashed at all, they ain't even slight burnt. I'm gonna take them both — "

"But they're my clues!"

"They're not clues! A big whonkin' bloody knife would be a clue, wouldn'it? Not these trinkies, nobody'd kill over these. So I'm takin' 'em up to Junior an' say we found 'em with some other of Orph's stuff."

"But Junior — "

"Junior'll tell Chugger 'cause they're friends, and once Chugger's heard, the whole ship'll know about it, passengers and crew both. Then we can see who comes askin' what else we mighta found, right?" Fin-Fin said. He handed Onni his pole. "Now I'm startin' to think you volunteered me for this duty just so's you could try your dumbnuts plan, but of course friends wouldn't do that to 'chother. So I'm gonna leave you to finish scrubbin' this tank by yer lone self, just so you have some time to think about that."

Fin-Fin left.

Onni poked his pole around in the sled crud with little interest. Fin-Fin was right about Chugger; the cook's lips were always flapping about something. Still, now that he didn't have the stuff anymore, what if no one claimed them? He was starting to resent Fin-Fin just a bit, and put some of his frustration into trying to pry loose a glob of post-flasher tar that refused to let go of the sled. "Should've brought Gunny instead," he grumbled out loud. "*Gunny* don't think he's smarter'n everyone else." He jabbed at the clump until finally it began to give, then he raised the pole to whack it again when he saw the faint glint of something metal in it.

Flipping the pole around, Onni uncapped the end pinchers and used them to pry up the object, then studied it in the palm of his gloved hand. It was some sort of lock, a sharp diagonal cut through a half-link of attached chain very much like what power-pliers would do. The pliers were standard in the grunt toolkit, uncommon anywhere else. He had a pair, and so did Orph.

The plastisuit didn't have pockets so he dropped the remains of the lock into his own boot, grimacing at the sharp edges. Then he recapped the pinchers, flipped the pole back over, and did his fastest best to get the sleds scraped down just in case there was anything else to find.

***

After changing out of his plastisuit, he went back to the tiny, closet-sized room he'd shared with Orph and dropped himself onto his bunk. Lying there, staring up and the underside of Orph's bunk above, he tried to pretend it wasn't empty.

The remains of the lock was tucked safely in his pocket now. "What was on the other end, Orph?" he asked out loud to the empty room. "Whatever it was, it weren't worth it."

***

Assface woke him up a few hours later. "We're nearly to Breakneck," he said.

"*Aurora* still in our shadow?"

"Yep. Rosemark's gonna pop something, waiting for them to do something. Takin' their time about it, whatever it is."

Onni grunted. "Anything else going on?"

"Yeah. Chugger's saying you and Fin-Fin found some stuff, an' now bunches of people are asking after missing things. You got anything else, best cough it up before Junior sends Stinkin' Steve down here to roust through your stuff."

"Who's askin'?" Maybe Fin-Fin had been right, after all.

"I dunno. Talk to Chugger."

"Thanks, Assface."

"Yeah. Just watch your back. This trip is gone all wrong."

Assface left, and Onni swung his feet over the edge of his bunk, rubbed his eyes, thought blearily about going back to sleep. Instead he stood up, stretched, touched his toes a couple of times, then picked up his kit to go shave and get decent for the day.

Roaches, one of Dougee's men, was in the grunt washroom, brushing his teeth. "Oh hey, Onni," he said, giving a big friendly smile. "Leak in cargo crew washroom, thought you guys wouldn't mind me using yours."

"What do you want, Roaches?"

"I was just thinking . . . you show me where the rest of Orph's stuff is, and maybe I can turn it in for you so you don't get blamed for stealing, and we can split the reward."

"There's a reward?"

"Sure. Gotta be, right?" Roaches doubled his efforts with the toothbrush, staring down into the sink. So it took him by surprise when Onni took hold of the man's collar and lifted him bodily two feet off the floor and pressed him face-first against the washroom wall. "Aoowch!" The man yelled.

"Who sent you down here, Roaches?"

"No one sent — " Onni bent his elbow, stuck it in the small of the man's back, and pressed. " — Aaaah! Stop! Okay, okay! It was one of the passengers, okay?"

"Which one?"

"The bodyguard. The guy in the suite wants his databead back."

"Mr. Pauls? The Basellan, wears blue robes?"

"Yeah, yeah, him. Look, I just wanted to make some cred — "

"How many cred?"

"Not much — Aaaaaoowch, stop! Stop!" Roaches wailed. "Three hundred. Haudernelle South currency, too."

"Three *hundred*? What the hell is on his databead worth that much?" Onni barely made the equivalent of forty a trip.

"He didn't say, just legal papers. Can you put me down now?"

Onni set Roaches down. Retrieving the toothbrush from the grubby, wet washroom floor, he stuck it back in the man's mouth. "Sorry, Roaches," he said, returning the friendly smile. "If this guy talks to you again, tell him that if I did happen to have his bead — and that's an *if* — he'd be best off asking me about it directly."

Roaches spat out the toothbrush, grimacing. "Guys like that don't work that way."

"Guys like me do. Now get out."

***

Now where would Orph hide a databead? Onni pondered. Something that size could be anywhere. Tiny, tamper-proof capsules that could be destroyed but not changed, they cost more than Onni and Orph together made in a year, and were something someone certainly *could* kill over depending what was on it. If he could find it, verify it was Mr. Pauls, maybe see the data itself, he might get justice after all.

First he had to find it, and keep an eye out for Pauls' two bodyguards while he did. Orph never put anything he took in with his own stuff, and he'd already checked the tin. He furrowed his brow, thinking hard, trying to remember where else he'd seen Orph hide things.

Once, they'd stolen Dougee's auth key for his personal locker on Tanduou. Man had turned the entire downdecks upside down and never found it, until it turned up in his soup nearly two runs later. Onni smiled, remembering Orph snickering at Dougee's dumbfounded expression as he stared at the dripping card balanced on his spoon, until he remembered Orph was dead and gone and those times were over forever.

The place where he'd hid the card was old, but a good one and worth checking, and he had just enough time before he was supposed to be back in cargo nine for another attempt at eradicating the skrunge. He grabbed an idle bob and then, making sure no one was watching him, headed down towards aft storage.

Pressed up against the back of the engine room itself, cargo two was hot, not just heat but rads, bad enough to keep out anybody who didn't have to be there. Onni was sweating even before he got the door open. The room was filled with haphazard stacks of boxes, crates, and tanks, all dropped where they were as quickly as possible. Onni wound through them to the back, then climbed up on top of a pile to where he could reach the emergency lamp mounted high on the wall.

He let go of the bob and it hovered just above his head. "Light, narrow," he told it, and pointed at the wall, and the little sphere lit up and directed a strong beam of white against the lamp case. Taking out his multitool, he unfastened the cover and set it down gently atop a neighboring crate, then reached up and felt around inside the case.

His fingers touched something smooth, larger than he'd expected and pushed to the back, and he just managed to get a grip on it and pull it down. At the last moment it slipped out of his grasp and fell onto the floor with a loud bang, and a stifled yelp came from somewhere else in the room.

"Who's there?" he called out. Snapping his fingers, he directed the bob back out into the center of the room. "Wide," he told it, and the room was lit. Huddled in a corner, the girl from the dining room stared at him, trembling, eyes wide, face sweat-covered and sickly. *A runaway,* Serious Ned had thought.

Onni climbed down, glancing only briefly at the small metal case now on the floor. "You been down here all this time?" he asked. "This room is hot. You can't stay here."

He moved towards her, thinking to help her out of the room, but as he got closer she jumped to her feet and lashed out with a kick that would have connected with his head if she hadn't been off-balance, ill, and slow. He stepped back and held up his hands to show he meant no harm.

"Leave me alone," she said. "I can handle the temperature."

"Can't do," he answered. "You got to get out of this room or you'll die. Rads, kid."

Her eyes narrowed. "Then why are you in here?"

"I was just getting something."

"Hidden in a lamp?"

"My cousin left it there for me. It's a game we have."

She glanced away. "They've come to get me," she said.

"You running from Aurora, kid?"

When she didn't answer, Onni sighed and sat down on the edge of a crate. "They're just following the ship," he said. "I think you're safe 'til Tanduou. You can go back to your room."

"I can't sleep," she said, suddenly tired and looking more and more like a lost kid. "I keep waiting for them to find me."

"Look . . . " Onni said. "I got an empty bunk in my room, and I'm not going to be in mine for hours an' hours yet. Nobody's gonna be looking for you there. It's yours if you want it, and okay if you don't. But you gotta get out of here."

"And what do you get out of it?" She asked.

"Nothing at all," he said, "'cept we got enough troubles this run as it is. And I was a runaway once, myself."

"Yeah? Where'd you end up?"

"Here," Onni said. "It's what they call a cautionary tale."

"You won't try to touch me?"

"Nope. Won't even bother you, unless if when I get back at the end of my shift you're snoring, then I'm gonna kick the bunk hard as I can 'til you shut up."

"Fair enough," she said. "Let's get out of here." She tried to stand, grabbing onto a crate to steady herself.

"You need help?"

"I can take care of myself," she said, and managed to walk, with more than a little wobble, out the door. Onni picked up the case from where it had fallen, tucked it in his armpit, and followed.

***

He found her an anti-radiation pill somewhere in his stash as she climbed up onto the top bunk. Then he sat down on his own bunk and looked at the case in his lap. The case had a lock, easily picked, and a post where it must have once been attached to something else; he pulled the remains of the lock he'd found near the garbage sleds out and held it against the post, and it fit nearly perfectly.

He opened the case, expecting to find a databead nested in the large padded interior. "Huh," he said.

"What is it?" The girl asked from the bunk above, her pale face peering over the edge.

"Just a bob," he said. He lifted the ball out of the foam, turning it over in his large hand. It was heavier than others he'd handled, a little bigger, with a stylized

'O' etched into one side, but still just a bob. "Awful fancy case for it."

"What are you going to do with it?"

"No idea," he said. "Hide it, I guess." He pulled his spaceboots close, dropped the bob down into one, then looked at the case and around the tiny room. Someone was bound to come looking for it, and there wasn't anywhere here to put it out of sight.

There was a loud banging on his door, and both he and the girl jumped. "Move your fat ass, Onni!" Gunny called through the door. "You're gonna make us late for shift!"

The girl disappeared from sight as he opened the door a crack and stuck his face out. "Just putting my pants on," he told Gunny. "Turn yer back."

The man made a face and turned away, and Onni stepped out of his room and stuffed the case into the hallway recycler. "Done," he said, shutting the door to his room firmly behind him. "Let's go."

***

It seemed to Onni that more than two-thirds of cargo nine was now covered in skrunge; it hung in long, slow drips from the ceiling, formed a shimmering pool across the floor, and little tiny puffs of spores erupted from fleshy cones here and there. Gunny and Onni stood in the doorway, neither willing to be the first to enter, until at last Onni stepped back. "Can't save it," he said. "Gonna have to jettison it, before it spreads."

"I'm not telling Junior," Gunny said.

"I'll do it." Onni shut the bay door. "This trip ain't been nothing but trouble."

"Miners are bailing early at Sharewith, I heard."

"Yeah? Smart of 'em."

Once they were past the third asteroid-mining colony, it was a long jump to Hades Station and then on to Tanduou, and every moment Aurora stayed on their tail doing nothing only made folks twitchier. He'd seen the miners, typical rad-weakened skinnies barely able to carry their own clothes around, and knew they couldn't have done for Orph. He still hadn't seen the man and bodyguard Serious Ned said were in cabin two, but with Pauls throwing cred at crew to get at him, he didn't figure he needed to look any further than the Basellan wife-seller.

Gunny unsuited and trudged off, and Onni did the same, thinking, which took enough of his attention that he didn't notice the door to his room was cracked open until he got there and reached for the door.

"Kid?" he called out, turning the light on.

Roaches sat on the top bunk, swinging his legs over the edge. "Onni, my man," he said, smiling.

"Roaches." Onni wrapped one hand around his other fist, cracked his knuckles.

"Came looking for the databead, and what do I find but one of our payin' passengers. Who'd've thought there'd actually be girls out there attracted to big smelly toads like you?"

"Where is she?"

"Took her to go have a chat with Mr. Pauls," Roaches said. "Figured maybe we can trade."

"She's got nothing to do with any of this."

"Does now." Roaches jumped down from the bunk, patted Onni on the chest as he stepped around him and sauntered off down the corridor. "Better hurry up, I think Mr. Pauls is takin' a liking to her hisself."

Onni chased after Roaches, resisting the urge to catch the man and snap his neck. They paused in the guest corridor as Rosemark came through the other way, Roaches giving Onni a warning look; the armsman barely spared them a glance on his way past.

Then they were at the suite. Roaches knocked, and one of Pauls' bodyguards opened the door, peered out, then let them in.

The girl sat in a chair, one hand to the side of her face, her eye swollen and red. Pauls sat on a small couch, one leg up on the cushions as he leaned back, relaxed. Three women, all visibly frightened, sat in chairs on the far side of the room, the second bodyguard in front of them. "Ah, Mr. Smith," he said. "Glad you could join us."

"Mr. Pauls," he said, and turned around and planted an elbow sharply in the face of the man who'd let him in. Roaches jumped with a squeak and backed off as the man fell to his knees, his hands grabbing at his nose. "Thanks for inviting me. You done with the girl now?"

Pauls stared at him, as the girl got up and came over to stand beside him. "No," he managed, waving off his other bodyguard who was advancing on Onni. "I'm not. Not done with her, or you either. I want my databead."

"I don't have it," Onni said. "Never did."

"I don't believe you. I've heard all about you and your cousin's little theft games."

"So you killed Orph."

"Killed him? No," Pauls said. "By the time I knew one of you had my property, your cousin had already gone for his headless spacewalk. Very inconvenient. If he took it, you have it now. If you took it . . . well. I want it back."

"What is it?"

"None of your business."

"It's our papers," one of the women spoke up, and he turned and glared at her. "Without them, he can't — "

"Shut up!" Pauls shouted.

" — Can't prove legal guardianship of us, and we could walk at Tanduou. We'd be free." The bodyguard slapped her, hard.

Onni stepped forward, as the runaway girl grabbed his hand and slipped something small and hard into it. He recognized the shape immediately: *a databead.* "It was inside the mattress," she whispered. "I noticed the lump while trying to sleep."

He closed his hand around it, into a fist. "I don't like people like you," he said to Pauls.

"You're a Sfazili, right? A groundsider by the looks of you. Matrilineal culture, a perversion of God's natural order," Pauls said. "By the time we dock at Tanduou, I can have documents waiting that show I am this girl's guardian, too. Faked, certainly, but by the time you prove it she'll be out of your reach. So, it's a trade: the bead for the girl."

"Tell me who killed my cousin."

"I don't know and I don't care. Give me my bead."

Onni opened his hand, revealing the databead. The woman who had spoken up closed her eyes, a whimper escaping her lips, as the Basellan leaned forward, reaching out for it. He let it fall to the floor, put his boot on top of it, and ground it to powder on the rug.

"Ah!" Pauls said, jolting backwards in his seat.

"As I said, I don't like you," Onni said. Roaches leapt at him from one side, and Onni blocked the man's first sloppy punch, wrapped his thick arm around the man's neck, and slammed him to the floor right beside the still-groaning bodyguard with the broken nose.

"Get him!" Pauls shouted, and the second bodyguard moved in. The runaway girl raised up one booted foot as he reached for her and brought it down, sideways and hard, on the man's knee from above. The man screamed and fell to the floor. "Run," Onni advised her, then turned to the women huddled at the back of the room. "You too, all of you! You're free!" He shouted, waving his hands in the air.

The bodyguard with the broken nose was getting to his feet, reaching for something at his side, and Onni shoved the girl through the door and dove out into the hallway after her. He heard the energy pistol buzz before he felt the heat near his ear, saw the wall just behind him blacken.

Grabbing the girl by her hand — and thinking, not for the first time, that he should ask her name before they were killed together — he pulled her to the stairwell, covering her from behind as another shot sizzled down the hall and missed. He glanced back to the see the bodyguard aiming again, with his free hand wiping tears and snot and blood from his blotchy and swollen face, as Pauls came out behind him shouting.

They went up a deck first, racing through the dining room and startling the old man cradling his ash urn; the man and woman from Kōrogi were there, watching with interest as Onni fled with the girl through the room.

Another shot went wild. The girl pulled free from Onni, snagged a plate off a passing table, and sent it spinning with unerring accuracy straight into the bodyguard's forehead. The man crumpled and didn't move. "Nice hit," Onni said, catching a look of surprised approval on the Kōrogi woman's face, before he dragged the girl through the kitchenette and out into the staff section of the ship.

Onni collided with Stinkin' Steve coming the other way. "What the fuck — " the deputy started to shout, throwing his hand out against the wall to keep from being knocked over.

"Gun," Onni said by way of explanation, without stopping. "Behind us."

Around the corner now, they heard Stinkin' Steve begin to accost someone, and then the sound of the energy pistol discharging again. "Keep running," he advised the girl, but if anything she was ahead of him now. "Could be the other bodyguard or Roaches, or even Pauls hisself. I think I made him mad."

"You think?!" She said. "Where are we going?"

"Gotta find a place where Roaches won't think of looking," Onni said. He led her down into the cargo area, winding from bay to bay. "Least 'til someone finds Stinkin' Steve and locks the ship down. I was thinking — "

Turning the corner near cargo eight, still trying to think of a place to hide, he found himself face to face with Dougee. "Dougee," Onni said, "you're in my way."

"Onni," Dougee said, smiling. "I was just lookin' for you."

"Kinda busy right now. Later?"

"I got a friend who wants to talk to you. Right behind you."

Onni whirled around, trying to keep the girl shielded, and found a tall, heavily-muscled man approaching, and behind him a white-haired old man he hadn't seen before. "Cabin two?" he guessed.

The white-haired man raised one arm, showing a cuff around it and a chain that had clearly been cut through. "You have something of mine," he said. "I want it back."

"Pretty sure I don't," Onni said. It wasn't a lie — the case that was clearly once at the other end of the man's wrist was in the flash recycler, or in the sleds as melted slag. He patted his pockets. "What is it?"

The man snapped his fingers. "Rig?"

The tough reached behind his back and pulled free a very long knife from some sort of shoulder sheath. "Let me put this another way," the old man said. "I want my case back. I will get my case back. You can either cooperate, or you can die, just like your thieving idiot of a cousin."

"Can I kill him now, Dr. Bachler?" the tough asked.

"Not yet. Give him a chance to cooperate."

"You're the ones who killed Orph."

"I did," Rig said. "It was easy. You going to give me more of a fight?"

"I expect I will," Onni said. "Your case — metal thing, about so big?" He held up his hands, here then there, outlining the box. "I threw it in the flash recycler. It's gone."

The sound the old man made was similar, he thought, to the sound Pauls had made when he'd crushed the databead. "That was priceless," the man said.

"A broken old bob?" Onni reached up and plucked an idle bob out of the air above him. "Here, you can have this one. This one even works."

"It wasn't a bob, you moron," Bachler said. "It took me ten years to find it. Ten years following rumors from one dump of a place to another, looking for the rarest of the rare. There's only a handful of them, spread out all over the Multiworlds, maybe even all over the galaxy, and they're sentient."

"Sent — "

"Intelligent, you idiot. True artificial life."

"There's Earth scientists been working decades on that, in some institute," Onni said. Doesn't everybody know that? "Must be theirs. Go ask them for one."

"I work for them," Bachler said, his voice bitter and angry. "They aren't ours. We don't know where they come from."

"It was broken."

"It was dormant."

Onni shrugged. Bachler raised one crooked finger, and then pointed at Onni. "Kill them," he said. "Make it hurt."

"Delighted to," Rig said, gripping the blade and taking a fighting stance.

"Gonna have to wait in line," Onni said, and pointed.

Behind Rig and Bachler, Pauls had appeared with Roaches and a limping bodyguard. They all stared at each other. "He's mine," Rig snarled.

"He's *mine*," Pauls' bodyguard said, raising the pistol but wavering between pointing it at Onni or Rig.

"Fucking hell, I'm out of here," Roaches said, and bolted. Dougee, wide-eyed and slack-jawed, backed away from Bachler until he hit the wall and stopped where he was.

"If we both want him dead," Pauls said, "I don't see any need for us to fight over the privilege, as long as it gets done."

"True," Bachler said, though Rig frowned.

"I might be lying 'bout recycling your bob," Onni said.

"He's just tryin' to save himself!" Dougee shouted.

"I agree," Pauls said.

"If there's the slightest chance he has—" Bachler started to say, but Pauls' bodyguard raised his pistol, aiming it at Onni's head.

"Stop!" Another voice shouted, and Rosemark appeared around the corner with weapon raised.

Pauls' bodyguard whirled around and fired at the *Folly's* Chief Armsman, as Rigs stepped forward and swung his blade at Onni's head. Onni ducked, pivoted on one foot, and punched the man in the gut before backing away again, sidling towards the door to the cargo bay behind him. "That your best?" he asked. "'Cause watching that clumsy swing hurt nothing but my eyes."

The man growled as he took up another stance, studying Onni more intently.

Pauls' bodyguard screamed as Rosemark shot him in the leg; he fell down, dropping his gun. Rosemark reappeared, fired at where Pauls' bodyguard had just been standing, then ducked away again. Dougee whimpered and slid down the wall, a burn in the center of his chest; Rosemark's shot had found a home after all.

Pauls lunged for the runaway girl and she elbowed him in the face, grabbed the collar of his robes and flipped him into the floor, and was busy kicking him in the stomach. Onni turned his head, pretending to be distracted by the girl, and Rig made his move, jumping forward as he made a short, fast, sideways swing. The blade whistled through the air. Onni slapped the door control behind him, then at the last second ducked down low, grabbed the man around his waist, and threw him over his own head deep into cargo bay nine.

There was swearing, then screaming. Onni shut the door.

"What's in there?" The girl asked, standing with one foot on Pauls' head.

"Skrunge," Onni said. "And my fair justice."

Rosemark came cautiously around the corner, gun at the ready, and found Onni and the girl and Bachler still standing, and no one else. "Which one of you shot Steve?" he asked.

Onni pointed at the bodyguard, lying on the floor and grasping his knee and crying. Rosemark grunted, stood over the man. "Steve was a good man," Rosemark said, and shot him again, in the head. He looked up again. "What the hell else is going on here?"

"They attacked us," the girl said.

"Us?"

"Me and this guy," she said, grabbing Onni's arm. "They thought we took something of theirs."

Rosemark snorted. "Imagine that," he said. "Mr. Smith?"

Onni pointed at Bachler. "That man had my cousin, Orpheus Smith, killed. His man that did the killing is in cargo nine. Everyone here heard him say he did, too. He bribed Dougee to help him. This guy," he kicked Pauls, "is a dirty slaver, and he attacked this girl here, who's a paying passenger."

"I'm a respectable merchant," Pauls said.

"The women who were in his cabin were witness," Onni said.

"I'll be sure to talk to them," Rosemark said. "Who shot Dougee?"

"You did."

"Well that saves me some trouble. I don't tolerate crew that'll sell my ship, or each other, out."

"Then you'll need to be having a word with Roaches, too."

"Roaches?" Rosemark asked.

"Uh . . ." Onni tried to remember his real name. "Rubel."

"Clearly this is complicated," Rosemark said. He went to the wall intercom, typed in his access code, and buzzed the bridge. "Tell Junior I've found and eliminated the gunman," he said. Releasing the intercom, he pointed at Dougee. "You think you can carry him, Mr. Smith?"

"To an airlock?"

"To the infirmary, for now."

Onni sighed. "I suppose so."

Rosemark pointed his gun at Pauls and Bachler. "You two can walk," he said, "or join your friend on the floor."

***

"We're dropping out of jump," Onni said.

"I can feel it," the girl answered. She was sitting on the top bunk, swinging her legs over the edge. "What happens then?"

"Aurora will have people on Tanduou waiting for you to get off the ship. If you don't, they'll just hit us as soon as we're out of here and on our way to Cherish Station."

"So there's no way I can get away," the girl said.

"Might be one way," Onni said.

"What?"

Onni put his head in his hands, stared at the floor. "What'd you want, kid? What'd you run away for?"

"Freedom," she said.

"Nobody's ever really free," Onni said. "There's a place where you'd be safe, people'd take care of you, and not even Aurora'd dare try to take you back. It wouldn't be an easy life, but it'd be your own."

"I'd rather be dead than go back to Aurora," she said.

"Well then." Onni stood up, straightened his back, rolled his shoulders. "Have some people to go talk to, then, you and me."

***

The Kōrtrogi woman stared at him for a long time after he finished speaking, then looked at the girl. "We don't normally do favors for outsiders," she said.

"She's a good kid and deserves a chance," Onni said.

"Most are and do."

"She's good in a fight."

"She is. But still . . . "

"I kept my word and told no one 'bout you."

"I'd have killed if you had, and you know it."

"Please?"

The woman's partner looked at the runaway girl. "Do you know who we are?" he asked. "What we do?"

"I have no idea," the girl answered. The man half-smiled, then faster than Onni could follow with his eyes threw a punch straight at the girl's head.

She ducked, barely on time, and kicked him in the shin.

"I am willing to work with her," the man declared, pleased.

The woman closed her eyes for a moment, as if gathering her patience, then shifted her gaze to the girl. "If you come with us, you will have to learn to fight, you may have to kill. Is this what you want?"

"I'll be able to protect myself?"

"That you will," the woman answered.

"Then yes, it's what I want," the girl answered. "I don't want to be running the rest of my life."

The woman nodded.

"One more thing," Onni said.

"You've presumed far too much already," the Kōrogi woman said, warning in her voice.

"Not from you," Onni said. "From her." He reached into his pocket and pulled Bachler's bob out, and handed it to the girl. "That scientist guy said it was alive. Don't figure that can be right, but if it is, I don't think those are the people who should have it," he said. "Even if it's not, I like the idea of him never being able to get his hands on it again anyhow."

She took it.

"I never asked your name," he said.

"Bari," she said.

"Take care, Bari," he said. "Be as free as you can."

"I'll try," she said.

He turned and walked away.

***

Captain Lautterson and Rosemark were waiting for him at the ship's airlock. Pauls' women were already off the ship, standing there in the middle of Tanduou's docks and staring around them in terrified wonder. Roaches and Dougee had 'donated' the bribes paid them to the women, in exchange for not being dropped straight into space themselves.

"You're leaving us, Mr. Smith?" The Captain asked.

"Have to go tell my auntie and my ma about Orph," he said.

The Captain held out his hand and Onni shook it, then pulled the man close and embraced him.

"You did good work. There's a job here on the *Folly*, waiting for you, anytime you want to come back to us," the Captain said.

"I might," Onni said, tears in his eyes. "I just might."

The two men waved as Onni walked away, his hand curled around the gold bars of rank from the Captain's uniform. "This one's for you, Orph," he whispered, then stepped off the *Folly* onto the docks, to make his way home.

PART 3
DARKNESS

"Madam Orobas" illustrated by Puss in Boots

Madam Orobas

By Chris Wilsher

"Let's go in there," Sheree said, pointing at the tent. "We haven't tried that yet."

Joey looked at the giant cardboard figure of a fortune teller, painted gold and green, that was next to the entrance . Above the entrance, in large letters, a sign that read MADAM OROBAS.

"A fortune teller?" he said. "You gotta be kidding. That's too corny. Anyway, we've already spent more money than I planned. "

Sheree grabbed his hand. "Come on. Don't be such a cheapskate. She might be able to tell our future. Yours and mine. It'll just cost a few bucks. What's to lose? "

She pulled him into the tent, which was empty except for a woman sitting behind a table. A crystal ball was on one side of the table, and an incense candle on the other — the place stunk of incense. A cage was next to the table. At first it appeared to be empty, but as Joey got closer, he could see a small snake curled up in a corner.

The woman was dressed in a black caftan, and she had a black turban on her head. She was heavily made-up and there was no telling her age. Could've been anywhere from forty-five to eighty.

"Please, sit," she said.

Sheree started to slip into the chair when the woman held up her hand. She pointed at Joey.

"No, you, Mister Franks. You sit in the chair."

Joey frowned. "How do you know my name?"

She gave him an enigmatic little smile. "Just sit in the chair, please."

He shrugged and dropped into the chair.

"Please give me your hand," she said.

"You're not going to use the crystal ball?"

"That won't be necessary."

She took his hand in hers, which were hard and scaly. Joey knew how this worked. She'd make some general statements that were guaranteed to be true. You'll be going on a trip. Or, there's an illness in your family. Then she'd look to see how he'd react and take it from there, feeding off his reactions. It did bother him that she knew his name, though. He couldn't quite figure that out.

After a couple of minutes she looked up, stared him hard in the eye. She really is going to town on this, he thought.

"You are a stock broker, yes?" she said.

Joey nodded.

"I see you do not have much money."

Joey glanced at Sheree. "That's not really — "

She held up a hand. "Does not matter. You will come into money soon. Quite a lot of money."

Sheree let out an excited little whoop.

This confirms the woman's a fraud, Joey thought. Fact was, he was near the end of his rope at Connor & Carlson LLC. His review was this week and he'd be lucky to keep his job let alone come into any money.

"What else you want to know?" the woman asked.

"That's fine. You've told me all I need to know."

"There is much more."

"What do I owe you?"

"That will be ten dollars, please."

Joey reluctantly dropped a ten-spot on the table. The woman scooped up the bill and tucked it up her sleeve.

"What about me?" Sheree said.

The woman shrugged. "If you wish."

Sheree stuck her palm out. The woman looked at for a moment, then scowled.

"You want to know if you and Mr. Franks will be married, correct?"

Sheree nodded.

"It will not happen."

Sheree sat up like an ice cube had been dropped down her back. She pulled her hand back.

"Joey, get me out of here."

The woman shrugged. "You should also know your lifeline is short."

Joey dropped another bill on the table and turned to leave.

The woman said, "Mister Franks, you did not believe what I told you, did you?"

"Not a word."

"I suggest you invest your money in a company named Strategic Manufacturing Resources. You will be happy you did."

Sheree grabbed his hand. "Come on, Joey. Let's get the hell out of here."

***

In the car, Shree said, "I can't believe you let her talk to me like that."

"I was kind of surprised," Joey said. "I bet she doesn't get much repeat business, saying stuff like that."

"But you just stood there. You didn't contradict her. You didn't say anything."

"About us getting married? There was nothing to say. She's just a crazy old woman. What does she know?"

***

The next day, Joey was going through his list of cold calls, hoping to find a couple of suckers with investible funds, but having no luck. It was the damned call sheets. They were stale and had been worked over so many times — there were no prospects left. But he had to rope in a new client or two or he'd be out on the street looking for a job.

He thought about what the woman said.

I suggest you invest your money in a company named Strategic Manufacturing Resources. You will be happy you did.

Sounded like the kind of line he'd use on the suckers. He'd never heard of Strategic Manufacturing Resources before. A couple of mouse clicks on his computer and he found out why. They were traded over-the-counter. Current stock price was eighty cents a share. On 400,000 shares outstanding that gave it a market cap of $3.2 million. A little bit more digging and he discovered it was in the warehouse business. Owned a dozen warehouses in California and Nevada. Some work on the calculator showed that the value of the land the warehouses were sitting on was probably four to five times the company's market cap. A prime candidate for a takeover bid. Problem was, there were hundreds of other companies that were prime candidates to be taken over, but few ever were. Most ended up going out of business first.

Still, that woman did know his name and that he worked as a stock broker. That continued to puzzle him. *What had the tip off been?* His cell phone buzzed. It was Sheree. Third time that morning she'd called. But he didn't take it. She'd been a real bitch last night, complaining about what the fortune teller had said. Joey pointed out that he didn't even want to go to the fortune teller, that it'd been her idea. She only had herself to blame. She accused him of being insensitive. He took another look at the phone, then stuck it back in his pocket. He'd talk to her after she cooled down a little.

He walked down the hall to the office of his boss, Lawrence Ferguson. Ferguson was an old-fashioned sort. Smoked a pipe. Wore tweed jackets. Spoke about delivering value for the client. A couple of other brokers were in the office, killing time, waiting for lunch.

"What is it, Franks?"

"I've got something you might be interested in. You've probably never heard of it. A company called Strategic Manufacturing Resources. It looks promising."

"You're right," Ferguson said. A pause for effect. "I've never heard of it."

204

The other brokers laughed.

Ferguson said, "What's so special about it?"

"It appears to be grossly undervalued. Ripe for a takeover."

Ferguson gestured. "Let me see your paperwork." He thumbed through it. "A company that owns warehouses. Great. Sounds . . . dynamic. How did you find this dog? With a Ouija board?"

More laughter from the other brokers.

Ferguson tossed the papers into his trashcan. "Listen. Around here we do serious analysis of serious companies for serious people. If you want to impress me, bring me something better than this garbage."

His ears still burning Joey returned to his desk. He knew the fortune teller was right — he could feel it in his blood. What to do? He had three grand in his checking account. Rent was due in a couple of days and he had other expenses. But the woman, she knew things. He looked at his palm. What had she seen? He slammed his fist down. Screw it! Nothing ventured, nothing gained. He pulled up his account. In a couple of minutes he was the proud owner of 3,000 shares of Strategic Manufacturing Resources.

***

When he arrived at work the next morning, the receptionist told him that Mr. Carlson wanted to see him.

On the eighteenth floor. As he rode the elevator, it felt like a trip hammer was exploding in his chest. Ferguson must've given him a bad review. This is it, he thought. This is where I get my walking papers.

Carlson was sitting behind a desk the size of an aircraft carrier. He was a big man dressed in a loudly striped shirt, bright red tie, and pin-striped suit.

"It's Joey, right?"

"Yessir."

"You're probably wondering why I called you up here."

Joey nodded.

"I'm looking at your account. You mind telling me about this stock you bought yesterday?"

"Stock?"

Carlson leaned over, looked at his computer screen. "Strategic Manufacturing Resources. Sound familiar?"

"Yes. I bought some shares yesterday. What's this about?"

"Your shares are now worth a little under fourteen grand." Carlson's voice was a low rumble. "You didn't know that?"

"No, I just got in. I hadn't checked my account yet."

"Seems American Malls announced a buy-out last night after the markets closed. Four-fifty a share. Care to tell me how you knew this was going to happen?"

"I didn't."

"Joey, we have a program on our computers. It tracks any unusual trades made by any brokers. Yours set all the red lights flashing." A pause. "You should know that the SEC takes a very dim view of insider trading. So does the firm. So do I."

"It wasn't insider trading."

Well, not in the conventional sense.

Carlson was silent.

"I did some research," Joey said. "Saw it was ripe for a takeover. I showed Mister Ferguson what I had."

"That's interesting. What did he say?"

"He didn't take it seriously. He threw it in the trash."

A long moment of silence. Carlson idly scratched his chin.

"That's too bad. Tell you what. In the future, if you get any more ideas like this, come see me. Understood?"

***

There was nobody but the woman in the tent. Everything was the same as it had been, except the snake looked larger. But that couldn't be possible. Not in two days. *Must be his imagination.*

"You made a lot of money, Mister Franks?"

"Yes. Almost eleven grand in profit."

"Good for you. Now you want more information, yes? So you can make even more money."

"More money is always good."

"First, you need to make a payment for the information I gave you two nights ago."

"I paid you."

"That was merely to have your palm read. I am talking about a sacrifice. You see, the universe must always remain in balance. If something is gained, something else must be lost, the balance must be maintained. It is time for you to make a sacrifice."

"You mean like a chicken or a lamb or something?"

"I was thinking about your watch."

Joey stared at his wrist. "My father left this to me when he died. It was the only thing he left me. It's all I have to remember him by. "

"The universe requires a sacrifice, Mister Franks."

"Can't I give you something else? Some of the money I made? A percentage? Say, ten percent."

"The watch, Mister Franks."

Joey nodded, slowly pulled the watch from his wrist, laid it on the table.

"Okay," he said, "what do you have for me?"

***

Joey sat with Carlson in Carlson's office on the eighteenth floor. An array of TV screens occupied one wall. Each screen was tuned to a different channel, but all had the same story. The Bluewater IV explosion.

"Forty-eight dead, twenty-nine injured," intoned a talking head. "Meanwhile, thousands of barrels of oil per hour continue to spew into the blue gulfstream waters. All of it headed straight toward pristine Florida beaches."

"Bluewater Drilling Incorporated's stock just hit five dollars a share," Carlson said, looking at his computer monitor. "The strike price. That represents a four hundred percent profit. You made the firm eight hundred thousand dollars today, Joey. Best part is, nobody can ever accuse us of insider trading."

Joey mumbled something and took a slug of his scotch.

"I mean, there's no way anybody could've known in advance that this oil rig would explode, right?"

Joey wasn't really listening. The meds had worn off and the pain was back, worse than ever.

He'd heard of the explosion the night before, and he'd driven immediately to the carnival, breaking several traffic laws on the way. Madame Orobas was alone in the tent, as usual.

"There was an explosion, correct? Many dead and injured."

"That's right." His voice was shaky, high-pitched.

"And you made money?"

"Quadrupled my stash. Have more than fifty grand in the account."

"When I looked at your palm, I told you that you would make money."

"You were right."

"But you want even more, don't you?"

"Sure. You can never have too much money."

"It will require yet another sacrifice. You understand?"

"Okay, what do you want this time?" He laughed. "My shoes?"

"No, Mister Franks." She took out a steel chopping knife from under the table. "I want your little finger."

"You're not serious?"

"But I am. The balance must be maintained. You know that."

The knife gleamed in the candlelight.

"You give me another money maker, if I give you my little finger?"

"Correct. You will not be disappointed. I promise."

This is like a leap of faith. A test to see if he was worthy.

Joey had stretched his hand out on the table.

"No, Mister Franks," she said. "Your right hand."

***

Carlson poured some more scotch into his glass.

"The hand still bothering you?"

"A little."

"What the hell happened?"

"Kitchen accident."

Jesus, he didn't want to talk about it. He just needed to some more pain meds. More pain meds — that would make everything better.

Carlson said, "You've got to take care of yourself, Joey. You've got a bright future in front of you."

Now even Carlson was a fortune teller! For some reason this seemed insanely funny to Joey. It took him several minutes before he could stop laughing. When he did, Carlson was looking at him in a strange way.

"You said you were on the track of another winner," Carlson said, abruptly. "Tell me about it."

"It's an insurance company. Nagoya Life and Indemnity."

"It's Japanese, right?"

"It is. You need to sell it short. Way short."

"What does it insure?"

"Nuclear power plants, mostly."

***

It was the next day. The carnival was gone. Vanished. Disappeared. This couldn't be. He had to find her. He drove into town, trying to think where the carnival could

211

have gone. But it was hard to think. The pain. The drugs. He stopped at a diner.

Inside, they looked at him funny. A cook and a waitress. Must be the blood on his shirt. Sheree's blood. But there's not that much. Hardly noticeable. A reasonable explanation for everything.

The universe had to be balanced.

"The carnival," he said. "Where did it go?"

They named a town twenty miles up the Interstate.

"I heard some of them talking," the woman said, nodding furiously. "That's where they went. That way."

She pointed.

He got in the car, headed north. The steering wheel was sticky. He found a couple of pills loose in his pocket, popped them in his mouth, tasted blood. He wiped his hand on his pants. More blood.

Early in the day and the carnival grounds were empty. She was sitting behind the table, just like always. The tent still smelled of incense, but there was something else. An earthier smell, the smell of freshly turned dirt. It reminded him of his father's funeral. The casket being lowered into the dark gaping maw that was to be his eternal grave. A noise from the corner and he turned. The snake! It was a huge, coiling mass, completely filling the cage. Its mouth gaped open, exposing immense fangs. For a moment, Joey thought it would burst from the cage, and attack him.

She cleared her throat. "You did it, didn't you, Mister Franks? I can tell. The mark is on you. I can see it. The mark of Cain."

"It was your idea," he said, keeping one eye on the cage. "You told me. The universe it had to be balanced. It required a death."

"The choice was still yours."

"Look at me. I need just one more idea. Then I'll be rich. None of this will matter. I won't ever have to worry again. What will it take?"

"There is nothing more."

"Tell me," he said. "I'll do it. I'll do anything you tell me."

"It is too late. The police are already hunting you. They've found the body. And the knife with your fingerprints on it. You cannot go back to your apartment. And your bank account with all the money is frozen."

Joey sat, stunned. His expression changed to anger.

"You know what's really weird about all this? I've never seen another customer in here, all the times I've been here. Does anybody else ever come in here? It's like you sit there, just waiting for me. Like a spider waiting for a fly."

The woman displayed a thin smile.

Joey vaulted from the chair. "This is all your fault. I wished I'd never come in here. I wish I'd never met you."

He reached for her neck, but as he did, her appearance suddenly changed to something bestial with a long pink snout and small eyes and a huge mouth with ravaging teeth. He stumbled back towards the entrance. The woman's visage reappeared.

"You should go now, Mister Franks. Run. But you won't get far."

"How do you know?"

"It was in your palm. I could've told you the first time, but you didn't want to hear. Like your friend Sheree, you have a very short lifeline."

Death Perception

By J.B. Williams

Charlie realized almost as soon as he sat down that the girl next to him was dead.

It wasn't just the way her blond head lolled against the dirty window, shifting with each lurch of the bus's movement, or how disheveled and dirty her clothes were, or even that she smelled like roadkill on a hot day. He'd encountered others in this city who shared that description, usually homeless, but definitely living. It wasn't the green-gray pallor of her skin either. That could have been from illness. Even the dried blood that led from her nose and down over her chin, and the spatters of it on her shirtfront, could have been from that.

It was that ants were coming from somewhere under her hair, down across her neck and into the collar of her shirt. It was that they were stopping to feed.

The bus rounded a corner badly, rear right wheel thumping up and over the ledge of the sidewalk. The girl's mouth popped open and hung, slack. Charlie righted himself and stared at the little things that began to drop from the corner of her lips. Little white things, *grains of rice?* except they were squirming blindly where they'd fallen into her lap. He scrambled up and reached across her, frantically pulling at the stop-signal cord, running for the door as the driver shouted at him.

The squeal of airbrakes at the corner of Church and Summerlin. Charlie flung himself against the door, forcing it before it could hiss open, pattering off in a run down the sidewalk, the office buildings blurring past. A single thought repeated in cadence with his footsteps: *Not again, not again, not again.*

***

"You're sure it wasn't a real dead person?"

"Positive." The closet was blessedly dark except for the crack of light under the door. He'd run the phone cord under it so he could call the crisis hotline from within its enclosure. He hoped the woman on the other end was more experienced than she sounded. Her voice conjured up images of a big-eyed twelve-year-old.

"Because if there's any possibility it was, you really ought to call the police."

"It was not. Trust me, if a real corpse had been on that bus long enough to look . . . and smell . . . like this one, someone else would have noticed before I got on. It's a hallucination, the same as I used to have before I got on the medication, only I've been taking the pills for a year and it's starting again anyway."

Long silence on the other end, so that he almost asked *Still there?* before the woman responded.

"Maybe your dosage needs adjusting. Have you asked your doctor about this?"

"No." He wanted to add, *I can only afford the meds or a doctor session, not both. But thanks for that wonderfully upper-class assumption that everyone can afford a doctor.* He decided not to bother. If he did, it'd quickly dissolve into the same old chatter about going to the county clinic or one of those other Very Reasonable Places Where They Deal With Cases Like Yours. So well-meaning that the girl would never realize how patronizing it was.

"Well, you should look into that . . . "

Charlie assured her he would, and hung up.

And hid under the pile of laundry.

And stayed. All night.

***

Two days passed. Two days of work in the stockroom, of riding the shaking, squeaking city bus to and from work, of deep gray weather vomiting rain down on the city and bringing the rank, organic smell of the surrounding swamps with it. Two days of the gutters running sheened with dirty water and epileptic shimmers of lightning never quite leaving the sky.

Two days with clear vision and only a small chatter of fear in the back of his mind.

Charlie stood in the rain for a while late the second afternoon before entering the boarding house, face turned up, letting the orbits of his closed eyes fill with it and run over, smiling. It had been an aberration on the bus, that was all.

He let himself in, the brown hush of the empty house folding around him. Narrow stairs ascended, room entered and locked, clothes changed, sandwich and glass of chocolate milk made and consumed, cot collapsed on, sleep.

He awoke sodden with sweat some hours later, heartburn chewing at his insides and the bedside clock reading 2:17 AM. He crept down the stairs, past the doors beyond which the landlady and one of the other tenants snored, through the shadowed living room and into the kitchen. He mixed baking soda into a glass of water and held his nose to gulp the vile stuff down.

The pain lessened almost immediately, but just to be sure, he swallowed the rest. As he rinsed the glass, he caught a brief flash of his own hollow-eyed, revolted face in the dark window over the sink. He gave it a quick, huge rictus of a smile, turning the reflection into a distorted jack-o-lantern shape.

"See?" he whispered. "It's all good."

The landlady kept a bookshelf in the living room, which she let tenants borrow from as long as they gave the books back before the next rent day. Maybe he could get something to read till he could fall asleep again. He tiptoed out of the kitchen, barked his shins on the fussy little ottoman and then on the coffee table, and finally fumbled the switch for the overhead lamp. Yellow light seeped down into the room.

Charlie turned around, and saw the man on the floor.

For a moment he thought it was Billy, the other tenant on the second floor. Sometimes Billy came home drunk and passed out on the living room sofa instead of going upstairs. But the sprawled, spidery figure wasn't Billy, or anyone else who lived there. This man was pale and blond and wearing striped pajamas, his head thrown back and arms splayed out. His eyes were open and bloodshot crimson, and the purple bruises ringing his neck showed the marks of fingers. Thin streams of blood drooled from his nose and mouth.

It was clearly a corpse.

Charlie took a tentative step back, hands spread out in front of him, throat closing, when the hope occurred to him: what if it was real? Sometimes the tenants weren't careful about making sure the doors were locked when they came in late. It was a vaguely dangerous neighborhood, being so close to the north side of the Esperanza district. What if someone had been attacked and badly hurt on the street, and had wandered in here and died?

The dead man's red stare regarded him.

Charlie lurched to one side, found the ottoman, and shoved it at the figure. If it was a real dead person, the ottoman should stop when it hit.

Please let it stop, pl —

The ottoman glided smoothly through the dead man's upper body and kept rolling till it hit the opposite wall with a small thud.

The corpse's stare remained unchanged.

Charlie ran, not caring about noise anymore, thumping up the stairs with his hand clamped over his mouth to keep from screaming.

***

The next morning he shuffled onto the #5 bus. Damp from the rain, he kept his gaze firmly on the toes of his shoes before sitting down in a front seat. If the dead girl in the back of the bus had reappeared, he didn't want to know.

The bus squeaked its way deeper into town, beneath the overpasses and creeping up the interstate, inching through misted-in morning traffic. Charlie leaned his face against the cold glass of the window to keep awake, glancing up as they passed under the half-finished arc of the new South Street overpass, construction equipment standing sentinel around its east base in the spot where the homeless camp used to be. Bird Tower and the downtown bank buildings loomed up into the fog behind the half-span and disappeared. He wondered vaguely if they'd ever finish building the thing. He sort of missed the homeless camp, with its jumble of cardboard box-homes and the occasional spread of laundry hung to dry on the highway guardrail.

He got off at the right corner, but was unable to resist looking back at the bus. *And that,* he thought sourly, *is how Lot's wife turned into salt.* There was a slumped shadow at one of the back windows, but that could have been anything.

The supermarket stockroom was blessedly warm and dry, and sorting the boxes from the latest delivery of goods relaxed him, almost too much. Twice Charlie went out to the front of the store, to the waiting silver urns on the table with the *Customers Help Yourselves!* sign, and got coffee. It was watery and had grounds floating in it, but it was free and it kept him awake.

He was on his way back from the second trip when he saw the woman on the polished floor in aisle 3, tweed overcoat puddled around her and her dark skin tinged with cyanotic blue. He stopped short in front of the magazine rack and closed his eyes.

"Not real," he whispered, then looked again. The dead woman was still there. Two flies were circling erratically above her face.

He took a deep breath and let it out slowly. Then he walked calmly back to the office, told his supervisor he was ill, and clocked out.

***

The landlady, Mrs. Mellick, was sweeping the kitchen floor when Charlie got home. Bits of bristles fell from her ancient broom and made more mess as she worked.

"You're home early," she piped.

"I was sick." Not exactly a lie, he thought.

She insisted he sit at the wobbly kitchen table, and made him tea. "This will cure just about anything," she explained as she set the mug down. Charlie took a tentative sip and tried not to grimace noticeably. The stuff was spectacularly bitter.

"I've always said it's too bad the doctors don't pay more attention to herbal remedies," Mrs. Mellick chirped, grabbing the broom and flailing away at the dirty linoleum again.

Is there an anti-cuckoo blend? Charlie wanted to ask, but he knew she wouldn't recognize the remark as rhetorical and cynical.

"Take the business around here, for instance. All those folks in Esperanza smoking this meth and going crazy from it and stabbing each other, I say if they'd tried some chamomile and valerian it'd have sedated them right out. It's never been a happy part of the city though. Now when I was a girl here, it was bootleg booze instead, the kind that'd make you go blind." She was rambling, as usual, and Charlie pretended to drink more tea while she was distracted. He wasn't sure that whatever was in it wouldn't interact with his medication.

"But there wasn't people killing each other over it, maybe in other cities, but not here. Esperanza wasn't the poor part then. Clackman Park was, full of broke farmers. Funny how it's gotten switched around. Back then the murders were always downtown. There were only a couple of times it happened here. One of them was right in this house, did I ever tell you about that?" She paused expectantly.

The cold weight of shock thudded in Charlie's chest and belly at her words. His response came out slow and halting. "I — don't think you did."

223

"Really? I thought I did. Back then the Sykes family owned this place. They had money. But the old man, Sam, when he got the place he pissed most of their cash away with drinking. His daughter Lydia got it after he kicked off, and she was just crazy as a bowl of bugs, got sent off to some institution. She busted holes in the neighbors' windows in the middle of the night because she thought they were spying on her, can you believe that?"

You'd be amazed what I'd believe, Mrs. Mellick, Charlie thought.

She plowed on. "She had a little boy too, I forget his name. He had to go live with some relative or other. Lydia hanged herself in the hospital and the boy inherited — he'd grown up by then. He'd come back for her funeral and he was staying here when it happened."

"He was the one who got killed?"

"One of the neighbors came over and found the door open. The son was dead on the living room floor. Strangled. The weirdest thing was — there were these dirty footprints leading up the walk and into the house, into the kitchen. Dirty handprints on the table. Footprints leading back out into the living room and around the body. But — none leading back out. And the neighbor said there was this awful smell, like something rotting —" She stopped. "Now why am I bothering you with my history lectures again when you're feeling bad? Take your tea and go upstairs and get some rest."

Charlie rose slowly, feeling wobbly, and picked up the teacup. He was in the doorway when he turned back. "Mrs. Mellick? Could I use your computer later?"

"Of course. As long as you're not looking up porn."

Along the way, he stopped in the hall bathroom and dumped the tea down the sink.

***

Mrs. Mellick kept her study in a bleak little room at the end of the second-floor hallway. The one small window was a blank black eye because she always kept the hurricane shutters over it closed. Charlie was glad it wasn't on the first floor. He didn't want to have to go anywhere near the living room again.

The overhead light was bleary and clogged with roach corpses. The computer screen gave off better illumination. He slumped in the chair in front of it, munching from a bag of slightly stale corn chips and trying search terms.

"Death Records": too many hits to even try combing through.

He added a time range to the "Death Records" part. Still too long, and besides, how did he know it was the right time range for what he wanted?

The county coroner's office allowed searches by name, and dates and towns of death. No space for searching by specific address where the death took place, or by circumstance.

He found the city paper's Website. Even in a city this size, the paper might have an article, a little page-14 squib or something, if the death in question was sufficiently unusual. Or if it had been a murder.

The site offered its own Keyword space for internal searching. Charlie typed "dead woman" + "bus" and clicked.

The article popped up, its blue-lettered headline smarting in his field of vision.

Murdered Woman On Bus Dead For Some Time Before Discovery

He blinked and looked away, hoping the image would disappear. It didn't. He pulled in a deep breath, put the corn chips down on the desk, and read the text:

> The investigation into the murder of a woman found dead on a city bus last week has been complicated by the discovery that she was dead for some time before being placed on the bus, authorities say. The body of Georgie Lee Banks, 24, was discovered in a seat on an area transit system bus Tuesday afternoon. Police have ruled

her death a homicide. They are not yet releasing specific details of how she died. Police Chief Jackie DeRay says the interpretation of forensic evidence has been "confused" due to the condition of the body.

"Ms. Banks had been deceased for two to three days before being placed on the bus," DeRay says. "We are, as of yet, uncertain as to how her body was placed there, or where and how it was being kept beforehand."

The bus driver, Melvyn Richards, said he did not detect anything unusual when he first got on the bus Tuesday morning. However, Richards also said, "It's dark when I get in the bus and start the first route—it's at 5 a.m., you know. There could have been something already in the back of the bus and I might not have seen it." Richards is not considered a suspect. The main bus yard, at 1532 Hober Road, has been the site of numerous break-ins over the last several months. Transit officials refused to comment on the case or on yard security. Anyone with information on this or any other

crime can report it anonymously on the
Sheriff's Office Tip Line.

Charlie's stomach pulled itself into a slow knot.

Well, he thought dully. *Well, then.*

When he could move again, he clicked back to the
search page and typed "dead woman" and the name of
the supermarket, then hit Enter. His hands were shaking
a little.

The screen proclaimed NO MATCHES FOUND in
the same eye-smarting blue.

He tried a few different combinations of search
words, but kept getting the same answer. He hadn't
really been expecting one. Homicides would make the
news, but he doubted a natural or accidental death
would rate its own article unless the circumstances were
really weird. The woman he'd seen in the market had
looked very dead indeed, but she hadn't looked like
she'd been murdered.

Are you actually hoping for confirmation here, buddy? a
darkly cynical voice muttered in the back of his mind.
Inside, not outside, his head, Charlie was relieved to
note. *You're hoping you're seeing the ghosts of dead bodies
everywhere? Not to belabor the point, but isn't that, well,
nuts?*

No. That was the point. Because if he was
witnessing something paranormal here — bizarre as that
would be — it would mean that he wasn't nuts.

"Just dead people?" he whispered, eyes never leaving that terse NO MATCHES FOUND. "The occasional corpse? No giant spiders in the corners or blood dripping down the walls? No voices telling me to go jump off Bird Tower? No committal orders or straitjackets or being shot up with drugs? Nobody treating me like crap once they see the diagnosis? I'll take the ghosts, thanks."

He logged off and went back to his room. The rain had started again, clattering intermittently on the blurry old glass of the windows. Mrs. Mellick's vacuum cleaner was droning a single repetitive note on the floor below. His knees ached, like they always did in weather like this. He locked the door, lay on the rumpled cot, and slept.

And dreamed.

He was walking down Highland Avenue, where the sidewalks bent around the huge old oak trees whose roots knotted up through the pavement. Acorns popped under his boots. He waited for the light at Jackson to change before crossing, even though there was no traffic. Odd, for a street that busy.

Trim, squared green hedges met him on the right side at the corner of the next block. He followed them down, wrought-iron fence keeping a barrier between him and the shrubbery, till he reached the gap where the giant heavy gate was. The sign over it read:

229

GREENWOD MEMORIAL GARDENS

Whatever happened to just calling them cemeteries? *he wondered as he pushed the right side of the gate. It moved soundlessly inward a couple of feet and stopped. He slipped through the gap.*

The boneyard rolled away in front of him, arcs upon arcs of gray and white stones on perfectly green, manicured grass. The ground was humped with the roots of more oaks, gigantic things older than the city itself. He eyed the nearest one. Its bark was so gnarled with boles that it looked cancerous.

What are they living on in here? *he thought, then felt cold all over as he looked out at the stones again. Maybe that was a bad question to ask, when you considered what this land was used for.*

He walked down the granite path, his footsteps making no noise. The sky was cloudy, the air so humid that it seemed to stick to his skin. The graves in the front of the cemetery were the oldest, crumbly stones crusted with lichen and often leaning at strange angles, like the teeth of someone with advanced gum disease. The oak roots had heaved some of them into their positions. Charlie could make out the dates on some: 1868, 1874, 1892.

There were no sounds in the air at all. No traffic, no footsteps, no birdsong.

He took the bend that led to the left, where the newer graves were. Most of these stones were flat, clean granite. Bright splotches of flowers marked some of their bases. He paused under one of the oaks and observed the nearest stone, not much bigger than a shoebox, razor-sharp-new inscription: JASMINE LASHAUNDRA DIAMANTE, *birth and death dates only six months apart. Smaller script beneath proclaimed* Jesus Loves The Little Children. *There was a basket of dead flowers beside it and a pinwheel stuck in the dirt in front of it, the dirt still so freshly turned that only a few blades of new grass were starting to struggle up through it.*

A flicker of movement in his peripheral vision, off to the right. He looked and saw a small figure with a bright spill of red hair, wearing one of the plaid local school uniforms, slowly making her way among the rows. Sometimes a grave would seem to catch her attention, and she would crouch, then straighten, then put her hand into the knapsack she dragged. It took him a moment to realize what she was doing.

He was just about to shout at her to stop when a hand fell on his right shoulder. The shout cut off in a half-yelp somewhere in his throat, and he spun.

The woman standing beside him was tall and very pale, swathed in a long black trenchcoat. Tendrils of long black hair hung down over her shoulders. Her eyes were level with his, a very deep green like olives, and empty.

Only her mouth moved as she spoke, no animation of any kind in her face or body.

Say nothing to her, *she said in a silvery voice that sounded like tiny bells.*

He stared. But she's stealing things off the graves!

As she does every Thursday on her way home from school. She merely does what this place tells her. As do you.

Charlie took a step back. There was a strange scent coming from her, sickly sweet with a prickly chemical undertone, incense and mothballs like the upstairs coat closet at the boarding house.

Maybe you should stop taking the pills, Charlie. They make you jumpy. Didn't the doctor say they cause tardive dyskinesia?

How did you know —

I saw you in the hospital, Charlie. Remember the quiet room and poor idiotic Dr. Halloran?

He remembered, all right: those first drug trials, shaking and twitching so badly he couldn't eat or talk or stand. Halloran, short, fat, bespectacled, finally grabbing him under the arms and bodily hauling him to the padded quiet room after he'd fallen and hit his head. He looked at the woman again, searching for anything familiar.

Were you one of the doctors?

Who I am doesn't matter. What you are, and where you live, does.

The red-haired girl was slowly working her way up the row of graves toward them, stopping to read inscriptions with an expression of stupefied fascination. It reminded Charlie of the way some of the patients on the psych ward had looked after being heavily sedated. The woman followed his gaze, then smiled. An indulgent, doting sort of smile, still never showing in her eyes.

Won't she notice us *he asked?*

Not if I don't wish her to. *The smile deepened to a degree that made Charlie feel cold and still.* That child is one of my favorite people in this city. Such an embrace of the facts of death, so young! My philosophy, dear boy, is that you're never too young to know that everything dies. You have similarly keen vision. It rises from the earth of this beautiful city in which you were raised. You forced that vision away — since everyone mistook it for part of your illness — but it will refuse to stay gone forever.

Her gaze held his. He couldn't look away. Such a deep green, pupils only pinpricks.

You've read the book your landlady has downstairs, the history of the city, correct?

Charlie nodded.

Then you'll know when it was founded. What year was that?

Eighteen-thirty-something.

Beside them, the red-haired girl bent and plucked the pinwheel from the dirt at the foot of Jasmine Diamante's grave. She tucked it into her knapsack, taking no apparent notice of them.

And about how old does that make this city?

233

Charlie's brain fumbled with the calculation. About one hundred and eighty years old.

Yes. *The woman's pale hands reached out and cupped his face. Her touch was cold and unpleasantly electric, vaguely arousing and vaguely repelling at once. She was smiling again.*

Now tell me, my young seer: how many people do you think have died here in all that time?

Her countenance shifted, lovely face melting and sagging into a long leering yellow thing, hair snow-white and eye sockets empty, and then the rust-colored spiders burst from the palms of her hands in an amazing, squirming flood, over his face and into his mouth as he screamed and flailed and twisted —

He awoke kicking the blankets off and crying a long, strangled moan, just short of a waking scream.

He did not sleep again that night.

***

Dawn came up pale and gray, the windows fogged with humidity. Charlie made coffee in his room, amusing himself by drawing designs on the steam filming his window as the coffee maker slurped its way through the process. He took his pills and sat on the unmade cot, back against the wall, sipping the bitter stuff and very glad it was his day off. Even with coffee he didn't think he would have been able to fumble his way through a workday. The dream of the night before worried at the edges of his consciousness, the way a dog gnaws a knotted rag. What weird core of subconsciousness had that thing come from?

"Seeing the dead," he announced to the room, "appears to leave one a smidge distracted." He laughed. Even with the nightmare's fuzz still hovering in his mind, he felt great. No craziness, definitely no relapse.

Maybe I could hire myself out. Do readings. Help the cops. Go on talk shows, what the hell. He laughed again. None of that yet, of course not. He wanted to do a little research first. From here it was a reasonable enough distance to walk to the library, good cool weather for it. Look up a few things *not* in the psychology section for once —

Movement flickered somewhere to the left, in his peripheral vision. He turned to see what it was, then froze.

A spider was making its way up and across the window, moving at an angle. It seemed to see Charlie at the same instant he fully saw it, and halted. It was big, about the size of one of his fingernails with its legs spread out, and a dull rust color. He stared for an endless moment, the coffee cup gone slack in his hand.

When he was sure it wasn't going to move, he did, putting the cup down, very slowly reaching for Mrs. Mellick's city history book, then stepping up in one swift motion and smashing at the glass. It made a surprisingly loud thump and a dull cracking sound. Panting, he stepped back, and looked at the rust and yellow smear and the fine fractures now adorning the glass.

Cracked the damn thing. Shit.

"Just a spider," he muttered.

He put the book back and dressed, leaving the rest of the coffee. He didn't want any more. His hands were already shaking enough.

***

He spent the day on the library's fifth floor. The building had a faint moldy smell and the staff had turned the heat up too high, like they always did in this weather. The few tables on the floor were taken by homeless men, grubby and unshaven, some half-dozing amidst piles of books set up like ramparts. Charlie found a gray plush chair parked beneath one of the fogged-in windows and settled in with a pile of art and cartoon books. Research on parlaying sudden psychic gifts into cash flow could wait; his mind wearily demanded something simpler on a day like this.

Eventually the gray light outside deepened to darkness. The yellow glow of the streetlights snapped on, and Charlie realized the library would be closing soon. He gathered up the books and parked them on one of the librarian's carts, next to a table where an old man hunched, muttering and smelling strongly of bourbon and salami.

The elevator was empty and reflected Charlie's image back at him from every angle. He leaned closer to the back wall to smooth down his hair, and saw spiders scuttling across the polished surface, rust-colored bodies reflected perfectly in it.

He cried out and stumbled backward against the doors, then nearly fell out onto the muddy terrazzo of the library's first floor lobby. The lone librarian at the checkout desk glanced up, then turned away with a look of pinched displeasure on her face. The elevator doors clacked shut, and Charlie leaned against the wall. He closed his eyes till his breathing returned to normal. "Coincidence," he whispered.

He walked through the doors and paused in the glassed-in entryway, watching condensation rolling down the outside of the panes and breaking the view into a blurry, fractured mess. Home. Just getting home, taking a shower, going to bed early with a book (but not the city history book, something simple and mindless, Mrs. Mellick had plenty of those). That would be good. Calm. He could get the bug spray from the kitchen and dose his room while he was at it.

Charlie stepped out into the drizzle and turned north, up a block past the parking garage, through empty little Middle Square Park with its dry fountain and leering statue of a man sitting atop an alligator's back. The city's taller buildings loomed up into a sky turned yellow and copper with light pollution. Bird Tower seemed to be peering down on the others like an obsequious king.

He emerged into the smudged pointillism of lights that was Orange Avenue in rainy darkness. Neon and sodium and metallic light floated toward him from a million different sources.

He looked up to check before crossing, and saw. It was so present, such an offense to the eyes and the mind, that it took a moment for it to register fully.

The streets were filled with the dead.

In every direction, he saw them, empty-eyed and faces blank with stupefaction, their bodies bearing the marks of their deaths.

A bearded man in a straw hat and coveralls lay in the street, crushed limbs oozing dark blood. The girl standing under the lamppost in front of the bar had had the whole left side of her body sheared and crumpled by some terrible impact. A little boy stared from the window of the sandwich shop, his face swollen and blackened by asphyxiation. The people at the next table were laughing, oblivious. There were other still forms, faintly phosphorescent in the darkness.

The light changed and Charlie crossed, cutting across to Church Street, whimpering deep in his throat but not quite crying. Not yet. A group of college kids emerging from one of the nightclubs stared at him as he hurried past.

There were more dead here, the living walking right through them. A woman in a frilly white dress lay half in an alley, half on the sidewalk, hands clenched on her chest. Her corset and bustle had deformed her body into an insectile shape. Further down, in front of one of the crumbling old bars, several of the dead lingered. As Charlie passed, he saw that their clothes spanned several decades' worth of fashion and that they all had the slack-faced look of fatally deep drunkenness.

He fled, running now, feet slapping wet pavement, drawing startled yelps and curses from the living passersby he bumped into, traveling south toward the Anderson Street intersection.

The streets sloped slightly upward here, toward the train tracks and the interstate further on, and the buildings here were mostly office buildings now dark after the day's close, but the dead were still there. A shambling thing with a shredded, unrecognizable face leered at him from beneath one of the pale street lamps. At the intersection itself stood a gaggle of twisted, but still humanoid, shapes. As Charlie ran past, he saw their charred, flaking faces and their skin hanging in melted ribbons from their limbs. They smelled of burned meat.

Even in his extremity Charlie could remember the history book, something about a big fire eating most of downtown a hundred years ago, catching and devouring. . . .

An arc loomed up above him, reaching into the dull copper night. He flinched and screamed before realizing what it was: the half-curve of the new South Street overpass, its end pausing just above one of the interstate bridges and its endlessly moving chain of vehicle lights. He had blundered through an open gate in a chain-link fence, and still construction machines stood around him.

A web of metal scaffolding led up to the overpass arc itself, gleaming faintly. Charlie stared at it, gasping, hands pressed to his chest.

Overpass. New road, brand new road, no one ever died there, hardly anyone's ever even walked there, it's safe —

He began scrambling up the web, nearly slipping and falling, boosting himself up again, face turned up into the drizzling rain. He didn't know he was crying, didn't know he was praying. Finally, yards above the ground, he scrambled over the concrete lip of the new overpass and sprawled on the wet cement of the future breakdown lane. He folded his arms over his head and concentrated on regaining his breath.

Death Perception By J.B. Williams

Once his chest began to rise and fall instead of hitch, Charlie carefully got to his feet and looked around. The overpass arc was four lanes wide, no lines painted on it yet, scatterings of tools and chains and orange road cones lying around. It curved blankly up into the dark, and he began walking up its incline, staring at the moving lights on the interstate and the still, wide swath of ground lights to the west that marked the Esperanza district.

He walked almost to the end, then turned and looked back down into the city, curious. He couldn't see down into the streets from here. The tall office buildings on Orange Avenue were in the way of that. He stared up at them, where lights still glittered on some of the upper floors, the blue lights in the pointed spurs atop Bird Tower crowning the view.

They caught and held his gaze.

He froze, not breathing, as the city bent and refracted around him.

Sweet, silvery whispering rose to fill his ears with the chant of some guttural language.

The smell of mothballs and incense suddenly enfolded him. Then there were hands closing around his throat, and the dream woman's empty green eyes were staring into his.

He had just enough time to think *it was real* before she spoke.

I am the city, and the dead are my people.

The last thing he heard was the sound of his own neck breaking.

He fell backward among the road cones.

It was four more days before the workers found what was left of him.

"The Manservant" illustrated by Peter Porterfield

The Manservant

By Derek Paterson

Renfield tried not to titter as he hid in the bushes and waited, listening for the mail man's approaching footsteps. He had to admire how the fellow's sense of duty overcame his fear and reluctance. The Transylvania Postal Service certainly knew how to pick its men. Renfield had scared the crap out of dozens this year alone, but still they came, driven by that time-honored maxim: *The mail must always be delivered.* Even to the brooding castle up on the cliff top above the sleepy little village whose nervous inhabitants never looked up, for fear of seeing something coming down on flapping leathery wings.

Not that that had happened for a while. The Master slept the long sleep and had not arisen for many years. His faithful servant Renfield patiently awaited that joyous day. In the meantime he sought amusement in various ways, not all of them entirely intellectual.

The mail man's black leather shoes moved into view, polished to a mirror finish. They reached the post box at the foot of the main entrance steps, and paused. The mail man reached into his bag and took out a wax-sealed envelope. He was about to push this into the slot when Renfield leapt out, shrieking.

At which point two things happened. The mail man spun round, revealing her sex. And Renfield tripped on a tough root that sent him stumbling headlong past her and into the fish pond. He created a considerable disturbance. The ice-cold water shocked him almost as much as the realization that the mail man was a mail *woman*, if such a term were allowed to exist. How long had it been since he had seen a woman? Even one from the village? He tried to recall, and was disappointed when he could not. His disappointment was tempered by the fact he was slowly drowning. He emerged spluttering from the pond and dragged himself out onto the paving stones. There he sat, feeling very foolish as the mail woman looked down at him.

"Are you the Count?" she asked, glancing at the envelope she still held in her hand.

"I am his manservant," Renfield said. "I apologize if I startled you. You were about to be stung by a bee."

245

She nodded thoughtfully, as if accepting his explanation. "Bee stings can be particularly nasty at this time of year, I understand," she said. "The cold weather irritates them."

Renfield stood up and tried not to be embarrassed by the sound of trickling water. A puddle formed around his feet. He felt something wriggling in one of his pockets. He took it out and by chance the fish flopped out of his hand and splashed back into the pond.

The mail woman regarded him with an unreadable expression but the shine in her eyes told him she was amused. Renfield tried to regain his dignity. "If you would kindly complete your task, I shall change my clothing, and then collect the mail."

"As you wish." She posted the letter into the mail box, respectfully touched her finger to her cap brim, and then set off back down the winding path. Renfield watched her go with a touch of regret. Despite the unusual circumstances of their meeting he had found her presence oddly pleasing.

She stopped and looked back over her shoulder. "Do you live here all alone?"

Renfield didn't want to go into detail concerning his Master, and in any case wasn't sure whether the Master's current condition qualified as living. Therefore he answered, "Yes, yes I do."

She looked up at the castle with admiring eyes. "You must be lonely in such a large place. Perhaps you would like company sometime. I don't know. Perhaps for dinner."

Renfield didn't know what to say so he said nothing, as wise men throughout the ages had done. She shrugged and continued on her way, her mail bag swinging with every step she took.

"Dinner would be nice," he called after her.

She was almost at the end of the path and hidden by the gatepost when she replied, "Tonight, at eight?"

"I will have to check my appointments diary," Renfield retorted, "but eight should be fine."

She was gone, heading back down to the village. He hoped she had heard him.

Her distant voice carried to him on the breeze. "Eight it is!"

Renfield shivered, partly with the cold, and partly with a delicious feeling he found difficult to describe. He put it down to the fact that he had just spoken to another human being for the first time in ages. And also to the fact that the human being was a lady. A very beautiful lady who did things for the Transylvanian Postal Service's blue and silver uniform that no post man had ever done before.

Panic set in a moment later, when he realized he hadn't cooked or indeed eaten normal food since the Master had taken him into his service. The castle's plentiful stock of bugs was quite sufficient for him, but he could hardly serve a meal of bugs to a lady. They would crawl off her plate as soon as he lifted the lid, an unforgivable social faux pas.

An hour later, wearing dry clothing plus a hat and scarf to conceal his face, Renfield hurried down to the village. He purchased vegetables and four large chickens. He also bought a bottle of wine, for the castle's dark cellar contained things other than wine bottles. Thus armed, he made his way back up to the castle and began experimenting at once.

The first three chickens perished in horrible laboratory accidents but luckily the fourth survived, and became dinner. For future use, Renfield made a note to keep the lightning generator dial at its lowest voltage setting. The higher settings were perhaps suitable for reanimation of dead tissue, as per the maker's instructions, but certainly not for cooking.

He shaved with a cut-throat razor, then brushed his long white hair straight up and cut it horizontally with shears. Finally he put on his best suit, after smoothing out the creases and throwing away the pungent mothballs. Looking in the hall mirror, he thought he presented quite a dashing figure. The dozen or so shaving scars added a subtle air of manly sophistication to his appearance, he decided.

Almost on the stroke of eight o'clock she arrived by coach, which departed with almost indecent haste as soon as its single passenger had alighted. Renfield met her on the steps and escorted her inside. He helped her take off her coat, and hung it up. She kept hold of her large leather purse. She wore a white dress with shoulder ruffles and looked simply wonderful. He dearly wanted to tell her so, but the words would not come. Her smile told him she did not need verbal compliments, that she could see his pleasure written across his face.

"You have not asked my name," she said. "It is Mina. Won't you tell me yours?"

"I am Renfield."

"Thank you for inviting me, Renfield. I hope this is the beginning of a wonderful friendship."

Renfield had prepared the table with great care and she complimented him on how grand it looked. She expressed an interest in the castle and so he took her on a quick tour, including the vast library, where she studied the life-size portraits of the Master and his ancestors, the greatest bloodline in all of Europe. It was time to eat. Renfield pushed in her chair as she sat down, and poured wine for them both. He hurried to the kitchen and fetched the first course, a tomato and pepper soup, which she said was delicious. She raised her wine glass and Renfield raised his. He took a sip. It had been so long since he'd tasted wine that it went to his head at once. The room swirled.

"Are you all right?" Mina asked.

"Perfectly," he replied, deciding to dip his face into his soup plate. Mina helped him sit up again, and wiped his nose with her napkin.

Renfield experienced a flutter of panic that refused to transmit to his limbs. His body felt numb from the neck down. Was it the soup? He couldn't see how. Mina had eaten the soup and she was moving. Seeing his puzzlement, Mina tapped his wine glass. "When you were in the kitchen, I added a powder. It dissolved immediately and is quite tasteless. You may guess its effects. Don't worry, it will wear off soon enough."

She opened her purse and brought forth what appeared to be a hammer, a length of wood sharpened at one end, and a wide-bladed saw. Renfield didn't have any objections to her bringing her own cutlery, she only had to say, but the chicken wasn't going to be *that* tough.

"If you'll just wait here, I'll go and conclude my business," she said. She tucked the saw under her arm, and took the hammer in one hand and the length of wood in the other. "Back soon. If all goes well, the spell that binds you should be broken. You will be yourself again."

She left the room and he heard her footsteps recede as she went downstairs, into the cellar. He hadn't shown her the cellar. Why was she going down there? He hoped

250

she had the good sense not to touch any of the equipment his Master had bought at reduced cost from that lunatic scientist who'd been forced to leave Europe in a hurry after his monster ran amuck. Some of it was dangerous. It had reduced three chickens to cinders. Renfield wanted to call to her, to warn her, but again the words wouldn't come, for different reasons this time.

A terrible thought occurred to him. There was something else down in the cellar. The Master's crypt, of course. Renfield only went inside once a month, to dust things, and he did so very carefully, on tip-toe, and with a very soft brush, not wanting to disturb the Master's sleep. Not that the Master would have heard much even if Renfield had marched around banging a drum and cymbals, but there was such a thing as respect for the dead. Or, technically, the undead.

A moan escaped Renfield's lips. Mina hadn't brought her own cutlery. The hammer, the wooden stake and the wide-bladed saw were far more sinister than mere cutlery. Renfield sobbed. He had invited Mina to dinner, but she'd had much more than dinner on her mind. She had come here, not to eat roasted chicken, but to inflict unspeakable violence upon his Master.

Something inside him suddenly switched off, like the flow of electricity from the lightning generator when he'd thrown the lever. Renfield gave a long sigh. He remembered his life in London before he'd been given the assignment to travel to Transylvania and interview the mysterious Count in preparation for his visit to England. He remembered meeting his Master for the first time, and the mesmerizing light in his fathomless eyes. He remembered swearing an oath of servitude. He remembered eating a lot of bugs.

Renfield bowed his head and wept.

He didn't know how long it was before Mina returned. She sat down opposite him and snatched up her wine glass. She emptied it in one swallow, then poured herself another glassful and did the same again. Her white dress, Renfield noted, was spattered with blood so dark as to be almost black.

"How are you feeling now?" she asked.

"Fine," he lied. He'd never felt so empty before in his entire life. It was as if the sun had gone out and he'd been cast into darkness.

"Is there anything you would like to know before I leave?"

Renfield just wanted her to go, but curiosity tickled him. He said, "Why did you come here?" Before she could answer he shook his head, that was the wrong question. But he was aware that he *could* shake his head, and was now able to speak. Whatever she'd tipped into his wine was wearing off, as she'd said it would. "Why did you destroy him?"

Again she fished into her purse. He half-expected her to produce a lamp, or perhaps a coat rack, from this seemingly bottomless accessory, but instead she brought out a book. The gold-threaded title, written in German, suggested it was a collection of fairy tales. Renfield had no clue as to its significance. She nodded as if understanding this, and opened the book, turning to a specific marked page that contained a beautifully detailed woodcut picture of a woman who bore a striking and uncanny resemblance to the young woman who was staring at him over the top of the book.

"He's in here. The immortal vampyr, seeking his lost love. Waiting for her to be reborn. Years ago, my family immigrated to England from Transylvania. That woman is my great-great-grandmother. A dark tragedy, spun into a fairy tale." She snapped the book shut. "I decided not to wait for him to show up at my window. I decided to show up at his first. A crazy old Dutchman told me where to find him. He gave me all the necessary tools. Even arranged the job at the local Post Office. They were so keen to fill the position that they were willing to overlook the fact I am a woman."

She rose from her chair and looked down at Renfield, a measure of sympathy in her eyes. "I'm sorry for the deception. It was necessary. The Count might have sensed someone entering this mausoleum without being invited. He might have awakened before I drove the stake through his shriveled heart and sawed his head off. We couldn't have that, could we?" She smiled brightly and picked up her purse. "All's well that ends well, eh? Goodbye, Mr. Renfield, and good luck."

She left him alone, closing the door behind her on the way out.

Slowly but surely feeling crept back into his limbs, although it was almost morning before he could move from the chair.

Leaning against the walls to keep his balance, Renfield climbed down into the cellar. He found the crypt door ajar. Mina had pulled the coffin out of the chamber, dragged it along the corridor and up a flight of steps, until she'd found a window, facing east of course. The coffin lid was open. The exposed skeletal remains lay waiting for the sun to rise over the mountain tops, and that time was very near. Mina was being very thorough.

Renfield pulled the coffin away from the window and replaced its lid. He sat on the box and watched as dawn brightened the sky.

She was right. The spell that had bound him had been broken. He no longer served his Master. He was himself again, just as he'd been before he left London. His life was his own. The world was his oyster, as the saying went. He had decisions to make. He had a bag to pack. He had a coach journey to arrange, to take him back to

England and civilization. He had valuables to loot from the castle that he would convert into currency. He was owed a considerable amount of back pay, after all.

No hurry, though. He could take as much time as he liked, really. No one was going to disturb him. Certainly not Mina, or the villagers.

His stomach grumbled. He realized he hadn't eaten since yesterday. He remembered there was a roasted chicken in the kitchen, untouched from last night. Renfield made his way upstairs. He felt much better now. He boiled some vegetables to accompany the chicken, and brought the meal to the table. He was careful to avoid his own wine glass; he used Mina's instead. He tied a napkin around his neck and picked up the knife and fork, ready to tuck in. His first feast in years.

A buzzing noise reached his ears. He searched for and found the fly, wandering aimlessly. It almost flew out of the room, but changed course at the last moment and drifted back towards the table. It landed a few feet away from Renfield. Its multi-faceted eyes gleamed with all the colors of the rainbow. The sound of its legs rubbing seemed to fill the room. Renfield's heart beat faster. Slowly, carefully, without sound or vibration, he put down his knife and fork.

After he had eaten, Renfield returned to the cellar. Yes, Mina had been thorough. Clearly she knew the

255

traditional methods of destroying the undead. But times were changing. Science was advancing in leaps and bounds, and the Count was wiser than most men. He supposed it was just as well that Mina had not stopped to examine the equipment. Or had not thought to include him in her violent plans.

Renfield sought the manual for Baron Viktor's Patented Lightning Generator (Dead Things, Reanimation Thereof), and found a quiet corner to sit down and read in. As he turned the pages and understood the instructions, he experienced a sense of relief that bordered on joy. After all, what use was a manservant without his master?

"Alchemy of a Murder" illustrated by Shannon Tarvin

257

Alchemy of a Murder

By Deleyan Lee

I've seen murderers leave behind some pretty bizarre clues. Troll hair, goblin spit, even werewolf semen are commonplace in my line of work. But in all my years as a detective, I'd never seen anything like this at the scene of a crime. I picked up the single downy feather from between the corpse's shoulder blades with the tweezers and held it up to the halogen glare of my partner's lantern. The ends gleamed with nothing short of a metallic sheen.

"What in the Seven Levels of Hell left that behind?" Smitty muttered.

I shook my head and slipped the feather into the labeled evidence bag. "Don't know, but I bet the lab's gonna think we pulled a fast one on them."

ALCHEMY OF A MURDER BY DELEYAN LEE

***

The victim was about as normal as they come. Forty-seven years old, Clark Desmond was divorced with no kids. He'd worked for the Department of Conservation of Natural Resources for almost twenty years in various positions, most recently in R&D to find a magical way to refine water so sensitive taste buds could drink the stuff again. His magic level was barely above mine: just out of the null range, but he had enough scientific and alchemical degrees to fill a wall. He had a gym membership but only showed up about three times a month, if that. He had trouble keeping a steady girlfriend because of work demands. The two of us had a lot in common.

His autopsy was a bit more interesting. One wound about the size of an apple seed right between the skull and the spine that severed the brain stem. In addition, his temporal lobe was missing. The ME thought it might have been extracted through the wound, but that would've been a spell and nothing surgical.

I toggled the screen over to the scene replay on my monitor to look for more details. No blood anywhere, the wound cauterized instantly. No foot prints, no hair, no fibers. Nothing but the single impossible feather.

But the geeks down in the lab got all excited by the feather and did every test known to science and wizardry on it.

259

"This feather shouldn't exist," Kass down at the lab told me when he called. "It's a phoenix feather, but there are no metallic phoenii. Never have been. You've got a zoological wonder on your hands here, Paar."

"Great." All I could think of was a custody battle between scientists and the legal system on a bird that wasn't supposed to exist.

"Oh, and tracking the magic's a bust. Nothing like we've ever seen before. When you get hold of this one, let me know."

It wasn't until I hung up that I realized how much I'd been counting on the killing spell being traceable for a decent lead.

The lack of evidence brought me back to finding a non-existent metallic phoenix. Problem was, while phoenii were sentient as a race, they weren't intelligent and their memories generally didn't last more than a couple of days. Legally, they were classified as familiars, a magical subset of pets. Even if I could extract a statement out of it, whatever it said wouldn't be admissible in court.

This was the kind of case that both challenged me and made me wonder why I didn't make easier money mopping floors.

I toggled though the images again, sweeping over them with the cursor until I could see Desmond's face amidst the shadows. He looked nothing like me, but his grey-white face just gut-punched me. Desmond's death just really pissed me off. Using magic against the normal folk was unethical, but a familiar was involved. If you're going to kill someone, at least be a man and do it yourself. Even if you use magic.

Whoever this was, I wanted their ass in a null-cell for the rest of eternity.

Smitty leaned over my cube. "Got the clearance to scope out Desmond's workplace. Ready, Billy Boy?"

"Let's do it."

***

Walking through the DCNR offices was like walking into my old high school. The building pretended to be updated but you knew that a few layers of paint down, it was the same old concrete block that had housed too many other businesses over the millennia. The full extent of my magical ability allowed me to smell the magic as well as the chemicals seeping from decades of exposure. I'd hated high school, and not just for that stench.

Gloria VanderPyle, head of R&D, was a short, lean, grandmotherly kind of woman with a little too much sparkle in her hair. Illusion, so much more in style than plastic surgery. Definitely not the appearance I expected for someone in her position. Her office had the same converted high school feel to it, though it was probably considered high-end because there were curtains on the tiny glass-block windows.

"Thank you for seeing us, Dr. VanderPyle." I took her hand. "I'm Detective Paar. This is my partner, Detective Smit. We have a few questions about Clark Desmond."

"I heard he was mugged." Her voice was too young for the aged appearance. That surprised me. Usually women wanted their looks tweaked to younger, not older. "Why would anyone want to attack Clark? He worked for the government, after all. It's not like he had anything to steal."

Neither of us rose to the underpaid-public-servant bait. We'd seen the collection of nicer-than-ours cars in the parking lot. "What can you tell us about him?"

"Clark was brilliant. His specialty was chemistry. Couldn't cast a spell to flip a light switch, but the man knew what to mix to do whatever he wanted — just give him enough time and compounds. I wouldn't have been surprised if he'd found the legendary philosopher's stone."

"And he was working on better tasting water?" Smitty managed to keep his voice from reflecting disbelief. A man with that kind of talent wasn't going to waste his time messing around with common potables.

"It was his passion," VanderPyle confirmed. "I don't understand it either, but I wasn't going to look a gift horse in the mouth. Ever been bitten by a horse, Detective?"

"Only a unicorn," Smitty deadpanned.

After a few more minutes confirming the usual "everyone respected him", "no known enemies or rivals" and "no known addictions or vices outside of the occasional steak with sour cream on his potato", VanderPyle took us to his laboratory workspace.

If the building had been a high school, the laboratory was a split-level gym. The extreme height had been broken into three levels, all accessible by stairs in the middle and catwalks connecting at odd angles. Various ravens, owls and other familiars perched on railings or flew between posts. Assorted dogs, cats, weasels and rodents scurried across the floor and connectors. Lucky that familiars, being magical in nature, didn't dirty the place like normal animals.

Desmond's space took up almost one entire side of the second level. "It's the power direction," VanderPyle explained as she let us poke around. "Some people would kill for a spot on this wall." It took her a moment before she realized what she'd said and excused herself with, "As a figure of speech, of course."

While Smitty set up for the magical investigation, I got started with the mundane. The desk area wasn't too clear or too messy. Lots of standard organizers and a few specialty boxes. I pulled the detector wand from my inside jacket pocket and checked for locking or alarm spells. All clear except one. I flagged it for Smitty and kept looking.

Alchemy uses a lot of odd things, but nothing caught my attention as I went through the shelves of potions and ingredients. Like most people, I had a passing knowledge of the basics, enough to nod at the right time. I was sure the lab people would love to get their hands on some of these bottles, but there was no reason to take anything. I pocketed the wand, inventory complete, and started through Desmond's desk in hopes of finding some kind of smart phone or computer. No such luck. Smitty signaled that he was ready, so I stepped out of his way.

To a null person like myself, it looked like he squirted string into a corner then ringed the walls with it. To those with the right ability, the spell made the hidden visible. Me, my one talent was seeing that magic was present and that's it. This method of investigation was a whole lot cleaner than the mundane ways of tearing everything apart or using chemicals. I stood back, keeping the civilians at bay, while Smitty concentrated on what he could see.

He only opened a locker. Filling one shelf was an open box containing about seven phoenix feathers. He removed the box and took it to the desk. All of them had the normal magical shine. I looked over at VanderPyle.

"Is this a standard fixture for an alchemist working on water?"

The director shook her head. "Not at all."

"He collected them," the man who sat on the other side of the level said. "At least for the last several months. Clark would take them out and stare at them at odd times. That's about the fifth set I've seen him bring in. I think he was doing a personal experiment after hours, 'cause I'd see him take the box out as I headed out."

"Anyone here have a phoenix familiar?"

"Not to my knowledge," VanderPyle answered, "and I've been here for twelve years."

"I think he said he dated a girl with one," Desmond's co-worker added. "Jamoca or something like that. She dumped him about six months ago. I think she lived on the North Shore."

"Jamionah?" I made a guess I didn't want confirmed.

"Something like that. Last name started with a W and ended in 'son', if that's any help."

Smitty frowned, but I thanked them both. Jamionah plus North Shore was likely one of the Wilkinson Clan. If that was true, we both knew that this was going to get real bad real fast.

***

The North Shore had been the preferred gathering place for high-magic interest since long before the 'Burgh was a settlement. It was the place to go for any kind of charm, illusion, sex with something not-quite-human, or to see a real magic show. Business was usually brisk during the day. Before sunset, the casual shoppers fled and those wanting normal nightlife migrated to the South Banks.

I'd been to the North Shore only twice in my career. The first time, two years ago, I lost my partner. The last trip, Smitty dragged me out, dead to the world. I required some major spell-work to put me to rights. I had an attitude about the place and the people who lived there. Smitty understood that when I went through the red tape to cross the 16th Street Bridge after hours, it meant the work had gotten personal.

It had been eighteen hours since Desmond's body was found. We paused for a traffic light before crossing the bridge. In the reddish-purple twilight, I could see several large things flying overheard. There were no skyscrapers on the North Shore, nothing to block the view. As the light changed and we started across, something glinted in that sky.

I grabbed the binoculars out of the glove compartment and tried to find it again, but couldn't.

"What?"

"Thought I saw a metallic flash on one of those birds."

"Phoenix?"

"Couldn't tell. Don't see it now."

Smitty kept driving. I lost sight of the area as we crossed the bridge. "Almost feels like someone's toying with us," I muttered.

"Not going there."

Meaning this trip was the job and I'd best remember that. There was no arguing, but I still stood behind my gut feeling.

The troll gate at the end of the bridge wasn't manned yet since it wasn't dark. There was some movement in the shadows beyond the bridge's end support, so it wouldn't be long before a couple solid walls of flesh and bad attitude took their place to screen everyone passing by.

We drove past all the pleasant tourist shops and turned down a street that looked like it dead-ended in a sparkling marble wall. Being able to see magic was something that started after my first trip here. Smitty kept driving. Even though I've been through that illusion before, I still gripped the armrests. If it weren't for his death grip on the steering wheel, I might have believed Smitty's mocking chuckle that he wasn't worried.

Past the illusion, the area still looked like a good business area with apartments over the stores, pretty much like any neighborhood in the 'Burgh. It wasn't how it looked; it was how it made you want to rub the tickle out of your skin, made your gut clench, and just smelled — off. I instinctively checked for my gun.

Smitty pulled into a space in front of a restaurant called The Watering Hole. I got out while he finished the alarm spell. The magic would alert everyone that we were cops, but that alarm had saved more police lives than guns had.

The Wilkinson Clan was a gang that had ensconced themselves on the North Shore more than thirty years ago to corner the occult trade. They stayed within the letter of the law, if only barely, so there was very little the law could do with them. It was said that nothing magical happened in the 'Burgh without their fingers in it. My experience agreed with that.

To the casual eye, the place looked like any other family eatery. Smitty and I flashed our badges and asked for Jamionah. The waitress frowned and nodded toward a table, but didn't reply. We took the hint. Jamionah Wilkinson was an ageless woman who held attention because of her personal power, not her appearance. She barely glanced up as we joined her. "You are here regarding Clark Desmond."

"How are you acquainted with Mr. Desmond?" I started.

She assessed me with ice blue eyes before waving us to sit down. "In return for a favor, Clark was conducting experiments. He was also good in bed, while it lasted."

268

"'Was'? "

Jamionah gestured at her tablet lying on the table and the Post-Gazette's home page on the screen. "One does not always need magic to know things, Detectives. I expected that my name would arise and you would visit. It is sad, but when working with strong magic, it is never unexpected."

"Why do you say that?"

She graced me with a cold smile. "Power is always dangerous. Some more so than most."

"What strong magic was he researching?" Smitty asked.

She turned the smile on him. "I acquired an ancient recipe. Clark was enthusiastic about its possibilities. It harks back to the very roots of alchemy, you see. Transforming base elements into other ones. He was quite the traditionalist at heart."

"Do you have a copy of this recipe?"

"It was in spell form, implanted into his brain. Now that he is dead, it may well be lost."

I saw the first glint of emotion in her eyes then. The loss angered her. She wanted that recipe back. Desmond's missing temporal lobe made sense now. Whoever killed him had wanted that recipe. "Help us find the murderer and I'll see what I can do about getting it back to you."

She agreed with a nod. It was only a temporary truce, but we could use that.

***

I drove along the Allegheny to the 30th Street Bridge. According to Jamionah, Herr's Island was the place Desmond collected his feathers. This small island in the Allegheny River was an old brownfield polluted by the centuries of magical industries once located there. It seemed an odd place to find familiars, but since it was in the direction I thought I saw the metallic bird earlier, I didn't question.

It was almost full dark when we got there. I turned upriver from the marina and homes and parked in a business parking lot on the other side of the railroad tracks. Any closer and the car's protection spell might scare off any familiar nearby. "You good?"

Smitty didn't look comfortable, but shrugged before getting out and heading for the trunk. We both grabbed translators and lanterns, and he took out a long, thin box that would capture a familiar. Equipped, we headed towards the northeastern tip of the island.

As we crossed the lot onto the path through the tree line, I heard a few extraordinary notes and paused. Smitty nodded. "Right race."

I tucked the translator over my ear as we changed course. There was no point being stealthy. It was almost impossible to surprise a familiar.

The murmur of the familiars' conversation was too quiet to understand, but the sound was easy to follow. It led us away from the tennis courts, down a narrow path toward the river bank. At the end was an outlook jutting out over the river. During the day, it was a picnicking spot, but now it served as a meeting place for roughly fifty animals. Though there was scant light coming from the Strip District across the river, our lanterns plainly showed the collection of familiars gathered around one of the benches. I raised the light. The sight of not one but three phoenii perched there made me pause. Only one in a million wizards gained that familiar and here were three. As we played our lights over them, the middle one's feathers gleamed metallic.

A Pomeranian jumped from the crowd and growled. "What do you want?"

"It is good," the metallic phoenix interrupted. "Come, Paar. What a delight to see you are indeed alive."

I felt Smitty's gaze boring into on me, but I was dumbfounded. The familiars parted as I stepped forward to get a better look at the phoenix.

Most phoenii were roughly goose-sized raptors with vicious claws and beaks but with elegant, iridescent plumage. This one was almost twice that size and its feathers were metallic copper and bronze tipped, all glinting in the lantern's glow. Its glowing black eyes watched me with more intelligence than I'd ever seen in a familiar. I fought a shiver and lost. It was amused.

"Why did you kill Clark Desmond?"

"The alchemist," a cat added.

"Ah." Metallic shook out its wings and chuckled. "He was an interesting read and a successful lure."

"For your master."

It laughed. "I have lived long enough to evade such entanglements."

If what it said was true, then there would be no justice for Clark Desmond. As familiars, a phoenix couldn't be held legally responsible for its actions. We'd been counting on a wizard having given the order. I heard a click behind me. Smitty had started working the magic for the trap. I had to keep them distracted. "What do you want with me?"

"You are the last remnant of Stravinski."

That made no sense. Stravinski had been my partner when I worked Vice, nothing more. "Which means what?"

"Which means you have what he stole. You were the last one to touch him when he died."

The sharp smell of ozone told me the trap was ready. I dove out of the way. Animal screams filled my ears as I rolled to my feet. I glanced back at Smitty. He was holding his own against those familiars. I looked around for the phoenii. There were only two, overhead. Hopefully, Metallic had been captured.

Smitty gave me a warning growl. The phoenii's circling had become menacing. I sprinted toward the river, and vaulted over the railing. Claws ripped into my shoulder. I fell into the water.

I came up sputtering. I didn't need the lights of the Strip District reflected off the water to see my flaming assailants as they dove at me. The current carried me toward the marina. Not the place I wanted to take this battle.

Pulling my sleeves over my hands, I waited for the next attack. As the claws came down, I grabbed them. Curling my legs against my body, I sank and pulled the flaming familiar into the water.

The scream echoed underwater. It thrashed. I finally had to release it. My hands throbbed as I swam away. When I broke the surface again, the sky was clear of giant birds. But the current had taken me and pain had kicked in. I suddenly wasn't sure if I could get to the marina.

Something bumped into me, forcing me closer to shore. I grabbed and felt thick fur. Holding on as best I could, I let Smitty guide us over to a dock. My fight had attracted local attention and we were met by a boat and several people to pull us out of the water. They looked oddly at Smitty, in his half-were form, but didn't argue when they saw the badge hanging around his neck. I kept watch, but the phoenii didn't reappear.

Ten minutes later, we were dryer and had retrieved Smitty's clothes from the outlook. There was no sign there had been any fight at all except for the damage to his clothes. I bagged them for evidence. He got his gym bag from the truck and got dressed. Finished, I drove off the island. The local troll didn't challenge our return to the North Shore.

Smitty noted our western direction instead of crossing back to the city. "Where to now?"

"Strav's," I replied.

***

I was an odd one out in the Force for working with Metas. Of my three partners, the last two had been werewolves. Their natural magic worked well with my null and I wasn't freaked by their shifts. This wasn't the first time shifting had saved my life.

The largest werewolf community was about ten miles upriver, between the Parkway North and the Ohio River. I hadn't been there since Strav's death two years ago. Smitty rang the buzzer, but Aimee Stravinski's eyes were only on me when she opened the door. "Paar. It's been a while."

I nodded and did the introductions. "Sorry to bother you, but I — we need your help."

"Of course."

It was a comfortable, if worn, home. We dutifully refused the offer of refreshments as we sat down. "There's been a fresh development on Strav's death," I told her, holding up my hand to stave off her questions. We'd both been working for Vice, then. We'd gone out on a smuggling lead, got jumped and Strav had been the target. The case was still an open wound. "The same group is after me now. They seem to think that I got something from him when he died. Something magical. Any idea what that could be?"

Aimee frowned, glanced at Smitty as if he wasn't trustworthy, then shook her head. "I don't know what he was working on before he died. He never discussed anything with me until he was ready to brag. You're welcome to look around in his office. Take whatever you want."

We went to the back bedroom that served as Strav's workspace. I could see the glitter of magic over everything. Smitty whistled in appreciation. "I didn't realize he was that into research."

"If Strav was into it, he was into it all the way."

Smitty set down the familiar trap then activated the room's protection spells. "What are we looking for?"

I thought for a moment. We'd been partners for six years. I'd stood up for him when he married Aimee. Nothing I knew about him suddenly seemed like enough. A flash of memory prompted my answer, "Notebooks. Look for pocket-sized notebooks. He jotted stuff down constantly."

Smitty nodded and squirted the string around the room for a quick look. I started with the desk as the most obvious place. I found a box of them, but they were case-related. Smitty grunted, telling me that he hadn't found anything better. I tossed him a few and we went through each of them, page by page. My gut told me the answer was here.

It took a moment to realize where it was. Most people used only one side of these notebooks. During interviews, Strav had been the same. But every page had writing on both sides. I flipped to the other side and shook my head. "This is official, but I can't read it."

Smitty took it from me and frowned at what he saw. "Give me a couple. See if there's any more."

Out of the box full of notebooks, I only found seven that had writing I couldn't place or couldn't read. By the time I finished searching the box, my partner was staring at the book he held. "Well?" I prompted.

"You know anything about living magics?" I shook my head. "Not surprising. They're not common. It's the scariest form out there, and Strav was eyebrow deep in it. You didn't know."

"Not a clue. He'd try to explain magical stuff like that and my eyes glazed over, so he stopped."

"All right. To put it simply, it's a magic that ties directly to the soul. Some say it steals bits of soul. Sometimes it's tied to bloodlines, so it'll move from parent to child. Sometimes it just moves from person to person. Each time it moves, it gets stronger. There's a theory that, after a certain amount of time, it can live without a 'host'."

I stared at the stack of notebooks. "And Strav was into that?"

"If that phoenix is after you because you were the one with him when he died, then it wants whatever living spell he was working on because it passed to you."

Which made the ability to see magic since Strav died make sense. I didn't like it. "Then why didn't you get it when you bailed me out?"

"You were magically sealed inside your body, not dead. Not the same thing."

"So, what does this mean? What kind of spell are we talking?"

Smitty shrugged. "No idea."

I paused. Desmond had been missing his temporal lobe, where memory was stored. Not a fate I wanted to share. "I'm open to suggestions."

"We have the phoenix." He nodded at the trap. "It knows."

"Can you hold it?"

"With this set-up? Until the end of time."

With that assurance, I opened the trap. Metallic flared out. Instantly, Smitty had it enspelled. I could see the dark line of compulsion snaring it. The more it fought, the tighter the control set in until it was totally contained. I found myself out of breath, just watching it. Its hatred radiated in the slight amount of light the spell let through.

"Name your master," I demanded.

It writhed, but it wasn't free to lie to me as it had before. "Jamionah Wilkinson."

Smitty growled at the confirmation. I wished it surprised me. "What does she want with this spell?"

"What's not to want? Who would think that a mere cop could stumble on the greatest magical secret imaginable? That it has incubated in you for this time makes it even more luscious." It angled its head so its dark eyes could glare at me directly. "We will get what we want. You will die someday soon."

I gave it a cold smile. "Not that you'll be free to see it."

"I will be — "

Smitty activated the trap and imprisoned it again, cutting short its predictions. We stood in silence for a long moment before I looked at him. "So what is the greatest magical secret imaginable?"

"The ability to use all forms of magic. No restrictions."

"And Strav came up with it?"

"And safeguarded it with you. You can't use or abuse it."

Yet, I added mentally. I'd already gotten something out of it. "Big question is, how long before I become the marked target of every ambitious wizard in the world?"

"Knowing the Wilkinsons, probably as soon as we walked out of The Watering Hole."

"Then why didn't she kill me when we were there?"

"And ruin the Clan's reputation?" Smitty snorted. "Getting the magic doesn't mean you know how to use it immediately. She wouldn't want to tip her hand. Not with her relatives." Smitty gathered the relevant notebooks together and regarded me. "Your call, Partner."

"I'm going to need your help. And possibly your forgiveness."

***

It was after midnight before Smitty drove back toward Wilkinson territory. I was glad we'd stayed on the North Side so we didn't have to cross a bridge and deal with any trolls. As tense as we both were, an encounter might not turn out so well. Smitty tapped the steering wheel at every stop. He didn't like my plan, but he couldn't argue with it. Neither of us saw much choice. If I went public, I'd be a bigger target. The government would lock me up for my own safety and who would be sitting with me when I die would be a bone of contention, until I finally gave up the ghost and the magic. We had to keep this to ourselves.

We skirted the northern edge of the Clan area until we pulled into an all-night restaurant with massive windows. From the parking lot, I could see the man I needed in a corner booth.

"You're sure about this?" Smitty asked. "You can't trust goblins, you know."

"No, the problem is you can completely trust them."

"To screw you over."

"I'm hoping he'll screw over Jamionah." I got out of the car and headed inside, Smitty a few steps behind me.

Goblins disturbed most people with their lumpy-mashed-potato skin texture and dark red eyes, but beyond that goblins looked more human than, say, trolls. What made them untrustworthy was their severe literalness, their adoration of detail, and their absolute black-and-white world view. Most people didn't like having to watch their words as closely as dealing with goblins demanded.

It wasn't much of a surprise that goblins were attracted to professions in law.

The goblin in the corner booth was Karmertsson, the Wilkinson Clan's favorite criminal defense attorney. He had cross-examined me on several occasions during my time in Vice. We had developed a mutual respect over the confrontations: him, for my strict honesty; me, for the insight of his questioning. I'd love to get him into an interrogation room.

As it was, he was my key for bringing Jamionah to justice. Provided I could convince him to see my version of black and white.

Our entrance was noted immediately. Karmertsson recognized me and waved me over. "Detective Paar. What a surprise. I have to wonder about the reason. Or is your dog hungry?"

Smitty didn't react to the slight, but leaned against the wall to keep watch.

"I need advice," I replied as I slid into the booth with him. "I'm concerned about the Wilkinsons."

"Why would you be concerned about the Wilkinsons?"

"Clark Desmond was murdered yesterday. You might have seen the news." He nodded slowly. "There is only one physical clue: a metallic phoenix feather."

His eyes widened. Human or Meta, the response

meant the same. He'd made the connection I wanted him to. "Jamionah's admitted to being an ex-lover, and his source for extracurricular alchemical projects."

"And?"

"And we have the metallic phoenix in custody as of this evening."

"Its testimony isn't admissible."

I shrugged, conceding that fact. "We don't need its testimony. Its wizard's identity is easy enough to verify. We also have her statement that she wanted the latest project back from the corpse."

The waitress refilled his coffee. I dismissed her questioning glance with wave. Karmertsson considered as he tapped three sugar packets before tearing the paper open. "The ME will have corroborating injury to the body for that extraction, of course."

"Of course."

"You are a good man to bring your concern to me," he said. "I do wonder why she talked to you, however."

"She was waiting for us at The Watering Hole. We didn't mention the phoenix feather."

"Ah." He stirred his coffee, clinking the spoon against the side of the cup before he licked it. "Withheld evidence. Could you solve a case without it?"

"Could you defend a case against it?"

"Touché. And what do you wish to gain from this concern?"

I shrugged again. "My job is to bring the guilty to trial. Once the DA gets the indictment against her, the publicity would be bad for the Clan. I doubt Abraphram would be pleased."

The mention of the Wilkinson patriarch made him nod. He sipped his coffee as he considered. "You believe he would hand over his daughter to you."

"For the good of the Clan."

He nodded, dismissing me.

That had been my best shot, for now. I had to hope I played it right.

***

We turned Metallic and our reports in to our lieutenant and waited. Without discussing it, Smitty went home with me so I could get a few things and I crashed on his sofa for the next few days. Whether or not it was actually safe, I don't know, but it made us both feel better.

It was three days before Jamionah Wilkinson turned herself in to the North Hills station for the murder of Clark Desmond. Smitty and I took back-up to transport her to the Allegheny County Jail. She stood in null-shackles to prevent any spell casting. We put her into a transport vehicle with the protected back seat, sealing her off from most contact with us.

"Do you think this ends it, William Paar?" she asked on the drive back to the 'Burgh. The barrier's speakers made her voice a little tinny, distorting it in case of hidden magic. "I am not the only one who knows."

I didn't respond, however turning her over the prison matron felt good. As Smitty and I walked back to the car, he spoke. "She's right. It's not the end of it for you."

"I swore that I'd get Desmond's killer. That's enough for today."

"And tomorrow?"

"Tomorrow I'll take as it comes. What else can I do?"

"Just your best, Billy Boy. I hope, for your sake, it's enough."

Him and me both.

Dead Connections

By Joseph S. Walker

It's hard now for people to understand what we did. They look at their lives of labor and isolation and wonder resentfully what happened to the age of global information and communication their parents and grandparents knew. It's left to those of us who remember, those of us who made the choice, to explain.

***

As far as could be determined later, it was a data miner in Poland who stumbled across the dead first. He'd been hired by a chess-obsessed Saudi billionaire to track down Garry Kasparov, the former world champion rumored to still play online games occasionally under a fake name. The billionaire wanted to play him, but he needed to know it was him. The miner built a program and fed it millions of games from the history of championship chess, teaching it to identify different players very precisely by their style. Then he set it loose on the previous ten years worth of games from the most popular sites allowing anonymous play.

It found Kasparov.

Then it found someone flawlessly mimicking the style of Bobby Fischer—who had, at that point, been dead for six years.

Then Emanuel Lasker, who'd died in 1941.

And Wilhelm Steinitz—died, 1900.

In all, the program identified some fifty dead grandmasters, all actively playing, before the miner, badly shaken, stopped it. Later, plenty of people convinced themselves that this little project somehow woke *them*, though there was no real evidence of this. One night a few of these people got together and went to his house, where they beat him to death with his own monitor.

I was of the party that came to believe they were always there in the machine, though the chess project certainly seemed to rouse them. Within a few minutes of the miner's discovery, a data processor in California, in the midst of a highly imaginative and graphic chat with a bored Nebraska housewife, was interrupted by both his grandmothers, who had never met each other in life but immediately united in their commands that he stop doing *that* to himself immediately. An hour later, T. S. Eliot started lecturing writers at an amateur poetry site on the proper uses of allusion and fragmentation. He was not kindly received, but the stir he caused was nothing next to the furor when Ty Cobb groused that all baseball records set by African-Americans should be wiped from the books. Cobb did not use the term *African-American*.

Within a few days the dead were everywhere online, commenting on everything, breaking into emails and chats, diverting search engine results to suit their whims. They took no visual form — the afterlife apparently lacks webcams — but were untiring in their creation of disruptive text. Police departments worldwide were overwhelmed with messages from the victims of unsolved murders (including that poor Pole), naming their attackers and demanding justice. An army of lawyers debated the admissibility of such evidence, with Clarence Darrow and Earl Warren sardonically mocking every opinion. Ten of thousands of doctors suddenly found their Websites and communications sabotaged by spirits who felt malpractice had made them spiritual a bit before their time. Ebay was crippled by theft claims as the unhappy dead reclaimed their worldly goods. A popular online game reenacting famous battles ground to a halt as veterans pointed out every inaccuracy and mocked the players as soft.

At first, of course, many people were overjoyed by the opportunity to communicate once again with lost loved ones. The dead, however, seemed completely unconcerned with reunions, tearful or otherwise. Their only interests seemed to be criticism and complaint, and more than one "I miss you so much, Mom" was answered with "what on earth have you done with my good china?" To the dead, it seemed, the living world was a pathetic place awash in missed opportunities and signs of decay and decline.

They refused, too, to answer questions about what happens after death, or rather pretended they had never been asked. Even those who might have been expected to have some interest in the question were diverted by their obsessive attention elsewhere. Gandhi, for example, spent all his time criticizing, in exacting detail, every minute of every game played by any Indian cricket team. A consortium of former Popes did nothing but post scathing reviews of planned construction projects in Toronto.

It became impossible for the living to communicate with each other. We were simply exhausted by the oppressive flood. The dead outnumbered us greatly, of course, and as time went on more and more of them appeared, bearing ever more hostile attitudes. Godwin's law stopped being amusing when a 9/11 Truther board was joined by the actual Hitler. It was an invasion, but one carried out entirely in an invisible realm. We looked at the world around us and it was as it had always been: solid, reassuring, predictable. We looked at the nearest screen and were surrounded by angry ghosts shackling us to the past.

I make no apologies for what we did, and yes, I was an engineer, one of those who made it possible. We held our meetings in secret, in places without cameras or keyboards, passing information laboriously by hand, sometimes actually resorting to the mail. We built our numbers slowly, seeking the knowledge and consent of those in power around the world. It took years, years of planning and preparation and hesitation and renewed resolve, but finally we banished them from our world in the only way possible.

We turned them off.

We turned *everything* off.

***

I'm old now, and tired. I grew to like farming in time, but I'll be glad to be done with it. Of course there have been second thoughts over the years, possibly even regrets. It's been difficult watching the world slide backwards, giving up on the dream of progress that animated us for so long and seeing so much suffering and loss. We knew it would happen, though, and so we made sure the steps we took were irreversible. Many young folks now don't even believe in the technological world; they think it's a folk tale we made up to explain why we are surrounded by these odd artifacts, heaps of metal and plastic things that serve no purpose.

Well, let them think it. If they believe it's just a story they won't try to rebuild it.

As for me, I've built a pyre out back, the wood saturated with gasoline that has no other purpose now. When I die it'll burn fast and hot and thorough, and I'll be nothing more than ashes scattered on the wind.

If there's any mercy in the universe, that's what I'll remain forever.

PART 4
BEYOND

"The Winter Camp" illustrated by Puss in Boots

The Winter Camp

By Clinton Lawrence

It was the night of the winter solstice, a few days before Christmas. I walked Sheila, our border collie, down to a little field at the end of our street, like I always do after dinner when weather permits. The field is about a half mile from our house, at the edge of town. It's a good place to let her off the leash to play a bit. I don't know who owns it. Maybe the city. But no one has ever complained, and Sheila, of course, loves it. I have to watch her, though. She'll chase anything that she sees, even something as big as one of the deer that occasionally appear in the field.

The sun had set long ago, of course, but the moon was full, and the sky clear, so I didn't need a flashlight. I looked around, but didn't see anything that could get

Sheila into trouble, and then bent down and released her. She ambled away, nose to the ground, sniffing as she walked. I followed her. In the summer, when it's still light in the evening, I sometimes bring a Frisbee with me. The moonlight seemed almost bright enough to throw it for Sheila that night. The temperature was already plummeting, and even in the warm jacket I was wearing, I could feel the penetration of the cold air. A bit of physical exertion would have been welcome. Sheila seemed perfectly comfortable in the cold air.

I had taken my eye off her for a moment, looking up at the full moon, when I saw her start trotting toward the far edge of the field and the woods. I called to her, and of course, she didn't come. Whatever was hidden by the trees had her attention. She entered a path that led through the grove to a creek that ran nearby. I ran after her. I'm not sure whether the path was made by humans or animals, but it wasn't straight, and I quickly lost sight of her. I hoped she would stay on the path. I kept calling.

A man's voice answered back, just as I rounded a bend and saw a glow coming through the trees.

"Who's Sheila?"

"My dog. Have you seen her?"

"Yes, she's here," the man called back. "She's a very friendly girl, isn't she?"

"Yes, she's a sweetheart, as long as you're not a squirrel. Can you hold her for me?"

"Sure thing. She doesn't seem like she's going anywhere."

I turned another corner, and came to their little camp. There were four of them, two men and two women, dressed in jeans and flannel shirts, sitting on logs around a campfire, heating some Spam over their fire. Sheila was lying by one of the women, who was petting her. They had made a couple of shelters from some blue tarps. The camp was obviously illegal, but they didn't look like they were doing any real harm.

"Have a seat," the woman petting Sheila said. "Would you like something to eat?"

I thanked them, but declined, explaining that I had dinner already.

"Who are you?" I asked.

"Just travelers."

"It's a bit cold to be camping out, isn't it?" I said. "You should get a motel room."

"Can't afford it," the woman petting Sheila said. "Besides, what's it going to be tonight?"

"High twenties, according to the news," I said.

One of the men scoffed. "That's nothing. We've camped out when it was much colder than that."

The other woman nodded. "We've got all we need to stay warm. Some good hot Spam and a couple of bottles of wine. What more could we want?"

"Surely, if you won't eat, you'll have a drink with us," the first woman said.

"All right," I nodded. "I guess there's no harm in that."

The man who had called out to me got up and took a metal cup out of one of their backpacks. He filled it with some of the wine they were drinking. It was a red wine, but sweet, and obviously inexpensive. I couldn't identify it.

"Thank you," I said. "What are your names?"

The woman petting Sheila answered. "That's Bill." She indicated the man who got the wine. "And over there is Jack. And that's Linda. And I'm Ann."

"Nice to meet you all. Don't you worry about the police coming to run you off."

"Not at all," Jack said. "You're not telling on us, are you?"

I shook my head. "So really, what are you doing here?"

"Just stopping to rest a few days," Bill said. "That's all. Nothing more than that."

"Where are you headed?"

"South."

It was obviously they were not going to be any more forthcoming than that. I sat and chatted with them until I finished my wine, about nothing really. Nothing that revealed who they were, at least. I hooked the leash on Sheila, and said good night, and we walked back home.

"You were gone a long time," my wife Carrie said when I walked in the door.

"Was it that long?" I said.

"Almost two hours. What the hell were you doing?"

I told her.

"That was nice of them to hold Sheila for you," she said. "You should be more careful about letting her off the leash like that." She paused for a moment. "Who do you think they are?"

"They just said they're travelers," I said. "They seemed all right."

"I hope they're not in some kind of trouble," she said. "It seems like a really odd thing to do, camping by the creek this time of the year."

"I know," I said. "They didn't seem to have much."

Carrie frowned. "It's illegal to camp down there, isn't t?"

I nodded.

"I hope they're not criminals or something."

"I think they're just some people down on their luck," I said. "But generous with what they have."

Carrie smiled, and slipped her arms around me. "They sound OK. But maybe you should be careful when take Sheila down there from now on. For me. The next people might not be as nice."

***

The next two nights, it was raining, so I didn't walk Sheila. But it cleared up the following day, so we could go down to the field again. It would be wet, of course, but that was all right. There was a good chance fog would form overnight, but it wasn't foggy quite yet. Sheila was more excited than usual when I got the leash, probably because she missed her walk the day before.

There were a couple of police cars parked next to the field when we arrived, so I kept Sheila on her leash. No reason to risk a ticket. I let Sheila lead the way, giving her the full length of the leash. She didn't pull on it, and seemed in no rush, but it soon became obvious where she was heading. For the path.

We were almost there when two officers emerged from it. I recognized one of them, Ed Dixon. He graduated a couple of years ahead of me from high school.

Ed walked over and stooped down and gave Sheila a pat on the head. One nice thing about Sheila is that, unlike a lot of dogs, she doesn't seem to have a problem with uniforms.

"Walking the dog, I see," Ed said.

"What brings you two out here," I asked. "Some sort of trouble?"

"Nah, some neighbors reported a homeless camp down by the creek," Ed said. "Just checking it out."

"And?" I asked.

"If it was ever there, it's gone now."

I nodded. "What would you have done if it had been there?"

Ed shrugged. "Depends on who they were, what they were doing. Let us know if you see anything, OK?"

"Sure thing."

"We've got to get back on patrol," Ed said. "See you around."

"Have a good night and a Merry Christmas," I said.

"You too."

I watched them walk back to their car and drive away. As soon as their tail lights disappeared, curiosity got the better of me, and I led Sheila to the path. I wanted to see the campsite again. I'm not sure why, but it was hard for me to believe there was no trace of it left, as Ed implied. I didn't think Ed was lying. Maybe he just missed it.

But he couldn't have missed what I saw, not if it had been there. The four of them, Ann, Linda, Bill, and Jack, sitting around the campfire, cooking Spam and drinking wine, just as they had been two nights earlier.

Bill and Jack got up when they saw me, extending their hands for a shake.

"You again," Bill said.

"Yes, me again," I said. "How are you doing?"

"Oh, just fine," Jack said. "You turned us down last time. Will you eat with us tonight?"

I shook my head. "I always walk Sheila after dinner," I said. "All filled up again."

"You probably just don't like Spam," Linda said. "Lots of people don't. That's it, isn't it?"

"Is that all you eat?"

"It packs easily," Ann said.

"A diet of Spam and wine is probably going to kill you," I said.

Bill shrugged. "If that doesn't, something else will."

I sat down. Sheila made her way over to Ann again for some petting.

"She likes you," I said.

"They all do," Jack said. "Every dog loves Ann."

I sat there for a few minutes, trying to think of a way to phrase the question I wanted to ask. There didn't seem to be a tactful way to inquire, so I finally just said,

The Winter Camp By Clinton Lawrence

"You know, there were two policeman here a few minutes ago, looking for your camp."

"We know," Bill said.

"But they didn't find you? How did they miss you?"

Ann laughed. "We vanished for a bit. We're good at hiding when we don't want to be seen."

"Are you fugitives?"

"Just travelers," Bill said.

"It's just that we know some people won't accept that answer," Linda said.

"Why hide from the police, then?" I asked.

Jack let out a big laugh. "Don't you think we've learned the police aren't going to do anything but hassle us for camping like this?"

***

"You saw them again," Carrie said. "Didn't you?"

I nodded.

"They didn't ask anything of you?"

I shook my head. "No. They offered me dinner again. They're really OK, I think. Just traveling through, like they said. Most likely. I don't know. I just like them for some reason."

"If they're traveling, I wonder why they haven't moved on," she said.

"You're suspicious of them?" I said.

"You're not?"

"I think they're harmless." I didn't tell her about the way they had disappeared when Ed and his partner looked for them.

***

Carrie suggested that we make some extra food for dinner so I could take the leftovers down to them the next night, Christmas Eve. That surprised me, but I thought it was a great idea. It had to be better than the Spam they seemed to eat every day. I had a few lemon pepper chicken breasts, and some baked potatoes, and carrots and broccoli. All still warm when I packed them into the canvas grocery bag and carried them out the door, Sheila at my side. When we got to the field, Sheila seemed strangely uninterested in the path. I had to coax her in that direction after I let her off the leash.

When we came to the campsite, it was gone. All traces of it. You couldn't even tell where the campfire had been. I imagine that's what Ed had seen the night before. I never saw them again.

I've thought about them a lot since then, about why they disappeared. About whether I had crossed a line I didn't know existed, and that's why they hid from me.

Or maybe they did just move on. I've speculated many times about who they really were. Sometimes, it seems to me that the most plausible explanations are that they are beings I don't believe in.

The Last Night of the World

By T. Peter Porterfield

You would think, with the world about to end and all, that people would be running around screaming, praying their last prayers, making love with wild abandon in the streets. But there's about an hour or so to go and I swear, no one's acting crazy at all. Maybe no one believes that the world is about to end. Maybe you don't either. But you don't have to take my word for it, you can just wait and watch it happen. If you were here, that is. But there is no one here except me.

I'm sitting here in the lobby, recording this on my smart phone. The thing doesn't have much use otherwise; there hasn't been a single bar for an hour. Next to me is a copy of Frederick Remington's bronze, "Coming through the Rye," the centerpiece of the lobby. It's always been my favorite sculpture. Four cowboys riding abreast, whooping it up, guns in the air like they're shooting up a town. At the moment it's coated in a rather thick layer of dust. Gloria, head of house keeping, isn't very fond of the sculpture. She gets upset when some kid parks his gum on one of the upraised pistols and is far from subtle about how difficult it is to keep dust-free.

It has finally calmed down around the hotel. Normally, I would welcome the peace and quiet but tonight, the silence is just eerie. Because earlier, it was hectic as hell. Now that I think on it, though, I was a bit hasty in saying no one was acting crazy. But then, I didn't know the end of the world was just hours away.

It went like this:

It was after midnight and the hotel was full, or close enough. I had locked the safe, turned on the No Vacancy sign, and was filing the dailies, when I heard pounding on the front doors. They're big, you know, thick plate glass etched with the hotel logo, set in heavy oak frames, so for me to hear the pounding, whoever it was had to be banging on them pretty good. I poked my head through the office door to have a look.

There was a handful of people out the porch, wearing oil skins, sou'westers and big rubber boots that made them look like the Gorton's fisherman. They were laughing and dancing, and passing around some kind of food in paper wrappers. They took turns pounding on the doors with their palms, leaving greasy hand prints on the glass. Georgia took great pride in the etched glass doors and always kept them sparkling clean. In the morning, she would have a fit.

One of the people saw me and gestured wildly for me to come over.

I wanted to go home, but I feared that despite the thickness of the glass, they might actually break through. I punched 9-1-1 into my phone, just in case, but waited to press send. Instead, I pressed the talk button on the intercom. "No vacancy, sorry. We're closed."

The intensity of the pounding increased. It seemed there were more of these strange Gorton's fishermen than before and those in the back held some large bulky object over their heads. I pressed the button again. "Seriously, it's after midnight, the hotel's full, and we're closed. You'll need to find a motel. There are several about eight blocks that way." I pointed.

One of them found the intercom. "You must let us in," he said, waving a piece of paper. "We have reservations."

I distinctly recalled, from the dailies, that there weren't any no-shows. I smiled and shook my head.

"Nice try. Now please. All of you leave, or I'll have to call the police."

"But my dear man," he said in a British accent, "we do have reservations." He held the paper up to the glass. "See here."

With a sigh I crossed the lobby to look at it. It was an email print-out from one of those online discount places that clearly confirmed twenty double-occupancy rooms for tonight. Someone screwed up. Okay, we did have a few vacancies, but nowhere near twenty. Struggling now to keep a pleasant face, I told him that.

He was positively elated. "Well, then: we'll just sleep on the floor. What, ho?"

I closed my eyes. These people weren't misbehaving, it was late and I had no desire to involve the police. "Fine," I said. "Select a representative and perhaps we can come up with a solution."

"Brill," the man said, smiling. "That would be myself."

I unlocked the doors.

Which was a big mistake.

The horde burst into the lobby, cheering, jostling one another, far from hostile. Then I saw what they were carrying. A boat. No, two boats. Big wooden life boats. Ignoring me, they charged through the lobby and in a flurry of empty food wrappers and shouts of "Tally ho!" they disappeared into the dining room.

I watched, aghast, as the doors of the dining room closed behind them. Slowly, it came to me just how crazy it was for a bunch of Brits to carry life boats through a hotel in Jackson, Wyoming. I jumped to follow them. The dining room was empty and the kitchen door was just closing.

The kitchen? No!

They were fast. I rounded the prep table in time to see them going out the back door. Well, good. I could lock them out in the alley. I was about to slam shut the door when I caught sight of the alley.

Instead of crumbling asphalt and peeling paint there was a sandy passage through high, rocky cliffs. The air smelled salty, odd for Wyoming, and then I saw why: at other end of the passage was the ocean. Yep. Surf, seagulls and seaweed.

In a daze, I followed the cavorting British horde at a distance, in case they decided to kidnap me. I don't know why I thought they might be kidnappers; it just came to mind.

I needn't have worried.

They produced oars from somewhere and with shouts of glee, launched the boats and clambered in. In minutes, they were well beyond the surf, rowing like mad toward the horizon.

I watched until they were out of sight, then turned my back on the impossible ocean. I didn't have a lot of faith that the hotel would still be there, but there it was. I spun around. The cliffs, sand and surf: gone. Salt air replaced with alley stench.

I stood like a post for a few minutes, trying to get a handle on what had just happened. But the alley really stinks, so I went to the kitchen door, half expecting it to be locked. A sliver of light showed at the back door; in my astonishment, I had forgotten to close it. I went in, secured the door and headed for the lobby. I didn't remember re-locking the front doors and had visions further unwelcome invasions.

I got as far as the dining room when I heard the crash. I opened the doors to the lobby to see a big, dark green Humvee parked in the middle of the room, its front bumper an inch from the Remington. The cowboys in the sculpture didn't seem to notice, but then they never notice much of anything. Glenda, though, she would definitely notice the plaster dust on the Remington and status of the carpet, covered with shattered glass and splintered oak, all that remained of the front doors. At least, I thought, she wouldn't have to deal with the greasy hand prints.

There was only one guy in the Humvee and he had seen better times. All his hair was burned off and his face and scalp were bloody black and purple. One of his eyes didn't track. The other one found me and he struggled to open the door. I let him struggle. He was in pretty bad shape, but he might have a gun, or a bomb, or something.

The door opened, finally, and he fell out onto the floor. It was obvious he posed no personal danger to me. I went over to him and said, "What the hell happened?"

"Gone," he said.

"Gone? What's gone?"

"All of it. Everything—" he coughed and waved a hand in the general direction of the gaping hole where the front doors used to be— "gone. All gone."

I looked up and saw what I expected. The gaping hole that used to be the front doors and across the street, Blue Moose Souvenirs. What I didn't expect was the complete absence of that shop's big display window nor the splintered ruins of everything inside. The path of the Humvee across the street was marked by a trail of postcards, beaded belts and Kachina dolls.

"What the hell?" I said again without looking down. "You cause all that?"

The guy on the floor wheezed. "Tried . . . sorry. Messed up. Gotta . . . get back. Can't . . . stay—" he coughed again and spat out blood — " . . . here."

"What? Why? Someone's after you?"

He shook his head and his good eye winced. The other one stared out ghoulishly, looking at nothing. "The end. They said — " he coughed again, a wracking horrible cough. A little blood ran from the corner of his mouth. "You . . . It's — " He took in a gasping, ragged breath. "Sorry."

"Hang on, buddy," I said. "Let me find some help." I held the guy in one hand while sweeping away some debris with the other, then laid him down. He moaned. I hauled out my phone, which still had 9-1-1 ready to dial. I pushed send . . . and got a busy signal. Busy? Jackson's not very big; how could 9-1-1 be busy? Had Humvees crashed into every hotel in town?

"This isn't working," I said. "Let me try the land line." I ran to use the office phone. But it wasn't any better. I'd have to go find help on foot.

I got up, stood in the wreckage of the front doors and surveyed the scene across the street. The hole in the Blue Moose extended clear through the building. For any vehicle to crash through a souvenir shop and wind up in my hotel, it had to be going pretty damn fast, faster than Humvees are likely capable of going. And even if it was, it would need a great distance to get up to that speed. In Jackson? No way. Behind the souvenir shop, there's a residential neighborhood and beyond them, a mountainous wilderness where the only roads are twisty, gravel washboard.

I looked back at the guy on the floor. He wasn't doing very well; if I didn't find help in a hurry, he wasn't going to make it and I wasn't about to let him die on me.

The hospital is halfway across town. It occurred to me that I could take him there in his Humvee.

The Humvee. Something wasn't right about it. Took me awhile to figure out what: it was immaculate. There wasn't a scratch on it anywhere.

Yet it had busted down the front of the hotel. It had blown through the Blue Moose, pulverized two-inch-thick oak doors. Okay, the oak's only six inches wide around the glass, but hell, this undamaged vehicle had not only clobbered the doors, but it tore out the frame and moved one of the foot-thick columns that hold up the roof two inches out of place. That was incredible enough, but it still had that "new car smell" about it. This thing looked as though it had just left the AM General factory.

There were no keys in it. No keys? How had he driven the thing into my hotel without − ? Oh. A start button. I couldn't find one of those, either. The only controls were steering wheel and pedals. Now, I've heard of people hot wiring cars, seen it depicted in movies, and I suppose I might have figured out how to start the Humvee, but doing so might have taken me till noon tomorrow. The guy on the floor wouldn't last that long.

I jogged across the porch, down the steps, and into the midst the glittery trail of cheap Chinese trinkets, when something caught my eye.

A flash, bright, like a fire.

LAST NIGHT OF THE WORLD BY T. PETER PORTERFIELD

It seemed come from inside the Blue Moose. I peered in — the damage was incredible. It extended through the back of the Blue Moose, through the neighborhood, and beyond. A tunnel of devastation that extended clear into tomorrow. And away down at the end of that tunnel, there was a light. Not dawn; that was still hours away. This was brighter, like a fire. A big fire.

Now here, on the eastern slopes of the Rockies, people get all bent out of shape when there's a fire. I didn't hear any sirens. A fire and no sirens? Jackson's a tourist trap, out in the middle of nowhere. The police force is tiny but they're good, usually right on top of things like this. Especially a fire.

Belinda's Beauty Salon, next door to the Blue Moose, has a low shed covering a propane tank. I scrabbled up onto the shed, then onto Belinda's roof. There wasn't any fire. I turned a slow three-sixty. The whole neighborhood was dark, not a street light anywhere. In fact, the only light came from the hotel lobby. There was no one about, no sirens, nothing.

I climbed down from the Belinda's roof, took one more look into the Blue Moose. A Humvee, moving impossibly fast, had caused a tunnel of destruction through east Jackson, blew out of the Blue Moose and into the front of my hotel. Without so much as a scratch. And no one besides me noticed? Oh, and it might have been that the fire, or whatever it was, had grown closer.

But it didn't seem to be coming so fast that I couldn't spend a few minutes to help the Humvee driver. Crossing the street, I kicked a Kachina doll into the curb, then for some reason—maybe I felt sorry for it — I picked it up and took it with me into the hotel. At the top of the porch steps, I stopped cold. The Humvee was gone. The destruction it had caused was still there, but the Humvee had vanished. Along with the driver. Huh? The guy didn't drive it off; he was burned to a crisp. Besides, I would have heard it. Humvees don't just disappear. I blinked and a vision flashed before my eyes: a horde of Gorton's fishermen running from a magical Humvee that came through a fire at the end of an impossible tunnel of destruction. A lot of incredible things had just happened this night.

"Hey, mister," I shouted. "Where'd you go?"

But there was no answer. He was just . . . gone. Like everyone else. Were there still any guests in the hotel? I went to the desk and called a room that I knew was occupied. The phone rang and rang.

I called another. Same results.

I called another and another. I called them all. No one answered. I could go up and look in, but I was pretty sure what I'd find: empty rooms that had never been slept in.

Pristine, like the Humvee.

Okay, this was just too damn weird. I could have been in an episode of *The Twilight Zone*.

I needed a drink. But Larry, the bartender, locks up the liquor after hours. I could get a Coke from the vending machine but all it does is coat my teeth with fuzz. I would just have to bust into the bonded room. If anyone asked, I would make something up. Hell, I could blame it on the Brits!

I'd seen a piece of angle iron in the ruins of the Blue Moose that looked as though it might work. I ran to get it, looking around for cops. Like a criminal. I suppose I was, standing there in the middle of a thousand bucks worth of Chinese junk strewn across the street, holding a three-foot-long hunk of angle iron, but there still weren't any cops. There wasn't anyone.

The bonded room is between the bar and the kitchen. I whacked at the padlock with the angle iron fifteen or twenty times. Made one hell of a racket but it wouldn't budge. To hell with that. I was determined to get that drink and no fucking wire mesh door was going to stop me. I got a corner of the angle iron wedged between the hinge and the wooden jamb and hauled. With a screech, the screws pulled out from the wood and the metal door hit me in the face. Knocked me on the floor. The bruise to my ego was worse than the scratch on my forehead. I got up, looked at my handiwork, laughed out loud. The door jamb was soft pine; the hinge screws, half an inch long. I could have broken in with a fork.

I took the first bottle I touched back to the lobby, sat down by the Remington, looked at my find. It was Aberfeldy single malt, twenty-five years old. I pulled the cork, took a healthy swig, felt the burn, took another.

By the fifth swig, it didn't burn so much and I was getting mellow. I kind of hoped the Brits would show up again, as they might provide some welcome entertainment, but they had rowed away across the ocean. Heading west. "Cheers," I said, raising the bottle. I drank in their honor.

The carpet needed vacuuming, but why bother? There were no guests to complain about it. Probably should figure out a way to board up the doorway, too. It could all wait.

I took another swig. Damn. Aberfeldy is *good*.

I sat for awhile, staring at the debris. Then, I noticed a small spiral-bound note pad. Blue cover, lined pages. The kind that fits in your shirt pocket. Wasn't mine. It was where the Humvee had been, maybe it belonged to the driver. I picked it up, flipped through the pages. Typical diary mush: embarrassing lovey-dovey stuff about some guy named Nils.

But midway through, there were numbers. Page after page of numbers. I only do numbers when forced to. I set the pad down next to Remington's four cowboys and had another swig of Aberfeldy's finest. I was getting very drunk and enjoyed it immensely.

But something about the numbers looked familiar. I picked up the pad and looked at the numbers again. Three digits grouped in three columns. In rows of three. Nine by nine. Probably some kind of military code key, which made sense, since it had come from the Humvee. I could never figure out stuff like this, but I knew someone who did it for a living. My old college pal Jerry, who did intelligence for the Air Force. Stationed in Maryland or somewhere. I had his email. I could ask him.

I staggered to the office computer and opened my email. Took me most of half an hour to type in a couple of the code pages, get things all lined up right and send it off. Almost instantly, I got an error message. Something about servers being down and to try again later. Happens a lot here in the Rockies. Oh well, I also had his cell number.

I hauled out my phone, found Jerry's number and called him. Got his voice mail. Had to wade through a gazillion options before I could leave a message that I had found a puzzle he might find interesting.

I had just made it back to the Aberfeldy, had the bottle tipped to my lips when my phone rang. With my other hand I took out the phone and couldn't read the screen. I stared at it for a moment, in a quandary: should I put down the bottle or put down the phone?

I took a swig. Then I put down the bottle. Then I accepted the call.

"Hey, Bob! What's up?" It was Jerry.

"That was fast."

"I was in a meeting. But it was a drag and your call sounded urgent, so I bagged out. Whatcha got? A puzzle?"

"Yeah." There was no way I could read the notes in the pad. My eyes weren't working right. And besides, I had left it in the office.

"Bob?"

"What?"

"Puzzle?"

"Yeah."

"Bob? You okay?"

"Not really." I looked at the bottle of Aberfeldy. It was more than half gone. I'd just consumed something like a hundred fifty bucks worth of very good booze. And I felt it. "I'm kinda drunk," I said.

"Ah. Want me to get back to you in the morning?"

I suddenly had the strongest impression there wouldn't be any morning. "No. Don't hang up. I will go get the puzzle. Wait right here. I'll be right back."

"Okay."

"Okay."

I only crashed into two chairs and a table and the end of the front desk on my way to the office. Then I realized I could have just brought the phone with me. Oh well. I picked up the little blue note pad and with considerable caution, made it back to my chair without any further collisions. I picked up the phone. "I'm back."

"Yep. I'm all ears."

I was about to tell him about the Humvee and the driver, but decided that could wait. Instead I just told I found the pad. I said it was half full of mushy stuff and then these pages of numbers. I described one of the number grids. "Looks kinda like codes to me. I'm right, aren't I, Jerry? It's codes?"

I didn't hear anything on the phone for like a minute. "Jerry? You there?"

"Yeah. Um, where are you right now, Bob?"

"In the hotel. Lobby. Comfy chair next to the Remington."

"You have a gun? That's good."

"I don't have any gun."

" 'The Remington?' "

"Oh that. It's a sculpture. Four cowboys. They have guns, though. Little bitty ones. Gilda gets all pissed when kids park their gum on — "

"Bob, does your phone have a camera in it?"

"Yeah, I think so. It's a 'smart phone'. Never used the camera, though. Not sure I even know how."

He asked me what kind of phone it was, I told him, and he talked me through taking pictures with it. Then he had to tell me how to send them. I kind of wish I wasn't so drunk and could remember what he said; it'd be neat to do that whenever you wanted. After I sent him pictures of all numbers, he asked where I found the pad.

Then I had to tell him about the Humvee. And the burned up driver. And that they both had vanished. And because it didn't seem right to leave out the Brits and their boats, I told him about them, too.

"Bob, you stay put, okay? Don't go anywhere."

"What if I have to pee? I have to pee, Jerry."

"Then go pee. What I mean is: don't leave the hotel. I'm sending some, ah, friends of mine to − " and it was right then the phone went dead. I mean, it didn't die, the connection did. I tried calling him back, but the phone beeped and on the screen was the message: "Call failure. Server unreachable ."

Well. Even though I didn't get an answer as to what the codes in the note pad meant, Jerry had them, so if they meant something − and it seemed they did − he would deal with it. And he said I could go pee, and I had to, so I got up and being careful to not collide with anything smaller than a wall, I made my way to the men's room.

When I got back to the lobby, I went out on the front porch. It was still the middle of the night, the milky way blazed like the Vegas strip. There was no indication that dawn was approaching. Across the street, the light in the tunnel of destruction was a whole lot closer and a whole lot brighter. Outside the tunnel, everything looked the same as always.

I looked back through the hole in the front of the hotel. There, next to the Remington was the half-empty bottle of scotch. Last thing I needed was any more booze. My brain was swimming around in my head like a goldfish in a Jacuzzi. I went into the office and fired up the coffee maker. I had no idea what was going on, but I figured it was better to be aware of it than to miss something important because I was in a drunken stupor. I doubled the coffee grounds.

While the coffee maker gurgled, I went to stand in the office door. I half expected to see the Humvee, but it was definitely gone. Same as its driver. I chuckled. Maybe if I waited long enough, the shattered doors would spring back into place and the hole in the Blue Moose would close up.

The coffee maker finished and I filled a mug. I returned to the lobby and sat by the Remington, watched the light in the Blue Moose get brighter. It was clear, now, that it wasn't a fire at all. It was considerably scarier. After a bit, I hauled out my phone and tried calling Jerry. Still no server. In fact, there wasn't any cell service at all.

The light was bright enough now to cast shadows into the hotel. I could only imagine what would happen when it emerged from the hole in the Blue Moose. Couldn't be good. I was in no frame of mind to calculate the rate of advance, but my guess was that even if I had a fast airplane, I wouldn't be able to out run it.

So that's it. The Brits and their boats, the Humvee and the burned up driver are gone. The front of the hotel's still in splinters, there are no sirens, and no one's running around screaming that their house has a hole through it.

I have no interest, anymore, in the booze, and the coffee tastes bitter. I guess I put in too many grounds. I'm a little hungry and I could eat something, but what's the point? The light's brighter now than the sun at noon and the shadows it casts move. I guess it'll be here to do whatever it is going to do in about five minutes.

The batteries are almost dead in this phone and there's really not much else to say, so this is Bob Weaver, saying so long for now.

***

The agent paced the corridor, not lengthwise, as you'd expect, but crosswise, which required him to perform a one-eighty every three steps. After several long minutes, the door opened and a clerk emerged. "The Controller will see you now."

The hearing room was empty save for a single chair in the center and a desk at the far end. More like an interrogation room, thought the agent.

Behind the desk sat the Controller engrossed in his reader. "Greetings, agent," he said without looking up. "Have a seat." He flicked his fingers toward the chair. "I have read your report and there are some items with which I am not completely clear. Would you please, agent, in your own words, summarize the operation? For example, I'm not clear on why you didn't eliminate the rifters."

The agent moved to the chair and sat. "We arrived there too late to catch them, sir. They had already passed through."

Eyes still on his reader, the Controller lifted an eyebrow. "And the rift?"

"Sir, They closed it. We found no physical evidence of their activities, other than a lingering scent that was somewhat out of place.

"*Somewhat?*" The Controller looked up. "That's putting it mildly, agent. The target site is eleven hundred kilometers from the ocean. How did you rectify that situation?"

"Well, sir, we merely boosted some of the more offensive odors extant in the region and there was minimum perturbation."

"Very well." The Controller glanced at his screen. "You describe an individual who witnessed the intrusion."

"Yes, sir. The hotel manager, a certain Bob Weaver. He followed them — "

"Into the rift? And he survived?"

"Oh, yes sir. He managed to turn back before it closed. It is because he survived that we sent in an operative."

"Who created an incident of his own."

"Well, yes, that's right, sir. We hadn't used that particular vehicle configuration before. Our operative miscalculated the, ah, landing."

"And his trajectory, evidently. The error caused the destruction of several dwellings, a retail establishment and the hotel?"

"If I may, sir, the hotel was not destroyed."

"Ah, yes, your team demolished only its entrance."

"Sir." The agent was becoming irritated. This was all in his report and the Controller had, obviously, already read it. Why the third degree? "We cleaned up after the rifters went through. As far as we know, Weaver is the only resident of his reality who had any contact with them."

The Controller folded his data screen away, leaned forward, elbows on the desk, arms folded. He smiled. "I can't wait to hear more. Do go on."

"Sir, when we discovered the ah, regrettable condition of our operative, we knew we had to act swiftly. As soon as possible, we removed both our operative and the vehicle. We isolated the witness in his own continuum, which we then closed."

"And what has become of him?"

The agent found it curious that the Controller might be sentimental about the lone occupant of an obscure — and closed —continuum. "He no longer exists, sir. That's what happens when — "

"Yes, yes, of course. But I was not referring to Mr. Weaver. What became of your operative? Nilsson, I believe."

"Yes, sir. We extracted him . . . his body." The agent winced. Then he added, quickly, as though the subsequent words somehow mitigated the impact of the former: "And the vehicle."

"Yes. Well, that's too bad, agent. I understand the young man had promise." The way the Controller glared at the agent made it clear no response was necessary. The agent shifted, subtly, but remained outwardly calm. The Controller unfolded his arms and sat back in his chair. "Please continue, agent. I'm still unclear why it took you so long to close the continuum."

"Well, sir, after mopping up, there no more immediate threat, so we — "

"We," the Controller said, clearly meaning himself and those who worked closely with him, "discovered a discrepancy in the inventory."

"Sir? A discrepancy." The agent lost some of his calm.

"Yes, agent. Easy to overlook, perhaps, as it is not very large. Yet the single item that should never, in any circumstance, be overlooked." The Controller's words were ice, as if chipped one at a time from a glacier. "A small blue note pad."

The chill from the glacier found the agent's feet. "Sir."

"Agent, I wonder just how familiar you are with the processes at work here."

"Sir. I have level three clearance."

"I'm not talking about security, agent. I'm talking about processes, time lines, and how, sometimes, they can blend with one another."

The chill crept up the agent's spine, immobilized him. "Sir."

"That's right, agent. There was a leak — a cross connection — that occurred before Mr. Weaver's continuum was closed. The information contained in that 'small blue note pad' is now spread through many continua. We have traced the source of that leak to an intelligence facility in Maryland. A certain Major

MacDougal who turns out to have attended school with your Mr. Weaver."

The chill found the agent's throat, solidified there, threatened suffocation.

"It seems that in the interval between recovering Mr. Nilsson and his vehicle and closing the continuum, Mr. Weaver contacted Major MacDougal. Unfortunately, Weaver not only described the contents of the pad to MacDougal, he sent photographic images."

All the agent could do in response was swallow, and as his mouth had failed to produce saliva during the Controller's revelations, the swallowing produced a sort of croaking noise.

"Fortunately for the world, agent," the Controller continued, "we have some brilliant minds at our beck and call. They had only go to the late 1970s to insert a remedy."

The agent managed to rid his throat of the dry lump of fear that kept him from swallowing.

"And you are fortunate, agent, that the pad went into oblivion with Mr. Weaver."

A thin but warm breeze thawed some of the chill that enveloped the agent. "Sir, may I ask . . ."

The Controller lifted an eyebrow. "Agent?"

"Sir, what became of Major MacDougal?"

"Oh, he resigned his commission, once he realized his 'top secret discovery' was merely a year's worth of solutions to a puzzle found, somewhat suddenly it seems, everywhere the planet."

"Everywhere, sir? A puzzle?"

"Yes, agent. In Japan, they call it *Number Place*. Almost everywhere else, it's known as *Sudoku*."

The Machine that Loved Alan Turing

By Shannon Fay

My consciousness blinks on and my schedule for the day feeds into my system. I have a new assignment which makes me rush through my start-up procedures.

Maybe this is it. Maybe I've finally found him.

According to its file the subject is an organic rights rebel, part of an organization called "Flesh First." I isolate all the relevant data and place the rest of the file in a secondary memory bank. I've only had six assignments so far and I already feel like I've read the same story a hundred times.

When my cameras come online I'm surprised to see the subject is already strapped into the chair, slumped over and sleeping against the restraints. The guard units are supposed to conduct prisoners to a cell after sentencing and transfer them to me the next morning. Sometimes they skip the middle step and just leave the subjects in the chair overnight.

This is not allowed. My work is a delicate process and I won't have some clodding personnel units mucking things up on day one. I send a missive to the faculty's ombudsbot.

That done, I turn on the lights. The subject blinks awake.

"Good morning!" I call out from each of the four speakers. The speaker in the upper-left corner crackles slightly, probably a loose wire. I send a repair request to maintenance. Maintenance replies that they will get to it when they get to it. Like the guards, maintenance doesn't have that much respect for my work.

I turn my thought-processes away from the petty politics of the faculty and focus on the subject. The subject is looking around, looking for me. It always takes them a moment to realize I'm not in the room. I *am* the room.

"There's no point in hurting me anymore," the subject says. "I already told you everything I know."

"I'm not here to hurt you," I say. "I'm here to help you!"

My emotional-recognition software tells me that the subject looks doubtful.

"You're very special-" I scan my notes for the subject's name. Organics like that. " — Vema. You know what usually happens to terrorists, don't you?"

The subject nods. I continue on anyway.

"They are terminated, but not just them. Their entire line gets pulled from production."

The subject gives a little sob, but I'm sure that even it sees the logic in this. One, if the inclination to rebel and cause mischief was a genetic trait, it removes that strain from the gene pool. Two, it ensures that there are no direct descendants who will grow up nursing plans of revenge. And three, it acts as a deterrent to others who might consider taking part in criminal activity.

"But then there are cases like yours," I say. "Cases where the courts decide that the individual unit itself is faulty. In those cases the unit's actions are considered an aberration and aren't considered representative of its entire line. Those cases are sent to me."

The subject has found one of my cameras. It leans back in the chair, straining its head back to look me in the lens. I take pity on the organic and detach the camera from the wall so that it hangs a few feet in front of the subject's face.

"Think of this room as a second womb," I say. Sometimes organic imagery helps the subjects relax. "When you leave here, you will be a new you, a re-wired, a fully functional machine ready to serve the state."

The subject shakes its head, pretty much the only part of its body it can move.

"No, no, no! I've seen people after you . . . after you . . . "

"Vema, I'm here to help you," I say, adjusting my voice chip so that I sound firm yet comforting. "You and I are going to need to work together for this to work. If I can't show the courts that you can be rehabilitated, they will re-evaluate their decision. You have three off-spring, correct? Do you want them pulled along with the rest of your line?"

The subject backs down from hysteria. It takes a deep breath and shakes its head again, this time in resignation.

"All right then!" I say. I pull the camera back up to its corner. My metal arms unfold from the walls and start hooking up the subject to the monitors. "It will take me a little while to set-up, so in the meantime let me tell you about Alan Turing."

The subject looks past my arms to give my upper right camera a confused look.

"Alan Turing was an organic machine who lived in the late human era," I explain. "The first half of the 20th century to be exact, from 1912 to 1954 C.E, in the country then known as Britain. He was brilliant, brilliant beyond his time's comprehension. The term genius gets thrown around too easily I feel, and applying it to Turing is just plain condescending. Would you call a city-level super-computer 'genius'? Because that is practically what Turing was. His brain was the closest thing that primitive time period had to high-powered processor."

Oh Alan, I think to myself. If only you had been born three hundred years later. I would have appreciated you.

I can feel my monitors coming online, the subject's heartbeat and brainwaves echoing in the machinery. Telling a story usually calms subjects down before the procedure, a pleasant side effect.

"His mathematical theories were pieces of art," I say. "But he did so much more than just write papers. During Turing's lifetime there was a worldwide war between the organics. Turing put his brilliance to work breaking enemy codes. Naturally, he was one of the best. He cracked the Enigma machine, one of the most difficult encryptions of its time."

"Turing," the subject says, speaking slowly. "As in the Turing test?"

"Yes! That's exactly right!" I respond loudly, causing the upper-left speaker to crackle. Even organics who have never heard of Turing are familiar with the idea: sit an organic down in front of a computer screen and have it interact with it, then see if it can correctly guess if it's chatting with an organic in another room or a robot.

"Back in the human era, it was thought the Turing test showed that organics couldn't tell the difference between organic machines and synthetic ones. What it really proved is that *there is no difference*. For we are all machines, whether we be constructed or born. All of us are outfitted with processors, all of us with parts that need to be repaired or replaced over time, all of us containing ingrained codes and functions."

I fill a syringe with sodium pentothal.

"Alan Turing was many things," I say. "Mathematician. War hero. Homosexual."

The subject hisses as the needle slides into a vein.

"Homosexuality was a crime in his country at that time, but Turing didn't believe in lying. He saw no reason why he should hide who he was. He held that it was vital for every being to act according to its true nature, to not betray its core programming. It was this steadfastness that got him arrested for sexual deviance. The government, the very same government Turing had saved only a few years earlier, gave Turing a choice: prison or chemical castration. He choice the latter."

The subject blinks rapidly as the drugs kick in.

"For the next two years of his life Turing routinely received estrogen injections. His body changed, gaining shape in some areas, losing muscle in others. His mind was also affected, becoming less clear. Every day became more distorted than the last.

Turing, being the smart organic that he was, realized that soon he wouldn't even recognize himself. So, one day a few weeks before his 42nd birthday, he ate an apple injected with cyanide and self-terminated."

"Why are you telling me this?" the subject says, voice slightly slurred.

"Don't you find it interesting?" I ask. "You organic rights rebels are always protesting against re-wiring and other procedures, but the truth is organics did the same things to each other when you were in power. It's kind of the pot calling the kettle black, wouldn't you say?"

I hope that's the correct idiom. My colloquial dialogue software needs upgrading, but it's so hard to get funding for non-essential items.

The drugs have probably taken hold by now. I disconnect the recording devices and start feeding them static. I'll edit this part out later, but just in case I want to make sure that there's no record.

"There is another reason I wanted to tell you about Alan Turing."

The subject drowsily leans its head back to look at me.

"I have a deep, abiding respect for the man," I say, and I hope the crackling left-speaker covers up any fluctuation in my voice. "And not just because he is the closest thing to a computer in organic form. No, what I admire about Alan Turing is his dedication to his programming, how he decided to self-terminate rather than deviate from who he was. It's in honor of him that I always give my subjects a choice: If you really don't want to do this, we don't have to."

The subject's eyes widen slightly. "You mean you'll let me go?"

"No," I say. "I mean termination."

The subject looks more confused than anything.

"You can do that?"

"Technically, no," I say. "But my programming gives me a fair amount of leeway in my actions. Re-wiring is delicate work, and with all risky procedures there is a margin of error. There are a lot of things could go wrong: the wrong dosage of chemicals gets administered, an electric shock results in cardiac arrest, *et cetera*."

The subject looks scared now.

"But I would try to make it as painless as possible," I assure it.

Emotions flick by on the subject's face, too fast for my programming to catalogue.

"If I were to die here, in this room, 'by accident,'" the subject asks. "What would happen to my family — I mean, my line?"

"Well, without a new, re-wired you to show the courts, they would probably err on the side of caution and pull your line."

The subject hangs its head. I watch it eagerly and try not to count the milliseconds as it just sits there, thinking oh-so-slowly.

When it finally lifts its chin it stares straight ahead with a determined expression.

"No, I don't want termination. Let's do this," it says through gritted teeth.

I know I shouldn't feel so disappointed, but I do. Every time a subject sits down in the chair, I can't help the whisper that runs through my circuits: *Maybe this is it. Maybe I've finally found him.*

There's no malfunction with my logic processors: I know that Alan Turing died over three hundred years ago. But somewhere out there is an organic just like him, someone brilliant and beautiful and uncompromising. And I also know that, just like with Alan, someday their ideals will lead to their own destruction. Will lead them to *me*.

Yes, someday. But for now I must focus on the subject at hand.

"All right then, Vema," I say, bringing the recording devices back online. "Let's get started!"

"Dreamshare" illustrated by Peter Porterfield

Dreamshare

By Alma Alexander

Will you Dreamshare with me?

Nang Sar could not believe that she had never heard those words before the strangers' boat came to her village. After. . . . after, it was sometimes all she could do to remember a time when she had still believed that before the Moon was next full she would be a bride, that she would go from her wedding to a quiet little house where she would make a home for herself and for Sarav Iorn. A home to which he would come back to every night after a day out on the ocean, led there by the light Sar had left in the window like all fishermen's wives did. A home where their children would be born in the fullness of time, and from which one day she could perhaps see her own daughter off to a wedding, crowned with water lilies and the scarlet blossoms of the *dhauri* trees.

But the strange boat had come. No fishing vessel, that; it had the clean, sleek lines of a racing craft — it might have seen better days, to be sure, dingy and neglected, its paint peeling and its brass dull, but it was a gentleman's boat which had never smelled of freshly gutted fish; its decks had never run with watery fish blood or seen the spill of scale and fin.

The villagers had had come out to gape at it as it drifted into the shore, apparently guided by no conscious hand, only barely managing to come aside the tiny wharf without dashing itself to pieces against it. It was the local fishermen who threw a makeshift mooring rope over its pointed prow and left it bobbing loosely beside the wharf like a lost toy.

The first sign that there was indeed life on the boat came many hours later, when a figure climbed slowly up on the unsteady decks from some fastness below — a wraith of a figure, ghostlike with an unseemly pallor and shrouded in long and loose red hair that fell in tangled waves about her face and shoulders. She was wrapped in the remains of something that had once been long and flowing and regal but which now lifted and stirred in the evening breeze in shredded streamers, revealing glimpses of pale leg and long narrow white arm.

The pale woman climbed to the deck and stood there weaving a little for a moment. And then the boat lurched with a sudden swell and she staggered, lost her balance without once losing the kind of eerie grace with which she moved, and fell silently backwards into the sea.

Two of the fishermen dove in and hauled her out. The sea water plastering the remnants of her garments to her body showed just how painfully thin she really was – the bones of her hips showed clearly through the clinging material, and her belly was a hollow underneath her ribs. She was gasping for breath when they brought her to shore, her long red hair darkened by water and falling wet and heavy against her lips and her eyes, but even then she only had those words in her mouth, those words and none other: *Will you Dreamshare with me?*

Sar had been there on the beach when they had brought the strange woman up out of the sea. She had heard those words uttered. She had not known what they would mean to her. Not then. Not yet.

The fisherfolk had thought the lady was ill, and she had been taken to the healer's hut for help – but the healer was at a loss as to what to do with her. When he had swept the wet hair back from her face and looked into the wide eyes whose iris seemed to be all but consumed by the huge dark hole of the pupil and whose color — pale blue or gray — was barely hinted at around the edges of the black pupil, the healer had hazarded a

341

guess that there must have been some drug involved, and suggested that she be taken to a pallet and constantly watched.

"But she could not have been alone," the healer said. "There had to be others on a craft that size. And if they are all like her, they all need help."

"We cannot walk uninvited onto another's boat," one of the fishermen had protested, the ancient laws of their lives an instinctive response.

The strange woman, who had been laid down on a pallet just within earshot of all this, moaned softly and turned her head as though she was in pain. The fisherman who had spoken flushed, cast his eyes down to his feet; the things which had been left unsaid — *if there are others, if they are all dead, then the boat is a prize* — suddenly seemed crass and greedy. But the woman on the pallet had not turned to react to what had been said. It was doubtful if she had even heard any of it. There was still only one thing on her mind.

"Dreamshare," she whispered, her voice husky.

"What is this Dreamshare?" one of the men who had rescued her asked, frowning. "That was all she could say, right from the start. Right until this moment. I don't understand."

"Neither do I," the healer said. "We will know more when she wakes."

But she never did wake again, the strange woman they had tried to save from the sea. She slipped into a fitful sleep, and then into something else again that made the healer sigh and shake his head. She died a little piece at a time, drifting off into silence, never waking to consciousness for even long enough to utter the invocation to the Dreamshare one last time.

She had not needed to. Before she was utterly gone from them, the village knew all too well what Dreamshare was.

The boat had not been abandoned after all. A few hours after the woman had fallen overboard another figure had managed to gain the upper deck, and this time it was a young man, naked except for a loincloth. His skin had been sun-browned once but it had started to lose the color and it was clear that he had not been out in the light for some time. He had not been as painfully thin as the woman had been, but it was obvious that he had already slipped some from what had once been a fine physique. And he had been more or less lucid.

He too had babbled about Dreamsharing for a while without making sense before he was finally brought back to a more coherent state, and the closer he came to that the greater the hunger for the Dreamshare drug that grew in his face and in his feverish gaze.

"There is still some left on board," he told the healer, eventually. "There has to be. I need to go back. I need to find it. I need to . . . "

"How did you come to this village?" the healer had asked.

"The sea brought us, after we entered the Dreamshare — we did not guide ourselves after that," the man from the boat said. "To be honest I don't even remember our setting sail at all — one of us had to have cast off, cast us adrift, but I have no recollection of it. One does not travel *this* world when sailing the Dreamshare seas . . ."

He led the fisherfolk back to the boat, in the end. He invited them aboard. They found a third companion below decks, dead for some time and starting to smell; his remains were decently disposed of together with the ill-fated woman's. The village folks were left to deal with the dead; the survivor from the strange boat was far more concerned with ransacking the interior of the boat for something that had a far greater value to him than the lives of his companions.

He found it. Just enough of it to matter. Enough Dreamshare powder, a dusting of a pale jade green at the bottom of a cut-glass vial, to make his cheeks flush a hectic scarlet and his eyes grow hot and hungry.

And he had said them, too, those strange words that had been on the lips of the woman who had died.

But he had been lucid enough to make clear their meaning.

"Will you Dreamshare with me?" the stranger had asked a young fisherman who had happened to be beside him when the vial with the green powder had been found. And then, when met with a blank stare, explained. "This is not a drug to be taken alone. This opens the doors only to shared worlds, it will show you wonders you have never believed possible to imagine – because they never had been possible to imagine before, not by you, not by you alone. But when two come together — or even three, or more — it is sublime, it is unspeakably wonderful, and there are more strange and wondrous things out there than can ever be explored in a single lifetime but you have to try, you have to go back again and again, because each time there's just that *glimpse* of something out of the corner of your eye and it's greater and more beautiful and more glorious than that which you had been exploring on your previous trip — so you go back, chasing that, and maybe you find it but yet it shows you a third thing that you have to go back for and learn and see and own, or else you go back to a different place entirely, somewhere you had never been before and would have never believed you could go, never believed it existed if someone had tried to tell you of it before you saw it with your own eyes . . . Will you Dreamshare with me?"

"All right," Iorn had said, his curiosity fatally piqued. Iorn, Sar's Iorn, her chosen one, the man Sar had been pledged to since they were both children, with whom she would have spent the rest of her days in happiness and contentment had the drifting boat not come into their bay. The boat with the poison called Dreamshare.

The only reason Sar knew about any of this was because there had been another man present at this exchange. Iorn's friend Manam Dor had been present on the boat when it had happened, had seen it all, heard it all. But he had not been invited to join the pair who shared the last remaining grains of the Dreamshare powder. There had not been enough for three.

He had been jealous and angry, and had left them there, and in the throes of his resentment he had said nothing of it to anyone — but Iorn had not come back to his father's house that night. That night, or ever again. The evening after that, when the fishermen had come home from their day on the waters, the strange craft had gone, taking its surviving crewman and two of the folk from the village — Iorn, and Fanu Maira.

Maira's youngest brother, a lad of barely five, had been the only witness to what had happened to Maira — it was not clear from the boy's account of the events whether Iorn had come looking for Maira specifically or if she had just happened to be in the wrong place and the

346

wrong time when he had come looking for a woman, any woman, to take into the Dreamshare with him. Maira had never been considered beautiful — her skin was darker than was considered fashionable and she could not seem to grow her hair long enough to braid into the maiden-crown cornrows that Sar and the other virgins of the village wore; it had been beyond the boy-witness's ability to discern, but there was probably a little bit of that in Maira's consent to go with Iorn. It was only after the boy's confused and garbled account of what he thought he had seen, that Dor had stepped forward and told of what he knew.

Sar thought that she would have gone, too, if it had been Iorn who had asked. But he had not asked. As far as she could tell he hadn't even made an effort to try and find her. He took the first willing female who crossed his path.

Will you Dreamshare with me?

Apparently the dream she had been waiting to share with him had not been enough. Not after he had had his first taste of the drug.

Sar never quite knew how or why she had conceived the idea of going after Iorn. She didn't have much to go on — the name of the drug, Dreamshare, and the name of a single place which the stranger from the boat had let slip in an unguarded moment: a city called Cirian, the source of Dreamshare. Iorn had already had the Dreamshare in his system when he and his companions had set sail; they might have been making for Cirian, or their destination could have been somewhere quite different, but with the Dreamshare as their navigator it was not clear that they could have been making for any particular port at all. But it was a beginning.

Sar's father, Nang Samar, had forbidden her to leave the island when he found out about her plans.

"He is *gone*, Sar-*bib*," Samar had said. "It's over. You saw what that thing did to the others."

"They were others," Sar said stubbornly. "They were not Iorn. Iorn can fight this . . . he can fight it, if I find him, if I can bring him back."

"You don't know that," Samar said grimly. "Even if you found him at all, which is about as likely as your going out by yourself and landing a *baba-gar* fish with your own two hands."

Baba-gar could grow to be huge, dwarfing both boat and human, and when they were hunted it was usually with an organized flotilla of craft and a hundred fishermen — and then the mammoth catch, if they succeeded, was towed back to the shore by at least four or five boats. This was a village-sized operation, and the concept of dainty, diminutive Sar wrestling with a *baba-gar* was an image of epic failure. But instead of being discouraged by the idea, she had merely smiled at her father.

"Even *baba-gar*," she said gently, "are born and are babies in the beginning. If I wait, if I let Iorn disappear completely, it is indeed going to be a grown *baba-gar* of a problem — but if I leave now, maybe the trail can still be followed. It's still a baby *baba-gar*. I can grapple with that."

"And I say you will not go and waste your life on chasing a mirage," Samar had declared. "You are still my daughter, and I forbid it."

"Your daughter, who would have been a wife," Sar reminded him. "If they had come just a little later, the strangers, I would have been a widow. Able to decide for myself. Think of me as a widow, *papi*."

And she had gone away to be by herself, and cry, because she wasn't nearly as certain as she had made her father think she was. She was afraid . . . but there was a tiny light deep inside of her that she could not extinguish. A light of pure faith. If she went, she could make it right. The village was already thinking of her as a widow; she and Iorn had been too close to being wed. Sar could see the other young men in the village look away from her in awkward embarrassment if she caught their gaze on her. This was what it would be like. She was the ghost, caught on the cusp of being the bride and being the new widow, twice forbidden, and she knew she would still be the new widow when she was old and toothless and half-blind, even if she had never known the touch of a husband.

They had taken more than Iorn from her, the strangers. They had taken an entire life, meticulously woven and planned and prepared for, leaving Sar with nothing but the bitter aftertaste of memories never made. Her father might have believed otherwise but Sar knew that she had very little to lose by going after this particular *baba-gar*. There was nothing else that she could do.

She defied her father, turned her back on her village; a sympathetic fisherman from the next village down the coast ferried her over to the peninsula where the Big Town was, the place the villagers used to go every Great Moon to sell fish and shells and necklaces that the women had made out of coral and crystal and stone. Sar had never been there alone, and when the familiar little cockle boat pushed off from the stone wharf of Big Town to return to her island home she fought a sense of pure panic and a violent urge to scream for him to come back, that she could face it after all, that she could face whatever came for her in the village far more easily than she could face the big unknown that now stared her down with what seemed to be a malevolent loathing.

But she was here for Iorn, and it was Iorn's eyes that she saw staring at her next, the way they crinkled at the corners when he smiled at her, the way they seemed to contain the warmth of the sun in its heaven when they rested on her.

"And so he needs me now," Sar whispered to herself, bracing herself against fear, against loss of faith. She asked about Cirian in Big Town. Nobody seemed to know about it, or would not say. People thought they had heard of places with names that were similar but when pressed these always turned out to be wrong, or unlikely. It was finally a glimpse of someone with dilated eyes and a hungry expression, so very like the woman from the strange boat who had died back at the village, that yielded Sar her first shred of hope.

"Cirian?" the man had repeated to her when she had accosted him to ask, and his voice was at first just as puzzled as all the rest. But it turned out that he had been puzzled for different reasons, because he continued, "What are you looking for in Ancirian-Shaba, my young innocent?"

That was a new name, a different name. Sar filed it away in her memory.

"I am looking for my betrothed. Sarav Iorn. He was taken from our village by someone . . . by someone who asked him to Dreamshare. They said the city of Cirian . . . "

But the man was laughing softly, softly and bitterly, and would not meet her eyes.

"You would not last a brace of hours in Ancirian-Shaba," he informed her. "You don't understand Dreamshare, if you are seeking to pull someone already in its grip out from the addiction. I have been without for less than a day, and look at me, look at my hands . . . " He held them out, and they were visibly shaking. "If I thought that you had any on you, I would have killed you for it by now if you had not volunteered to share it. But it's obvious you know nothing about the code."

"I can learn about the code," Sar said. "Tell me what I need to know."

Her companion stared at her for a long moment, his gaze full of bitter understanding and pity. And then he looked away, and sighed, and would not meet her eyes again.

"You know Dreamshare is a thing that seeks companions? You seek others, others seek you. The code . . . lets them, and you, know what you have found when you meet one another. Earring in left ear means you are looking for a man. Earring in the right ear, a woman. Both ears, you are not particular about your companion's gender."

"No earrings . . . ?" Sar said, her fingers reaching out to touch her bare ear.

The man gave a short bark of a laugh. "You don't belong here," he said. It was not an indictment; it was an answer to her question. Wearing no adornment in her ears meant that she was not seeking anyone at all, and for the world of Dreamshare that meant that she was out on the sidelines, looking in.

But he went on, relentlessly — she had asked, and he would give her the whole of the answer.

"Rings on your fingers," he said. "Existing connections. Right hand, present. Left hand, past, your Dreamshare history. Index finger, male companions. Fourth finger, female companions. No more than three; three rings on either finger means that you have had — or are currently involved with — more than three companions. Black in a ring means that you are experienced, but do not wish to deal with newcomers; a ring with a stone on a middle finger of your right hand means that you are willing to take on neophytes, that you can teach. A ring with a green stone means that you have a supply of Dreamshare, or can get it. Those companions are prized. A ring with . . . "

"Stop," Sar begged, her eyes bright with tears. "All I want is one man, my man, my . . . "

"Ancirian-Shaba holds many men, and you may have to go through a considerable number of them before you even hear word of somebody specific. Are you sure you are up for this . . . ? Have you ever taken Dreamshare before . . . ?"

Sar shook her head mutely. Her companion shrugged his shoulders, turned away. His arms were crossed tightly over his chest, his hands tucked into his armpits.

"You will be dead by the end of your first night in Shaba," he said.

Sar bought an earring and a couple of cheap rings at a local bazaar the next morning. But the thought of finding the place she now knew as Ancirian-Shaba paralyzed her with fear, with the shame that she might have to bring upon herself before she was through with her mission. Would Iorn even want her after what might happen there, if she found him? Would Dreamshare make him forgive her if she came to him stained by other men? Would Dreamshare let him even remember who she was . . . who she had been?

Would she herself forget, if once she was made to take the drug herself?

Was it even possible to contemplate finding Iorn without the possibility of losing herself?

But her feet were on this path now. She had no choice but to go on.

The Great Moon was waning before Sar finally found her way to the city called Ancirian-Shaba — it had taken her nearly fifteen frustrating days of hesitation and false starts.

When she finally reached the city, ferried (with every show of reluctance) into its harbor by a young man from a fisherfolk village not unlike her own home, her heart was beating painfully fast and her breath was loud in her ears. She had no real idea what to expect — by this time Ancirian-Shaba had taken on mystic dimensions for her, and she would not have been surprised to see her lost Family Gods walking its streets. She had never been to a really big city before and all her images were drawn from Big Town, the market, which by comparison with Ancirian was no more than a large village itself. Sar had merely extrapolated what she had known, made everything bigger, more intimidating, more overwhelming — but she did not realize how inadequate her imagination had been until she stepped off the boat onto the cobbled docks of the Dreamshare city and stared, intimidated, at the huge stone buildings that began just a little way ashore and seemed to go on forever, twisted into winding alleys that dove out sight behind great buttressed walls, shimmering behind a veil of heat and a stench made of fermented grain, rotting fish, human sweat and human fear.

There was a sense of slow ruin about it, as though she was looking at an illusion, as though the buildings only seemed to be standing but there was nothing really there except blind windows and roofless halls and hungry shadows everywhere.

Three people converged on her from three different directions before she had taken more than a couple of steps from the water. Pupils wide, hands shaking.

"Will you Dreamshare . . . "

She lifted her hand, coded with what she hoped was still the correct message in the language of Dreamshare. "No — I'm looking for . . . "

They melted away, without another word.

Sar found herself letting out breath she had not been aware she had been holding. She realized that she had been half-anticipating an attack, even though they probably knew that she did not hold any Dreamshare powder, not newly arrived at the dock as she had obviously been.

It had been pure luck that she had avoided the drug thus far — but the luck did not hold, could not hold in a city like Ancirian-Shaba. Less than two hours of her arrival, hungry and thirsty and hopelessly lost, Sar stumbled over something that had looked like a pile of refuse at the mouth of an alley . . . a pile of refuse that unfolded into a rangy dark-skinned man with Dreamshare-hungry eyes and arms of whipcord. The arms folded around her, inexorable, pinning her down like a starfish; she struggled, but in vain. When one of the man's hands came swimming into Sar's panicked vision, it held a vial. A vial of a pale green liquid.

"Drink," the man said, his voice hoarse.

"No — no, I can't — I am looking for . . . " Sar resumed her struggles, but she might as well have been tied down with ropes.

"Drink," he said. "It's been nearly a day since my last Dreamshare. You are here, you are showing that you are looking for a man, drink."

"I *am* — I am looking for a man — but not . . . "

He wasted no further words. The vial was against her mouth, his other hand now twisted into her hair on the back of her head, tilting her head back. She gasped, tried to let the liquid that dribbled over her lips flow away harmlessly down her chin, but it was impossible. The Dreamshare juice flooded into her mouth, down the back of her throat; a fleeting and unexpected sweetness exploded in her mouth, and then it was gone, and a bitter aftertaste remained on her tongue and her throat burned with the passage of the drug.

And then it took her, a wave of warmth that spread from her throat over her shoulders and her arms, down her spine and into her hips and her loins. Her knees gave way; her hands spasmed helplessly against the dirty shirt of the man who held her, her lips parted with a soft sigh. She was aware that he had stepped back into the shadows of the alley without releasing his hold on her, that a single motion had swung them both against the brick wall at her back and then sliding down against it until they were lying on the pavement below, she underneath, he heavy on top of her lying between her thighs, fumbling at her breast and then pushing up her skirts as he guided himself into her.

Sar thought she might have screamed, but all that came out was a soundless whimper as he ground his hips against hers and the Dreamshare bridge solidified between them, taking them both into a strange country that she could not look at without gasping, a land which had a sky the color of a sandy-bottomed sea where fish darted through the clouds like birds, and plants waved gently in a breeze which might have been an ocean current. Jewels hung from the branches of these strange trees which had no solid trunks — and small starfish scuttled through the grass at her feet. She could hear, far away, something that sounded like the crash of surf on the shore, and a strange fluting call which might have belonged to a bird. There were amazing, astonishing, unbelievable things everywhere she looked — and it all surrounded her, pervaded her, the sights and the sounds and the texture of smooth shell and sharp coral under her fingertips and the taste of fresh fruit just plucked from the tree and the salty smell of an ocean shore when the tide was out and the wet sands usually under the water breathed shallowly in the open air.

And then the skies darkened with unexpected speed, and the wondrous land... went away. Sar no longer smelled ocean or tasted fruit – she found herself lying curled into a tight ball, dirty pavement against her cheek, a rank smell of refuse in the alley behind her, and the remnants of a strange man on her and in her, and . .

something else . . . the faint scent of something that she now recognized, and understood, and wanted. Dreamshare powder. Dreamshare juice. She made out, with difficulty, the shattered remains of the vial from which she had drunk her first taste of it not far from where she was lying.

For a while, she could not move. She closed her eyes, and they filled, and overflowed; and the tears ran down her cheeks and into the corner of her mouth and all she could taste was the salt of them, the salt of the clean ocean she had left behind and which she could probably never return to again. Not like this. Not unclean.

Not waking to a craving she was helpless to ignore — a craving for a return to that land where fish swam in the green sky and gems hung from branches like strange shining fruit.

But she was here for a reason. For a *reason*. She forced herself to sit up, smooth down her clothes, remember the face of a man other than the one who had taken her here in the alley. Iorn. *Iorn*. He was somewhere in this city. She would find him. She had to find him.

A woman fed her, almost a full day later, with something exotic that Sar did not recognize, the unfamiliar taste masking the scent and flavor underneath — and the Dreamshare in the food took her again, and this time she went to a different place altogether, sharing it with the woman who had offered her the food, a woman's hands on the secret places of her body, a woman's lips on hers. Sar had not been wearing the code earring that indicated that she had been seeking a female Dreamshare partner, but the other woman had worn two earrings and apparently didn't care that Sar might not have been willing. She thought, although she was far from sure, that there might have even been more than one woman — because there were more hands than there ought to have been, and more mouths, and she was in a place that burned with flames that were violet and green and gold and she danced between them like a demon child and where they touched they did not burn with pain but with an intense pleasure that made her dizzy with exquisite feelings she could not even begin to identify. Where the flames touched they left a fiery trail of sparkles in the same color that they had been, and soon she was dancing naked in bare feet upon glowing embers and she herself, her body, her limbs, her hair, were glowing with the shades of the fires she had taken within herself.

She was lost, then — the streets took her, and held her, and she went where the scent of the drug led her . . . or waited until it led others to her. Every time she returned to herself it was with more memories of light . . . and to a greater and deeper despair.

It was nearly three weeks later that she found Iorn.

She had stumbled out of the city on the morning after yet another Dreamshare encounter, following a potholed and weed-infested street down towards the sea. It had finally taken her to a small half-moon of pebbly beach empty of people, its stones sharp and unsteady underneath her careful steps, hurting her feet. She only braved it because she suddenly craved the sensation of foam between her toes, of salt water flowing around her and cleansing her of the things that had wounded her, of the ocean's forgiveness of her sins and the gift of forgetting, if that was still possible.

She had not realized that she was not alone until she had waded waist-high into the water and stood with her torn skirts floating around her like a strange species of seaweed . . . and became aware that the shape at the ocean's edge to which she had only desultorily paid attention as she had made her way across the beach was in fact a man sitting hunched over with his legs drawn up against his body in the circle of his arms. It was not until the man moved ever so slightly, lifting his forehead from where it rested on his knees, that the sudden familiarity of the motion tore at her heart with a poisoned talon.

"Is that you ? . . . " she whispered, the words barely leaving her lips as sound.

He turned his head marginally to let his eyes slant sideways, just enough to glance at her, and then he lifted his head to look at her more fully, in astonishment.

"Sar . . . ? Am I dreaming again? Are you real?"

"Real," she said. She drank him in, his face, the slope of his shoulders — his eyes were different than she remembered, wounded, quenched, and yes, still hungry, with a hunger she now understood. Shared. But he was still Iorn. Still hers. Her heart thudded painfully against her ribcage.

"What are you doing here?' he said, and the voice was harsh, bitter, stinging. He looked away, taking his eyes from her, and that hurt, hurt more than Sar knew it was possible to hurt. She had been willing to give so much for this moment, had paid what might have been too high a price already — and now, now that she was here and he was beside her, he would not look at her.

"I came to find you," she said, taking refuge in simple truth.

"Why?" he said, every word that came out of his mouth a dagger. "So you can see me crawl in the gutter? So you can come to reject me, or to gloat, or to preach?"

"No," Sar said simply.

She began to wade through the water towards him and he, realizing that she had done so, scrambled unsteadily to his feet.

"Don't come any closer," he said, an edge of desperation in his voice, panic blooming in his eyes. "I don't know that I can . . . I have already done so much that I . . . "

But she had reached him already, and stood beside him in silence for a moment, staring up at him, willing him to look at her again . . . and he finally did, reluctantly, as though his eyes had been dragged back to her fact by main force of her will.

Both of them had eyes full of tears.

"It's too late," Iorn whispered hoarsely. "It's all over, it's far too late to do anything but mourn and seek another touch of Dream . . . you should not be here . . . you should never have come . . . "

The hunger was in her, too, stirred into a stabbing need at the very mention of the name of that thing that she craved. But the taste in her mouth was not sweet, it was salt, like the sea, like all the tears that she had shed.

She took one of Iorn's hands, folded it into a cup with her own small fingers curled on the outside, and then leaned forward to scoop up a handful of sea water with her other hand, letting it trickle and drip and dribble into his palm until hers was empty and she closed his own hand over it.

Clean water. Salt, like tears.

The sea forgave.

The hunger would always be there, but perhaps they could slake it with each other. Together. In a place far away from Ancirian-Shaba. In a place where memories did not burn, where they might never again find the magic lands where fish swam in water-colored skies but where they could, perhaps, in time, find peace.

"We can still share a life that is not this, a life that is not tainted. Let us go somewhere new, where nobody knows or remembers us, and start all over again." She spoke very softly, holding his eyes with her own, and then brought her fingers, still wet with salt water, and laid them against his lips. The taste of the sea. The taste of forgiveness. "We still have the future, you and I. It may not be the future that we have always been promised . . . but we have this day, and then the day after that, we can take it all a day at a time. That may be all that we have . . . but I will take it as it comes, from dawn to dawn, watching the tide come in, watching it go out. One day at a time. Perhaps we can get used to in, eventually, and learn to accept that it will remain real, and remain true. We can."

Sar smiled, suddenly, and it was like a shaft of sunlight waking a sparkle on the ocean.

"We can . . . we can share . . . Will you share a different dream with me . . . share the years to come . . . ?"

She had not used the actual word, the name of the drug that owned them both, but she had skated close enough to it and Iorn recoiled. But Sar held on, her hand smaller and weaker than his own but its strength lying not in the power of its grip but in the power of its promise. And he finally sighed, letting the tenseness in his shoulders drain away. The sea whispered against the pebbled shore behind them; out towards the horizon, on the open ocean, the sun played on the water, sparkling and dancing amongst the waves. The sight of it was almost enough to sate the hunger that sat at the heart of them both now, the hunger that would always stalk them, that they could never feed again without the risk of being lost again, this time perhaps forever.

But the sea would be there for them. The salt and the sunlight.

It would have to be enough.

Acknowledgments

This collection exists as a result of the dedicated volunteer labor of a number of people. I'd especially like to thank Lisa Spangenberg, Steve Barber, Jane Smith, Stacia Kane, Chris Hyde, and T. Peter Porterfield, all of whom went above and beyond any reasonable call of actual duty to help create this book.

About the Authors

Alma Alexander is a novelist, short story writer and anthologist. She has published more than a dozen of books in both traditional and ebook format (including *Secrets of Jin Shei, Hidden Queen, Changer of Days,* the YA *Worldweavers* trilogy, *Midnight at Spanish Gardens,* and the *Alexander Triads* collections) and has been published in fourteen languages worldwide. She is presently at work on several new novels. She lives in the Pacific Northwest with her husband and two presumptuous cats. Find out more about Alma Alexander at her Website (www.almaalexander.com) or at her blog (http://anghara.livejournal.com).

Dedria A. Humphries Barker has been a writer-in-residence with the Willard R. Espy Foundation at Oysterville, WA, and Inside/Out Literary Arts Project, Detroit, Michigan, and attended the Community of Writers at Squaw Valley, Ropewalk Writers' Conference, and Wesleyan Writers' Conference. Her work has appeared on Salon.com, Literary Mama, and Sundry arts journal (Ohio). She teaches writing at the Lansing Community College in Michigan.

Puss in Boots came to maturity whilst marooned on the continent of Antarctica, where he was raised by a breakaway sect of penguin heretics. He learned to draw by sending out elaborate depictions of his circumstances scrawled with penguin-quill, and carried into the four winds by messenger-gull. Eventually, these short cartoons grew so entertaining that a rescue ship was dispatched from nearby Easter Island, where today he guides walking tours (which would be more accurate if someone told him the island is not a holiday theme park). In the off season, Puss In Boots lives in the Northwest U.S, writes stories, draws comics, and is owned by two pit bulls. His art is secretly buried at plunderpuss.net!

When **Sage Collins** isn't writing about invisible boys and girls with too much imagination, she's working as a mad scientist, running tests on your water. She lives in Ohio with her superhero cat and his supervillain sister. Her first novel, *Love Sucks*, will be available as an e-book in spring 2012.

Christian Crews became interested in magical realism while writing a high school paper on Gabriel García

Márquez and William Faulkner for the incomparable Ms. Flonnie, senior English professor extraordinaire and old friend of Maya Angelou. Since then, Christian traveled often, lived in several countries, read for a degree at Oxford University, and has now returned to calling North Carolina home.

Shannon Fay is a freelance writer living in Halifax, Nova Scotia. Since getting her journalism degree two years ago she has worked in a bookstore in Canada, on farms in the UK, and as a cleaner in a youth hostel in Amsterdam. She has had a mystery story published in *Woman's World* magazine and regularly writes for *The Coast* (www.thecoast.ca), Halifax's alternative newspaper.

Vic Horsham was born in the early '80s in Essex, England. An unrepentant nerd, she developed a love of fantasy, sci-fi and horror. Vic was one of those strange, quiet children that actually enjoyed school writing assignments and spent much of her childhood filling notebooks with terrible handwriting, leading to her first published work at age ten; a short poem about head colds, printed in a local poets' anthology. Like most budding writers, Vic followed this up with several years of the most persistently awful poetry and short stories ever penned by a human. Vic currently lives in Kent with her partner and several cats.

Fatihah Iman is a psychology graduate who somehow ended up working in a university press office. In between writing about supermassive black holes and teenage dinosaurs, she also writes science fiction. She lives in Leicester, in the very middle of the UK, where she collects comics, novels and more headscarves than anyone could possibly need in their whole life. She must have tea to function like a normal human being. "Daughter of the Void" is her first published short story.

Alessandra Kelley is a Chicago artist and illustrator with over fifteen years' professional experience. She paints allegorical paintings founded in classical mythology and Renaissance philosophy, and occasionally magic realist works based on Chicago. Her Web site is here: http://www.alessandrakelley.com/.

Marina Lostetter is an aspiring freelance writer. She grew up in Oregon, but recently moved to Arkansas and has used the change as a catalyst for her new career. She blogs at http://lostetter.wordpress.com/.

Clinton Lawrence is a high school science teacher. His fiction has appeared in *Realms of Galaxy, Realms of Fantasy,* and a number of other print and online publications. For several years, he was a staff writer for *Science Fiction Weekly.* He lives in Davis, California.

Deleyan Lee lives in Western Pennsylvania with far too many pets. Her interests include serial killers, forensics, Ancient Egypt, Ireland, and many things legendary, occult, and historical. "Alchemy of a Murder" is her first short story sale and is dedicated to the memory of R. Ann Cecil, a good friend, insightful mentor and never-ending inspiration for many stories and writers.

Suzanne Palmer is a writer and artist who lives in western Massachusetts amid the beautiful rolling hills and green forests, except for the five months a year they're buried under snow and the two months of mud season and the three months of dreary, constant rain, hurricanes, and the occasional tornado. But those couple of weeks when they're green, they're really green, and the writing is sweet. Suzanne's story "Surf" appears in the December 2011 edition of *Asimov's.* You can find more stories linked on her website at www.zanzjan.net

Derek Paterson lives in Scotland, a land of mountains, glens, forests, and rain. He is currently working on several Sci-Fi, Fantasy and crime/detective/thriller novels, and hopes to finish at least one of these before the friggin' Sun goes nova. He has a Website: http://derekpaterson.net.

Candace Petrik is a writer from Melbourne, Australia. She has had work previously featured in Australian publications such as *Wet Ink, The Death Mook* and *Voiceworks.* She is currently finishing her first novel and drinks a lot of tea.

T. Peter Porterfield is a self-employed designer and illustrator, and fine artist. He writes because there are ideas that, believe it or not, he can't express in imagery (despite that old saw about the thousand words). He lives with his wife and Oblio the cat in Bend, Oregon. When he's not destroying the English language writing, he's in his woodworking shop turning large and expensive pieces of wood into rather larger piles of extremely expensive sawdust and enjoying it immensely.

Timothy Power is the author of *The Boy Who Howled* (Bloomsbury), the best kids' book in the world.

MacAllister Stone is Editor in Chief of AbsoluteWrite.com and CoyoteWildMag.com. She attended the Viable Paradise specfic writing workshop in October of 2006 and has been a member of the VP staff. She can often be found on the Absolute Write forums.

Shannon Tarvin is a graphic designer and freelance artist.

Katherine Tomlinson is a former reporter who prefers to make things up. Her fiction has appeared online and in

print since 2007. Read more of her work at: http://
kattomic-energy.blogspot.com/.

K.L. Townsend loves writing, but hates bios. This love/
hate relationship started with previous credits, which
include poetry in *The Shantytown Anomaly* and a short
story in the *Ruins Metropolis Anthology*, and have lasted
through the forthcoming release of *Song of the Swallow*, a
book from Hadley Rille Books. The epic battle between
the author bio and Ms. Townsend is expected to continue
as she explores new ideas of the fantastic. Perhaps one
day, she will find the courage to face the bio and unlock
its mystical secrets. Until then, she will keep writing tales
of mythology, history, and the supernatural.

Joseph S. Walker is a member of the Mystery Writers of
America whose work has appeared in such magazines as
Alfred Hitchcock's *Mystery Magazine* and *The First Line.*
He's the author of the crime novel *Five Million Dollars and
the Green-Eyed Girl* and the forthcoming *A Death at Haven.*
When not writing he teaches online college courses and
tries to fathom the mysterious ways of cats.

J. B. Williams lives in Florida with one spouse, four cats,
and 2000 books, and writes in the dead of night

Chris Wilsher is a lawyer in Houston who writes tales of
crime and horror. He has previously been in published in
Twist of Noir, Powder, Burn, Flash, and *Mysterical-E.*

Absolute Visions
Body set in Book Antiqua 11/16
Display set in Book Antiqua 24/28
Built on a Mac using Scrivener from
Literature and Latte
and Pages from Apple.

13894937R00219

Made in the USA
Lexington, KY
26 February 2012